Fiction

WWW.INDEPENDENTLEGIONS.COM

KYLA LEE WARD

THIS ATTRACTION NOW OPEN TILL LATE

STRANGE SIGHTS AND SHADOWS

ISBN: 979-12-80713-41-4
SEPTEMBER 2022

COVER ART: ALESSANDRO AMORUSO
PROOFREADING: KAREN RUNGE

RECIPIENT OF HWA SPECIALTY PRESS AWARD

For my teachers.

With thanks to Belinda Kelly, Kate Orman,
Evangelos Paliatseas, Gillian Polack and Lynne Roberts.
Also, most especially, to Mrs Bowra and Mr Tome.

"Kyla Lee Ward has long been one of the leading weird poets of our time. Less familiar, perhaps, is her weird fiction, but This Attraction Now Open Till Late displays her many talents in prose narrative. The variegated settings of these tales (Prague, Venice, Australia, and elsewhere) match the diversity of weird motifs. Her vibrant prose, her engaging characters, and the keenness with which she finds strangeness in the most commonplace scenarios of contemporary life make every one of these stories a thrill to read. And what can we say of 'A Final Masque,' a rich and complex novella of ghosts and necromancy set in the decades following the French Revolution? No devotee of the truly weird will want to be without this book."

--S. T. Joshi, multiple award-winning literary critic, author of *I Am Providence.*

"Kyla Ward is one of my very favorite contemporary writer-poets. In this collection, she puts her macabre spin on stories with twists and turns smooth as ectoplasm. Find out why a young pianist has a secret fear of a black cowled figure. Four unusual youths run a tourist attraction, but things go awry when the tourists are gradually replaced by barely discernible monsters. In one of my favorites, the color cordovan on a canvas takes on a whole new meaning for an artist's dealer friend. There are stories of necromancy and black magic 'Pain is the stain of a ghost's fingers, which unseen, may still be felt.' Discover what happens to a young girl with a lifeless hand when the world begins to die. Of particular literary succulence, there's one about gargoyles. Surreal nightmares may be a side effect of reading this collection. Beware! Kyla will have you in her spell, as she did me! Buy it, it's a keeper!"

–Marge Simon, Multiple Bram Stoker Award-winner, co-author of *Satan's Sweethearts*

"Take a tour of the world, through an alchemy of exotic curiosities, the much-acclaimed Kyla Lee Ward as your guide. Wholly magical and gritty with realism, This Attraction Now Open Till Late beckons patrons with thirteen lush and lyrical tales to intrigue and inveigle. Beware, though, the compelling little sideshows, those unexpected detours through dark passages and dusty backroads since nothing good can come from those. An extraordinary collection of numinous curios, This Attraction Now Open Till Late, is well worth the ticket price."

–Lee Murray, four-time Bram Stoker Award-winner and author of *Grotesque: Monster Stories*

"Kyla Lee Ward's work is darkly lyrical and poetically prompt, with gentle humour drifting through it like smoke. She brings a macabre beauty to horror that is hard to ignore and harder still to forget. These stories will get under your skin, and stay there."

–Alan Baxter, award-winning author of *The Gulp* and *Sallow Bend*

"Kyla Ward's collection of dark stories moves through different countries and different times, revealing dark and horrific events, lost characters, and strange beliefs. Each is presented in carefully chosen writing styles. It is uniquely Ward's and is certainly worth your time. "

–Rob Hood, award-winning author of *Peripheral Visions and Fragments of a Broken Land: Valarl Undead.*

KYLA LEE WARD

THIS ATTRACTION NOW OPEN TILL LATE

STRANGE SIGHTS AND SHADOWS

AND IN HER EYES THE CITY DROWNED

I came to Venice in June. As the brilliant days collapsed slowly into August, I began to hear. Then, I began to see. Now I'm scared, to the point of actually shaking, that the woman will appear again tonight in the mouth of the Calle di Pignoli.

At first, I was as arch-dazzled and spire-smacked as everyone else. Marty calls it the Venetian brain-freeze, like you've just guzzled a massive gelato flavoured with sunshine, marble and brine and flecked with gold like the glassmakers do their goblets and bowls. Fresh off the water taxi, that's exactly what the tourists go for: gelati or glass. Then, after staggering around the Piazza San Marco, gawking at the basilica and the belltower, and the clock where the bronze man strikes the hour on a bell, they collapse into chairs outside the Doges Café, and listen to us.

Cameron Keesey is a name nobody has heard. That's because Marty and I are refugees, from the culture drought currently afflicting Sydney, Australia. Marty plays clarinet, though he prefers the tenor sax. I play keyboards, which here means a top-of-the-range Yamaha on 'grand piano' setting. A sweet platform like this has a vast menu of Voices and can handle even more exotic uploads, as well as multiple tracks. It can channel woodwind, strings or a full choir: it can construct octaves from the sound of breaking glass. But for two solid months now, it's been stuck on grand piano. Our cellist is Lise, who usually plays in a Czech Goth metal band, and the violinist is Soho Stevie, who patched this outfit together in London last winter. God knows summer in Italy sounded like a good idea, and I had some vague idea that Venice might inspire me to write my breakout piece. The history of music—of all the arts—is full of people travelling to Venice and creating masterpieces, and I am classically trained. So now we are the Doges house band, one of two which old Cavinato has engaged for the season. The other group are local, and they play twelve to two, four to six. We get two to four and six to eight or nine every day, excepting the occasional appearance of special guests, and every single night.

When I mentioned what I saw to the others, Stevie said I was crazy: that even if the woman is into skinny redheads of her own gender, nobody ever goes for the keyboardist. As a violinist, he would say that and believe it too. Marty said we were all a little crazy by this point, that anyone would go crazy after the five thousandth repetition of *Speak Softly Love*, *Santa Lucia*, *Oh Solo Mio* and *That's Amore*. And this is true, but I cherish a special hatred for *Que Sera Sera*. It's not just the whiny, see-saw melody; it's the attitude. What kind of teacher, what kind of parents tell a kid that it's not worth trying? The short answer: mine. My mother, pushing me to practice and gain grades all the way through school, and then fully expecting me to pack music away in the box where she keeps my Pretty Ponies. My father, refusing to pay for my ongoing tuition, let alone my equipment, and going apeshit when I persevered. Threatening to throw me out of the house if I didn't attend interviews at this friend's insurance firm and that friend's real estate office, right up until the day I flew out. Now he's getting drunk over the barbeque back in Cherrybrook and telling those friends that I'm begging on the streets. I didn't tell him about Venice: why would I? He'd be saying that if I was headlining at La Scala.

Here's the routine. At one pm, we eat our panini in the kitchen. Marty and Stevie change into black suit and tie. Lise and myself wear little black dresses with subdued make-up and no visible piercings. Our outfits are laundered and pressed between every shift, which is a blessing. Our first time all dressed up, Marty and I took photos for his parents. I stared at my image, thinking that the dress made me slim rather than skinny, tall rather than a beanpole: that even my stringy, red hair approached the glamour required for album sleeves and foyer photographs.

Then Marty said, "Cam, you're going to make one hell of a waitress."

I told him he looked like a monkey.

But once we're up on stage out the front of the café, there's no danger of being asked to get some tourist *"a proper cup of tea, please, not that lukewarm yellow stuff!"* The chairs and tables are spread out across the cobblestones and acres, whole acres away, we can glimpse, like a reflection, another set of chairs, and another stage fronting another café. Cafés surround the piazza as completely as the marble arches. There are three levels of these arches, all white, all columned, on every side except for the insanely intricate façade of the basilica, which is comprised of every colour of marble except white. From two to four we play, with short breaks between the scheduled coach parties. To mix things up, we sometimes add the *barcarolle* from *Les Contes de Hoffman*, which is partially set in Venice, and variations on the theme of a certain secret agent who keeps trashing the place. If Giuliano's on shift, he puts vodka in our water.

We drink espresso in the back alley and play cards, and at six we're back up there. Gradually the light softens, as though the gelato is melting, running through the cracks between the cobbles, mingling with dirty water and spilled wine. The crowds roaming around the square thin out, though the chairs are all still full. Then, as the sky cools towards a soft indigo, the lamps come on: huge, branching glass-and-wrought-iron things that in any other place would be restricted to ballrooms. I haven't seen anyone dance in the Piazzo San Marco, but then, *Carnevale* is in February. The only masks I've seen worn have been cute, glittery things on children and the occasional plague doctor on some guy who has contrived, despite Venetian prices, to get drunk.

As the lamps come on, sharpening the shadows and blanking out the sky, it begins. The first thing I hear is a medley of the other bands, who are all playing the same things as us, but on different cycles. It's maddening. I have always been unusually receptive to the sound of places, to their Voice, if you like. It was one of the things that made me realise I was a musician. After the medley comes the sounds of the audience, the coughing, the scrape of chair legs, the painful shifting of old bodies. The hiss of glass globes heating, and a stray breeze dragging its fingernails along the colonnades. I hear wood creaking, stone grinding and the lapping of dark, dark water, and these are the things that conjure her from the shadows beside the clock tower, with her mask-like face, her long and flowing hair. I could not say when was the first time I noticed her there, part and parcel with the darkness, the sea and the stone. But I do know that having done so, I cannot stop.

She seems to listen to us and us alone; raptly, intently, though God knows there's nothing separating our performance from all the others. All her attention is directed towards the stage and, as I came to realise, towards me. Why is this terrifying? Because no one accompanies her, no one ever acknowledges her. Because she seems, night by night, to be drawing nearer, yet I never see her move. I sit at the keyboard in my black dress, back straight and hands in position, and play:

she stands and listens, and we continue like that until the bronze man has whacked his bell eight times, or as long as it takes the tables to clear. Then I'm off the stage and into the water taxi with the others, and back to the hostel at the rail terminal. Not even the Venetians stay the night in Venice.

At the hostel, some of the terror fades. We eat Chinese or Mexican, turn on the soccer and zone out while Lise skypes Stanis, her boyfriend back in Prague. She leans her cello against the table and plucks out little tremolos as they discuss lyrics like *"in the catacombs of alchemy, love lies bottled"*. Or else it will be Stevie I can hear in the background, chatting up another of his universal contacts, hustling for the next gig, the one that's sure to be our big break. We've got auditions, he's promised, for a new supper club the instant we're back in London. Or was it in Helsinki, or Lucerne? We'll be a trio, anyway, because Alchymistickou is heading to some massive Goth fest in Germany.

I have no one to Skype. I left my useless boyfriend in Sydney, twice over. Usually I talk things through with Marty, but he's been monosyllabic since Stevie played the never-with-another-band-member card on him. I think that, in his own way, he's afraid as well. Maybe at the root, it's because we all know that this place where we're sitting is sinking slowly into the sea. Cavinato says that for the past few years, the winter tides have rolled over the very spot where we play.

We used to rehearse in the mornings, experimenting and improvising. Sometimes Lise would fit an amp to her cello and I'd 'play' samples from my laptop, looping the sound of steps passing through an arcade into a rhythm track, turning the cooing of pigeons into notes, and otherwise annoying the crap out of Stevie. I started recording samples the moment I arrived, because that's what I do. I use a hand-held digital recorder with inbuilt stereo microphone and good compression rates, that loads straight into my D.A.W. The whole setup is last-gen, but it's served me from the time I started handing in 'experimental' pieces to my composition tutor, and it's not like I can afford to upgrade. You can call it synthpop, electronic fusion, *musique concrète* or a dozen other things and, yes, at its most rudimentary, it is playing secret agent themes in pigeon Voice. But, with just a little imagination, you can conjure a bass line from the crackling of a bonfire, lift a melody out of the sounds of a train journey, and much, much more.

One day, I successfully captured the Voice of a motorboat tearing down the Grand Canal, lashing the deep, green water to a dirty white. The wake scrapes the ancient stonework like a knife. I caught the Voice of a glassblower's kiln, leaning through the doorway of his shadowed workshop. Lise likes that one: she says it's what Hell would sound like, approaching the gate. Over these past two months, I have captured all the sounds of hissing, creaking and lapping, and filed them away. But the rehearsals faltered, then stopped, as the soccer heated up and the humidity increased.

So this morning, I did what anyone I told about my secret fear would surely have recommended. I walked down the Grand Canal to the Piazza San Marco and approached the Calle di Pignoli in broad daylight.

I had half-packed the night before. Had been ready to desert the others and break my contract by jumping on a train back to London. Only what that really meant was a plane back to Sydney, and what that really meant was that I wasn't a musician at all. Not even one who worked the tourist circuit while trying to develop her own sound, to find people to share it with. God knows, as a keyboardist with tits, that's always been doubly difficult for me, but this was my second summer, only my second of hostels, cafés and playlists that were my own opinion of what Hell sounded like. Could I really have burned out so quickly?

It was another perfect Venetian day with cobalt in the sky and copper in the water. Stallholders lined the bank, spruiking their masks and T-shirts in a polyglottal din. The gondola companies fought for space, adding a layer of splashes and shouts. As I passed into the piazza, queues shuffled through the arcade of the Doges palace and into the basilica door, where a whole new theatre of echoes awaited.

The Calle di Pignoli was packed with people in T-shirts fresh from the rack, balancing smartphones and dripping gelati as a diminutive local woman herded them along with a tinselled cane. My gaze snaked up the tottering towers of brick, the cream and ochre façades that made the place a winding canyon. I was hoping to see a votive Madonna or decadent caryatid that might catch the lamplight by night: instead, I saw shuttered windows and red geraniums blooming on ornamental balconies. Nor did any dummies in *Carnevale* costume stand outside any of the shops, which was another possibility that had occurred to me. Engulfed by shuffling, snapping and cries of *"Rapidamente!"*, I passed the furthest point that I could possibly see from the stage, and a bridge over a canal appeared with no more fuss than an alley in London or Sydney. I escaped the crush to stand at the crown, peering over the water at the gondolas winding yet further inwards.

I could hear the strains of *Santa Lucia*, hollowed by the stone and diluted by the clucking and lapping. The passage of the slim, black boats struck me as percussion. I set my recorder going and leant out over the rail of the bridge, inhaling sour green and listening. Listening.

Whatever Byron may have heard on the Rio Zullian when he gave its bridge its popular name, I heard no sighs here. Instead, the echoes from the gondola passage below me and the omnipresent roar of the crowd came to resemble groaning, as though the speed of the playback was slowed right down. The water sounds were all combined in weeping, as clearly as I ever heard my mother through the bedroom door. Through the same spectral engineering, the gondolier's pleasant tenor voice accelerated into a wail that scraped my skin: in my bones I felt other sounds, pitches and vibrations trailing off the aural scale but still a part of this, this symphony. It was impossibly vast, inconceivably deep, and both a part of what I heard at night and as far beyond it as the development from the exposition, or even an entire new movement.

Then I saw that the wall across the canal had crumbled away—for all I knew, it had happened as I stood here, the tourists passing as oblivious to me as they were to the curling paint and splitting bricks sloughing away to reveal carious timber bones. Whatever the case, the gap running down to the water was now a good metre wide. The music was pouring from a gate to Hell like nothing I nor Lise had ever imagined. I could see everything, though the cyst beyond was as dark as the day was bright: could see because I could hear. Synaesthesia is supposed to be beautiful, sensual—like stroking velvet with your ears and music pouring down your throat like honey. But I could hear the stairs, plunging from the floor above into utter blackness. A humming stagnancy lay there, the kind of vibration that cancels sound, devouring the blood-red walls whose tops still showed gilded wreaths of laurel. But descending, the garlands became beards of algae, thickening into a talus of black slime. Salt extrusions swarmed the plaster like maggots. I couldn't breathe, couldn't move; my heart was beating but it didn't keep my body's time. I felt intrusive, culpable: this wasn't something to be seen, by me least of all! And in the deepest part of it, where nothing could possibly exist, a ruinous, black-cowled thing was reaching *out.*

I heard it say my name.

I fled the bridge, then completely at random I pushed through streets where the crowds swore at me in the lyrics of pop songs. The next moment I was crossing a plaza where the only occupants were the pigeons I had chased with my recorder. But as hard as I ran, the sounds stayed with me, as if each step I took was down those stairs, hurtling towards the darkness. Finally, I found myself running down another canyon-like street towards a burgeoning roar. I thought of a tsunami, swelling out of the sea to wipe the horror away—I burst out into the throngs of the Piazza San Marco and here, finally, the dreadful chorus dissolved into the din.

I had been recording the entire time. When, eventually, I played back just a portion, all I heard was lapping, clucking, and *Santa Lucia* giving way to *O Solo Mio*.

Synaesthesia is supposed to be beautiful. But schizophrenics hear voices, and see horror in the most ordinary things.

I cornered Cavinato before the start of shift and described, in muted terms, the place I had found. I asked him what it was. He scrutinised me for a moment, then said, "any of a hundred bars". So I asked Guiliano and he told me about the pilings. When the merchant princes raised their palaces, they first sank pilings into the soggy soil. Whole trunks of trees were roughly planed, embalmed in pitch and sent splashing into the ground water at the bottom of narrow shafts. Then they sealed the shafts with marble.

"There's no air down there," Guiliano told me, stubbing out his cigarette on the Doges' back step. "So they don't rot. They go all stony, like bodies in bogs. When the water started coming over San Marco in the winter, the pavement started shifting. Some of the shafts opened. The air got in and the pilings started to rot. All the buildings you see leaning against each other with cracks in their faces, that's what's happening inside. In some places, the pilings are *rising*." He actually shuddered, though the air was as hot as smoke.

"What did you hear?" I whispered.

He shrugged, flicking his neat, brown cowlick, and smiled. He routinely charms jet-lagged Americans, who *"Just want a real coffee for Christ's sake!"* with that smile. Then he asked why I was asking, and I couldn't even speak. Couldn't say, *Because I hear what I should not hear and see what I should not see, and her eyes never leave me, not when the customers pass between us, not when the music stops and we reach for our glasses. Do you see her? Do you hear her? Do you just ignore her screaming, day after day?*

That was this morning, which the clocks assure me was mere hours ago. Now it is night. Now I am back here on this stage and, as *Que Sera, Sera* seeps from the Café Florian into our *barcarolle*, I feel sick. My stomach is cramping: I haven't drunk enough, or just maybe I've already drunk too much. Is Guiliano on tonight, or is it that other waiter with the bad bleach job?

A nudge at my elbow: Marty's eyes are bulging over his puffed cheeks and mouthpiece. We're both still playing, fingers dancing across our respective instruments, but now I realise something's wrong.

Oh dear God, I'm playing Que Sera Sera.

A few bridging chords and I'm back in the *barcarolle*. The audience hasn't noticed: the silver-white and artificially red heads are swaying, and one woman is flapping her lips along to the melody. The men sit grey, stout and unmoved, for the most part, waiting for their drinks, although an elderly gay couple are holding hands and getting misty-eyed towards the back. You can see that they've always dreamed of seeing Venice. And then, without warning, I see her. At the mouth of the street, I see the un-white pallor of her face. Whatever she wears is as amorphous as her hair, absorbing too much light to be black alone. My stomach twists into a knot of wrought iron, but I keep on playing, listening as the symphony unfolds. Picking out the instruments and analysing every line.

She is closer now than ever before. No one in the audience reacts to her, even though she is near enough to touch the gay couple, to reach out and brush their exquisite quiffs. In the tired slump of Marty's shoulders, in the nonchalance of Lise and Stevie, I see equal insensibility and it's just not *fair*! Venice was supposed to inspire me, to give me a way out of my own private pit! I should never have come here. My parents knew that I'm not a real musician; all my tutors, they knew I was just someone who stands outside a café playing *That's Amore*. Just as I used to stand on the steps of the Sydney Town Hall mixing birdsong into *Waltzing Matilda*, busking to get the money to undertake my next grading. To buy my recorder and D.A.W. To save up the fare to Europe, where all my dreams would come true.

Lise catches my eye this time, with just a flicker of a smile. *"When you're down by the sea and an eel bites your knee, that's a moraaay..."* she mouths. Something else from our rehearsals. I try to smile back, but water leaks down my cheeks and stones grind in my stomach. Another few cycles of that seasick riff and it'll be *Que Sera Sera*, and I know that I'll look, and I'll see her, and this time I'll break down and scream, and scream, and I won't be able to stop.

No.

No, I won't. I may be going schizoid or synaesthetic, or home, but first I'm going to show that woman, whatever she may be, what I'm *worth*. I'm going to show all these people, the deaf, the blind and the denying, what Venice truly is, and I'm going to do it as only I can.

I don't remember cabling my recorder into the Yamaha, or fiddling with its programming. Seems like I may have been doing it night after night, a little at a time, so that the local band wouldn't notice the difference and blab to Cavinato. Seems like I've uploaded some of the files from this morning as well as from our rehearsals, and one or two from a commercial FX site, creating a set of Voices I can play just as easily as grand piano. In any case, everything is now prepared.

As Marty performs his opening flourish—a flurry of notes he is rightfully proud of—in the very instant that the front row begins to sway and smile, I bring up a Voice I've labelled 'canal funk'. For the moment I'm still playing my part, but in notes of stone and water.

Marty's face goes macaque red. He repeats the flourish, darting glances at Stevie and mouthing at me to *"Wake up!"* But it's too late: the worst song in the world is already dissolving, as *O Solo Mio* dissolved beneath the bridge. I glissade pigeons, I hiss like lamps and then, in an ascending choral progression, I shatter glass. Marty has frozen, the clarinet dangling from his neck strap. The violin and the cello are faltering, and the faces in the front row are starting to whisper.

Then I hear a low and resonant thrumming. It's Lise, and I'm damned if she isn't doing her best to sound like a glass-blower's kiln. Gladly, I bring up the effect for her, easing the double bass into the mix. A moment later, even as the violin ceases completely, the clarinet joins in with an uneasy tremolo. I flick the rhythm track over to gondola percussion.

Music without a name comes leaping and swirling into the Piazzo San Marco, scouring everything else away. Like a tsunami, like a real band is playing. I started the improvisation, so it's up to me to set the pace, gathering the contributions of my band mates into the overall structure. I keep it classical: now that the exposition is through, I develop the basic theme with basso sucking and treble weeping. Then, as the clarinet begins to wail, I marry it to the sound of screaming. As Lise's elbow thrusts like piston, I bring up the groaning and yes, yes, I can hear it! And so can they.

I see it in their eyes. I've brought this to them, not the whole symphony but at least this fragment! I've brought it to them here and now in front of the Doges Café, and they cannot ignore it. Nor, it seems, can Venice itself. As though I have hit that one, sympathetic pitch which can bring down bridges, the towers around us are shaking, the arches are rocking, the water is slap-dancing in the canals. In the crumbling palaces, every empty chamber resounds like a violin's bout. There's no one who can ignore this! For a moment, the piazza is La Scala, it's the Albert Hall and the Opera House, and stages all over the world. The bronze bell is chiming and I am performing in Venice.

There's only so long we can sustain it, especially with Stevie standing there like the Death of Paganini. Lise begins to recapitulate and I follow, returning once more to my stone-water melody, allowing the worst song to reappear briefly before the motorboat scything up the bank devours it all.

Rapidamente! Rapidamente!

As I let the crowd sound trail out, I hear scattered applause and *bravo*! Guiliano is standing there with his mouth hanging open. The couple at the back are the ones cheering, along with the old woman who was singing before. The rest of the audience just sit there, staring.

"You bloody idiot!" hisses Stevie.

But for the first time in months, I feel alive. For the first time ever, maybe, I'm not just hoping I can make it—I *know*.

Then *she* is there. Between me and the audience rises a wall of darkness and cold. I breathe stagnant black as she reaches out her salt-encrusted hand. Her mask is marble, blue and grey, and in the crumbling sockets of her eyes

and in her eyes

are dancing sparks, particles of gold as the glass is flecked with gold, as her gown is brocaded in every possible colour, and every one a sound that the symphony weaves together.

In that moment, a future coalesces before me. I see myself shouting at Cavinato and Stevie, refusing to apologise, and a midnight train journey to a place I have never been. But then I am on another stage with Marty, Lise and Stanis, facing a sea of black shoulders and white faces, all roaring, roaring for us. I see the downloads page crashing under the demand, the single and the first EP. I see red hair splashed across black and white photos, close-ups of my hands on the keys, webzines giving way to glossy print. Stage after stage, audience after audience and then the first album with its title track and cover of a drowned city.

The nightclubs and festival tents give way to auditoriums and amphitheatres. The audiences wear gowns and suits, their faces change colour again and again. We play reflected in water. As each scene shifts, I know I am in a place called Venice. Little Venice, Venice of the North, Venice Beach, Venice of the East— there seems no end to them, in London, Amsterdam, Los Angeles, Suzhou. To each of them I bring the sounds and in each of them I make recordings, attempting hybrids, seeing what traits will carry through. Seeing if the sounds will take. As album follows album, each encompassing more of the symphony, I understand how a city can survive collapse, how its essential soul can escape and flourish anew, but only when given the right foundation.

I see myself sinking, friends and helpers, managers and lovers dragged down by my obsession. Lise, Stanis and even Marty are stripped and blackened, descending into illness, madness and shame. I feel their pain, hear their screaming as all at last are buried. And I am buried too. As I slide down into my final resting place, the water thick and black, and chill, the echoes boom from above and my shaft is sealed.

I see it all. And I reach out and, as her fingers crumble in my grasp, I feel sparks beginning to dance in my blood.

The wall is gone. I face my first audience, sitting and waiting for someone to take them in hand.

I shoulder past Stevie and take the mic. "Thank you, everybody, for listening to us tonight. We are The Pilings, and I hope you enjoy what's coming."

Who Looks Back?

Who looks back on the Waimangu track?

Not Kelsie Munroe, running light over gravel, the slope gentle but the surface potentially foul. The track's made for walking, not running or driving. There is a road proper for that, for ferrying tired tourists back from Lake Rotomahana. You're meant to walk one way down the length of the valley, taking in all its steams and smokes and weirdly-coloured sinter. But Kelsie never walks where she can run and Lewis jumps.

Lewis Zabri keeps her pace for now: brown skin abreast of freckles, black stubble beside red hair. They dress much the same; singlets, shorts and runners, packs strapped into the small of the back. Kelsie is taller and can beat him over short sprints, but this is four kilometres of up and down, winding, and in places rough. Lewis keeps himself loose and breathing easy. He knows she's planning something.

The valley of Waimangu, New Zealand, is the youngest landscape on earth. Nothing here, not the trees, not the streams, nor the cliffs themselves, existed before the eruption of 1886. The ground split, swallowing everything, then spewed it out again as boiling mud. Forest and farmstead, whole villages died. For kilometres around, there was not a single living thing. On the walls of the Visitors Centre, blurry black and white photos show weirdly peaked hills and plains of ash. It's gone green now: first the extremophile algae, then lichen and ferns, then melaleuca spilling down the slopes in a long, slow race—the reclamation marathon. The algae was first to reach the bank of Frying Pan Spring. But Kelsie, or maybe Lewis, will catch up soon.

You're not meant to run, and definitely not to leave the track, risking a scalding, broken limbs, or damaging the unique terrain. But Lewis and Kelsie leap, climb and throw themselves off things as a matter of course. The terms of this race have been agreed: first to the lake via the Mount Haszard lookout ahead of them, and still a serious drop below is where the track and creek first cross. The climb to the lookout begins there, but Lewis sees no reason to wait. Running straight at the guardrail, he extends hands and flips himself over the cliff in a perfect *saut de chat*. He doesn't so much as glance over his shoulder.

Kelsie is not impressed. She trains in parkour herself, but this isn't the terrain. Lewis can say what he likes about the zone and the flow, but terrain is king. She knows this and that's why she'll win. He's risking a spill for a gain she'll more than make up at the lookout, if the map approximates reality. Worse yet, this close to the Visitors Centre; he's risking the rangers seeing him.

Three metres below her now, Lewis adjusts automatically to the crunch and mealy slide beneath his feet. So long as he stays off the algae, he'll reach the start of the climb seconds ahead of Kelsie, and that gain he'll keep. Ribbons of colour unwind beside him, pink rock and water a startling green. Steam sifts across his field of vision and there is frantic noise around him, an all-encompassing bubble and hiss. One part of his mind feels the heat and moisture and yes, some fear; the other only registers angles, surfaces, opportunities. He is in the zone, feeling the flow. The goal of all his training is to clear his mind of the artificial clutter of modern life and here, now, he is almost free. That's why he'll win.

Kelsie burns on down the track. Despite his pretensions to this or that philosophy, Lewis never really thinks—or else thinks that everywhere is just like London, where no one gives a damn. But sometimes people do care. They care about travelling together. They care about sleeping together. By God, a whole lot of them care when someone tic-tacs on the shrine at Tanukitanisan Temple, and what was the point of that? They had to leave Japan overnight, and it didn't even make the blog. Then again, nor will the stunt she's banking on today, for which she's carrying an extra kilo. Twenty metres, ten: Lewis vanishes ahead of her into the steam. She can hear the creek: Is that the creek? It sounds like voices. It's like from out of the ground, from the weeping black ferns and deliquescent rocks, there rises a deep and liquid dissension. The warmth envelops her, damp upon her arms and face, sulphurous in her eyes and nose. For a moment she runs blind.

Lewis rejoins the track, and not a moment too soon: Kelsie is coming up fast. Here, the valley narrows sharply and the banks seem to be rotting a foul, yellowish slough, choking the creek bed. He peers ahead for the turn-off and sees only the wildly swirling fog. Is he motion then, with nothing to mark his passage? Can there be motion in a void? Yes, there can: so long as Kelsie comes behind. Grinning just a little, he eases, anticipating her sight of his back. She takes all their games so seriously, even in bed. Then something shifts beneath his feet. The gravel is suddenly live as well as warm. The fog billows and the noise of the creek rises sharply around him: *Is* that the creek roaring? He does not stop, cannot, as directly in front of him, something forms from the white.

Kelsie knows that sound isn't the creek. Its voices have not vanished, merely retreated behind the encroaching rumble of a truck on gravel: she has Australian ears, accustomed to country sounds. A bank of wind hits her face, clearing the steam. She sees Lewis running slow, and beyond him she sees a large, white utility bearing the park logo. Coming straight at him, at her. Behind the cab she glimpses ridiculous things, white and shapeless with reflective face plates and Lewis is—*oh no, he's not!* Not slowing or swerving, Lewis guns straight into the path of the moving vehicle and vaults. Hands and foot on the bonnet, next step against the windscreen. Even though the truck is jerking, skewing to a stop, he executes the move with perverse bloody brilliance. Straight over the top he goes and through the white shapes, revealed by their reaction as men in thermal suits. In the instant of their shock, before they even imagine her presence, she shifts balance and angle, and leaps out across the water.

Lewis sees angles, shapes, the moving flat of the truck bed. His pulse sings as he leaps to the ground and keeps running, unfaltering. *Yes, yes; that was perfect!* Did those guys even *see* him? By those shouts and grinding, clunking gears, oh yes they did. A grin splits his face as he rounds the bend and sights the turn-off.

Kelsie grinds uphill through ferns and bushes, wincing as she pushes on her right ankle. Her leap covered the distance as she saw it, but seeing isn't believing down here. Solid is slurry, ferns anchor foam. Her ankle stings and she's not sure if it's a burn or a graze. Either way, she's committed: their rules don't compensate for accident, pursuit or even biohazard. It's win or lose and she is not losing today, there's too much at stake. So she climbs a bad climb. Exposed rock to a fallen log: it's an obstreperous sign of her progress that the plants get bigger. The pink and yellow cools into grey; spindly trunks and spiking tussocks block her view of the stream, but she can still hear voices. And not shouting scientists and squealing rangers; the old voices, that the Maori tribesmen must have heard to mark this place as the realm of monsters. While Lewis was psyching himself up, she read the placards in the Visitors Centre. Then suddenly, startlingly, she is out of the bush with hard-pressed earth beneath her feet. Before her the path to the lookout swerves up a steep defile. But she is alone and whether Lewis is ahead or behind, she has no idea.

Lewis would say he was ahead: ahead of the utility and its shrouded occupants. *What the hell were they doing, dressed up like that?* The cluttered part of his mind noticed machines in the back of the ute, the monitors, and probes. It made sense they'd check the valley regularly, though he would have thought they'd use the access road for that. But here he turns up the hill and here the Ku Klux Rangers cannot follow him, if that's what they're shouting about. It's true they could reverse all the way back to where the climb rejoins the main track and wait for him there, but surely they've got somewhere to be! Another blast of air strikes him from down the valley. He hears a new note in the creek; a warbling, high-pitched sound.

Kelsie ploughs up the path, but she's spent her best. If by some miracle Lewis is behind her now, she'll abandon her plan and take the track down to the lake. But how to tell? The vegetation here is thick. Strange flowers rise aside the path: purple trumpets on stems like giant foxgloves. Huge tree ferns, the biggest she has ever seen, lip over her head and reach for her feet with long, black tendrils. Branches bristle with inch-long thorns. Still, a faint whispering rises from the earth, punctuated by the rasp of her feet and controlled breath. Then suddenly, by screams.

Lewis looks up to see the white utility, with its doors swinging and machines falling as the vehicle flies through the steaming sky. Rangers fall too: foolish, flailing space men, mission aborted. One remains braced in the driver's seat: Lewis sees him clearly as the truck rotates. That's a whole truck up there, spinning slowly as though something wraps it, carries it amidst shifting coils. And as the nacreous mist thickens, something does.

Kelsie all but stumbles towards the lookout. She's made it: there's a bench concreted firm into the ground, and there's the cliff. Ferns, flowers fall away: the valley lies before her, a snaking, smoking rift down to the metallic sheet of the lake. Nothing in that view suggests a source for the dreadful sounds, the mash of flesh and branches. It was behind her then, the accident. *Lewis, oh my God.* And she turns. She begins to turn back, as branches crack and the wind flattens, and something huge and whistling like a train churns up the hill. Into her view drops a white utility. It drops from the sky right before her eyes, crashing, sliding away down the cliff as something in the air loosens and billows, shooting away with a furl resembling the feeding fringe of a coral polyp as much as steam or clouds or a weather balloon: what the Hell is she *seeing*?

Lewis hasn't stopped moving down the main track. This was where both truck and terror came from, but they aren't there now, and he can really put on some speed. His is the discipline of pure motion, but maybe there's something in this headlong rush of a small, brown boy being hunted through the London alleys. The track bends and bends again; on his left Mount Haszard and on his right the creek, bubbling with increased vigour. And his cluttered mind suggests that if what he saw *was* an explosion, the freakish herald of a volcanic event, then in all likelihood he's running right into it. Where is Kelsie? If he was so far ahead that she didn't see the horror, then she might well have continued on up to the look-out. He's closer now to the exit than the entrance: when he reaches that he'll head up and meet her. They're bound to be safe on the mountain.

Kelsie had the rope and carabiners in her pack. This was her plan: an assisted fall from the lookout, ten metres down onto what they called the Terrace, then a straight though possibly scalding sprint to the shore. She'd take risks when it counted.

Confined to the remainder of the path, Lewis would have lost minutes and been lost in wide, white-grinning admiration of a stunt so worthy of himself. Then she could have told him she was through. Now she goes through the same motions, to deadly purpose: there are people down there, she can hear them. Anchor on the bench and on the largest tree, though that wouldn't be worth much: quickly, quickly pull the sleeve in place so the cliff doesn't cut the cord as she goes over. Climbing was her first love, in the erosion gullies around the farm: her first attempt to escape. Her second took her to London, and where hasn't she been since then? Stepping off into air, she looks down.

Lewis hears another rumble. A thrashing, boiling, torrential sound: in the direction of the lake, pure white striates the sky. There's been no geysers in Waimangu since just after the eruption, when they claimed it held the largest in the world. What's this then, what is this? It's *incredible!* In all his travels, running round and round the world in search of its edges, he's never seen the like! The entire lake must be rising, and even as he runs, as the track beneath him starts to shake and the outrunners of the wind hits, there's as much delight in his *whoop* as fear. Until he realises that the wind and the whistling is coming from behind him.

Kelsie drops into ruin. The valley floor is made up of smashed sinter, broken rocks, raw scars scraped through the undergrowth and white wreckage steaming, all of it steaming. A white figure flails, caught half in metal, half in water the same unearthly green as the spring. Rumbling, roaring, human screams: a tenuous thread of sound. Kelsie is shaking, everything is shaking and as she lands, nice and light and square, she's nearly flung off her feet. Not even unhooked she is turning, stumbling, drawing the rope across the heaving pink and yellow ground. Inhaling an overwhelming smell, like eggs boiling in a rusted kettle, she reaches down and hauls on wet fabric.

Lewis slithers in blood-warm water popping and stinging against his skin. There was nowhere else to go, from something that wasn't a trick of the light, nor a current of superheated water, or anything else but a creature came hunting. His entire body knew it, and that wracks him beyond the heat and acid. He keeps himself loose and floating: going with the flow, but he isn't alone. Slick like rubber and obscenely buoyant, white corpses follow the current, floating swiftly towards white Hell.

The ranger's name is Ahere; her skin darker than Lewis where it isn't burned, her eyes a brimming brown. Crying and hugging Kelsie, she tells her things: a seismological blip, a bloom on the thermal map, an early morning expedition in full heat-wear down to check the lake. A new vent had opened, yes, but there had been nothing to suggest more until the thing emerged.

"*Hīanga*," she says. "We put the lines down and it comes, we put the lines down and it catches us!" She points frantically to a strange, circular mark in the sinter, a circle at least a metre across with five deep indents that Kelsie assumes was caused by some part of the utility.

All Kelsie really gets from Ahere's story is that the lake is dangerous. But there's no going back the way she came: the whole cliff looks unstable, and she doubts Ahere could make it in the best circumstances. Whatever Ahere saw, whatever *she* saw, they have no choice and apparently there's a reason. Ahere is saying they'll be safe.

When Lewis was a little boy, he loved dinosaurs (raptors, hunting him through the alleys). Ruins too, the temples and tombs of all the ancient civilisations—but keep digging and you reach dinosaurs, their big, stone bones tomb and temple both. To go back further takes more than science or even imagination, but clawing at foam and slurry, Lewis realises that this isn't the youngest landscape on earth: it's the oldest. Go back further and it was all like this or near enough, a fury of earth and water. Near enough for that thing, maybe; that primal, elemental thing. Maybe life on earth did not begin with cells, but with fire and air. The cluttered part of his mind runs on like this, the other is crawling in the sludge, out of the creek but keeping low. It wants to find a hole and crawl inside: the other is telling him he needs to find the widest open space, where the rocks won't fall on him. That's what they said in Japan. He can only hope Kelsie is safe.

Kelsie was going home. From the North Island of New Zealand, Sydney is a hop across a puddle. She was going home and not like she swore to her father she never, ever would. She got the news two days ago in Wellington: her grant had come through and she had a whole new life of work and study waiting. But how to tell Lewis she's sick of living in hostels, tired of waitressing in shitholes to fund the next leg of the trip while he blogs and preaches *parkour*. She knows he wants to climb Machu Pichu, has tagged Easter Island and Antarctica as stations in his quest for who knows what, and perhaps he will. But she's going to die in New Zealand with a stranger staggering on her arm. As the earth shakes beneath their feet and through the steam, the whistling rises once again.

Lewis runs. On the path but hunching, nearly on all fours. The hunter is still out there: he hears its whistling, its rush. He pushes, burning all his last and, miraculously, there is Kelsie paralleling him through the steam. All this, and neither has gained so much as a step! He lopes along the gravel, she jogs across the world-famous Warbrick Terrace, deep crimson bleeding under her feet. Her hair flashes: she is magnificent, she would be flying were she not hampered by a pale and lumbering thing. A monstrous form, a homunculus or golem with gleaming white skin. And fly she must, for through the clouds the hunter is coming: he feels its wind, sees the mist clear. And as it comes, his shrieking, cluttered mind shears clean away. He sees angles and surfaces. Instinctively he understands that little warm-blooded things scuttling through ferns don't interest this hunter. How could they threaten it? How could they even feed it? It's the monster it seeks, with its unnatural contours: he yelps and changes course.

Kelsie hears Ahere shriek and feels her suddenly sag against her: thinking she's stumbled, she yanks her up and then sees her face plate is shattered. Her nose and eyes have vanished behind a web of cracks, and there is blood. Are there stones in the air now? She grabs Ahere, reaching into her core for one last effort, and oh my God there's Lewis sprinting towards her, Lewis with his stubbled head, arms and legs pumping crazy. She lets go of Ahere's arm and sees Lewis raise his—a sharp, black rock in his hand. It freezes her brain. She can't comprehend what she's seeing, match cause and effect. Only when the second flint strikes the helpless woman, opening a gash in her thermal skin, does she leap to intercept him, grabbing his arm, hauling at him, her height and weight costing both their footing and bringing them down.

She's in his arms now, rolling and thrashing; he laughs and rolls with her, all heat and sweat and hair. Slipping, sliding, seeping crimson; he's hard as a rock, licking permanganate from her skin. He's below her and she strikes him hard, no longer thinking of Ahere but rather of his grasping hands, his grinning mouth, of being dragged and used, and assumed. Of needing to win so she can finally, finally not need him.

Something passes over them, the two little mammals rolling in the mud. Something screams in agony and the crimson drenching them is at blood heat.

Kelsie stares down at Lewis and things click back into perspective. He's still grinning, but he's shivering, and what comes out of his mouth isn't words. She could leave him here, she really could. In light of what he did and the trouble she'll have, perhaps she should. But she can't. Somehow, she has to get them all to the lake. Looking around, she can no longer see Ahere, so presumably she's followed her own advice. Aching, weary, but somehow no longer terrified, she staggers up and then offers Lewis her hand.

He'd rather lie here, wet and happy, but everything is shaking and they had better find shelter. Somewhere quiet and dark where the water makes no sound. He stays close to his mate, gaze darting through the undergrowth and ears peeled for the hunting cry of the things below, that strike from above. Their voices are everywhere, but only the whistling counts.

Up ahead, Kelsie sees black and white. Black the fringe of unbelievably stubborn vegetation; white the boiling lake. There's no escaping there. Then part of the black resolves into a roof and windows, wheels, and she realises what Ahere must have meant. Running off from the dock, directly ahead of her and Lewis lies a road, and parked upon it is a small bus. The access road and the bus that takes tourists out of the valley! A broad and stable slope, solid walls and engine: this is their way out and always was. *Where is Ahere?* There's no sign of her here. *Oh please, let her not still be back there....*

He knows the artificial hollow is a trap. They can't go in there: he takes hold of his mate to pull her away. She resists him, chattering shrilly as though it's he who doesn't understand. He does understand, the hunters are waiting for more white monsters! Now she is grabbing him, dragging *him* towards the unnatural planes and sharp angles, and what is that dark substance streaming across the ground like water, yet solid? He twists out of her grasp, makes a blow of it, a stunning blow to the side of her head—and misses. She has jumped clear of him, landing on the black.

Kelsie screams as the bus explodes upwards in a geyser that holds a shadow, a writhing, tubular shadow that crushes windows and seats. Shrapnel scatters but she is already running, uphill again, but she will not give in to what she saw and will not die in the grip of a nightmare. Lewis pursues her; she hears him ploughing through the bush at the side of the road, chuckling in his madness. She veers away from him, though it costs her speed, and now she is shrinking from the whistling in the air, from the steam-shadow hurtling, coalescing into solidity right above her.

He gathers up all his strength, all his superbly honed muscle, and makes his leap. Although he no longer considers it as such, this is the pinnacle of parkour: a *passe muraille* such as hearsay finds impossible to believe, that makes the witness gasp and the practitioner sigh. Not to scale a wall, but to interpose himself between his mate and the thing with the whiplash body, the grasping tendrils, the five-pointed sting. It is not fully material, not at its full strength when he hits, so the impact sends that sting plunging into the tar. But it solidifies around him, lifts him up with a billow and swarm, and does not fade as it carries him out, over the edge of the world.

At his yell, his triumphant scream, Kelsie glances over her shoulder.

Who looks back on the Waimangu track? Anyone who does will never really leave.

When the rescue team finds Kelsie, she has painted herself with sulphur and antimony, and is using her pitons to punch the five points into the road, again and again.

A Whisper in the Death Pit

Dr Jessamine Wiung was lead archaeologist on the expedition conducted earlier this year, by the Department of Oriental Studies, at the site of Kayalyk in south-eastern Kazakhstan. The following email was received by the head of department on August 16. It was the final communication from the expedition camp before the assault by as-yet unidentified persons, which claimed the lives of two of our colleagues.

The university, in consultation with the families of the deceased and the missing, has decided to release the full text, together with a draft translation of an important inscription from the site. Please bear in mind that the latter has not yet been officially published and contains clear errors, as well as a degree of fancy. But her reflections on Kayalyk may well constitute Dr Wiung's last written work. It is hoped that the free circulation of this material, as well as honouring the members of the expedition, will stop the spread of rumours which, as well as ludicrous, are disrespectful to their memory.

***

To the world at large, those first images of the Death Pit will forever represent Kayalyk. But I retain a different picture. Situated between the mountains and the river, the site is indeed remote, yet also spectacularly beautiful. This morning, I saw wild ibex grazing not twenty metres away from our encampment. As I write, the last light of the sun is still visible behind the peaks, and the excavated courtyard of the monastery is a pool of shadow. Soon, there will be nothing to see but the unbelievable plenitude of stars. The lights of Koilyk village do not reach us here.

I first saw the city ruins as a graduate student in 1998, when I assisted Dr Aliyu Aliyev in the first of a series of beneficial exchanges between the university and the Institute of Archaeology RK. We were studying regional dialects and collecting folktales—she always said the two were inextricable. It was in these circumstances that I heard the legend of the monastery of Ak Araw, the name translating roughly to 'Pale Tree'. I ask that you permit me to reiterate the relevant details, so that you will understand the precise nature of this latest emergency.

From the eighth century onwards, Kayalyk was a major hub of the Silk Road. Parties from China, having survived the Taklmakan Desert and the Tian Shan mountains, would frequently take the opportunity to on-sell their goods to Middle Eastern and even venturesome European traders, and pass the winter here before daring the return journey. This collision of cultures, doctrines and technologies made, as in Taraz, for a unique and dynamic milieu, persisting until the city was abandoned towards the end of the thirteenth century.

Koilyk #34 (Aliyev, 2000) recounts that, in the years before the coming of Genghis Khan, a 'jade demoness' came out of the desert and corrupted the abbot of one of Kayalyk's Buddhist monasteries with promises of immortality. Soon the entire community, including a formerly segregated order of nuns, had abandoned all regulation in favour of orgies, alternating with torturous rites of abnegation and the brewing of strange potions. Caravans were plundered to provide ingredients, and children disappeared at night. Corruption entered the river and the crops failed. In desperation, the citizens appealed to the Khan, offering the unconditional surrender of the city if he would but rid them of this terror. A contingent of Mongols marched upon Ak Araw, only to find it an empty shell. Its occupants had become immortal and flown to the western paradise.

I first noted the correspondences between the folktale and the Chinese alchemical parable in my paper 'The Jade Demoness: a journey of motifs' (*JoOS*, 2001). The thirteenth century Héxī'āshū lù ('Dew Writings'—see Van Galen, 1972) preserves the tale of Yù Sōngshù, a princess of the Jin Dynasty who shunned marriage and the court to become a Daoist practitioner and disciple of the Sage Pang Liu. 'Jade Pine' (the name collates two traditional symbols of longevity) had long been thought to represent the elixir of immortality, arising from the death of her master (the proper combination of the elements) at the successful conclusion of the Work—in this, Chinese alchemy is indeed similar to its western counterpart. In this paper I proposed that, setting aside the typical folkloric flourishes, it was not hard to picture a disciple or group of disciples who fled beyond the northern border during the purges conducted by the Jin, settling in Kayalyk and pursuing immortality through the accepted means of meditation and alchemy. The destruction of the monastery by Genghis Khan was at least theoretically possible, placing the conclusion of the story around 1220 C.E.

But the Death Pit presents a grimmer ending. Confronted by an army known for its atrocities, the inhabitants of the monastery entered the subterranean meditation chamber and collapsed the passage behind them. In classic Daoism, ascension as a true immortal traditionally involved immurement in a cave for a period that might last centuries. This may have been a final attempt to grasp the crown of their practice, or it may have been the mass suicide which was certainly the result.

There were many reasons to conduct a fresh investigation of Kayalyk, not the least being the site's elevation to World Heritage status in 2014. This expedition was always cast as an adjunct to the excellent and ongoing work being conducted by the Institute of Archaeology RK, and initially I welcomed the participation of my old mentor, Dr Aliyev, with great enthusiasm.

It was her translation of the stela we found in the courtyard that confirmed the identity of our discovery—Ak Araw was myth no more! This, too, has largely been submerged in the spectacular footage of the naturally mummified bodies and the chamber, with its stellar patterns upon the roof and brilliantly coloured floor mosaics featuring plants and animals of the region. But the stela's importance cannot be overestimated in terms of cultural history and the context it provides to the larger find.

Not a classic sutra, it nonetheless must have been important to the practice of the monastery. I reproduce here the full translation:

What, then, is the day?
  Eternity is the day.
What, then, is the night?
  Everlastingness is the night.
What, then, is the roof above?
  The never-ending sky.
What, then, is the floor below?
  The boundless realm of earth.
What, then, of the pillars?
  The mountains ever-rising.
What, then, is thy meat?

The presence of my sister.
What, then, is thy drink?
The presence of my brother.
How good, how pleasant to join thee in the garden!
How fine, how fragrant, the thousand-petaled rose!
How fine, how pleasant, to feel the coiling dragon!
How good, what sweetness, to hear the phoenix sing!
What, then, is thy breath?
Knowledge of the truth.
What, then, is thy blood?
Perfection of understanding.
What, then, is thy life?
To speak the sacred words.

One morning in early July, a student volunteer from the Institute insisted to me that one of the bodies sighed when she touched it. Several of her fellows claimed to have heard whispering while in the pit which could not be traced to any person present. These rumours spread and were augmented to such effect that some of our personnel refused to return to the pit or to handle the remains, placing the burden of logging and conservation on our contingent. This loss was in no way remedied by the increasing presence of the curious and pecuniary, to be sure, but also by belligerent groups from Koilyk village—the subject of previous reports—who drove around the outskirts of the site by night shouting threats, and whom I suspected in the subsequent rash of thefts and sabotage of our equipment.

Initially, Dr Aliyev found it fascinating to observe how the discovery of the Death Pit was being incorporated into *Koilyk #34*, and she attempted to engage the volunteers in the process of study as a means of exorcising their own fears. The locals used the old tale to forecast the consequences of our disturbance of the bodies, but for the main seemed gripped by a non-specific dread.

There are forty bodies in all, in varying states of preservation. Many remain in an upright, meditative posture. Both male and female, the sexes alternate, although male/male and female/female have been confirmed. All subjects wear robes of coarse grey silk, and the heads are shaven. Although all may be assumed as residents of the monastery and the majority are surely from the Kayalyk area, the variety of ethnicities is apparent to even the most casual eye. There is no trace of coercion in the array, or in such bodies as have been properly examined. Their tissues contain a substantial presence of alkaloids and metals—standard ingredients of the elixir—which may have contributed to the exceptional preservation of some of the mummies. We have not yet touched the central pair, who kneel opposite each other as if this were a marriage ceremony rather than a funeral. Those two are in truly incredible condition. I make no rash claims, but the woman displays an ethnicity consistent with Northern China: her companion is a Kazakh with possible western traits.

Daoism today is a lively religious expression for millions of people across the world. It approaches contemporary life with both continuity and a wonderful flexibility of tradition that has always focused on development of both the community and the individual. We have received expressions of interest and support for our work from many Daoist communities, even though the practice of this monastery appears to have been truly unique. In any case, religious scruples are unlikely to have contributed to the unrest amongst our volunteers or in Koilyk, where the majority of the inhabitants are Sunni Muslims. No, I fear it is the example of Hollywood that sparked this surge of 'mummy madness', with a more worrying possibility that I will come to soon.

You may well believe we have all been under a great deal of stress, and the physical labour is taking its toll. But I had believed the professional archaeologists were coping. This was an error of judgement for which I take full responsibility: as the expedition leader, I should have been more aware. But despite being in her sixties, Dr Aliyev was shaming the rest of us 'youngsters' with her energy and commitment. She had been spending a considerable amount of time down in the pit, recording and identifying the various symbols incorporated into the mosaic. When she confronted me during today's lunchbreak, I was truly surprised. She said that it had never before struck her that these people had believed, had been utterly certain of their ascent to paradise. Should we not recognise this? Could we find some way to conduct our work while respecting their decision? Although she said this all in a reasonable tone, her hands were shaking.

At this, I abandoned my retort about thirteenth century Kool Aid and told her much the same things as I had said to the Kazakh media: that we were treating the mummies with the utmost respect and bringing them to 'life' in a world they could never have imagined. In turn, we were learning invaluable things from them. At this, she sighed and said in her opinion we should remove no further material, bodies or otherwise, from the pit. The reason she gave was the encroachment of autumn and the attendant risk of storms, but as she said this, her hands shook even harder and she gripped the notebook she carried strongly enough to tear it.

I thought she might have been threatened. There is no question that antiquity thieves are circling, and in this part of the world such operators are both organised and armed. Indeed, I now suspect their hand in the demonstrations of the villagers. My subsequent enquiries amongst the local personnel turned up nothing in this regard, but a student did let slip that after speaking to me, Dr Aliyev had returned immediately to the pit.

This struck me as contrary, given her outburst, and I was thunderstruck to discover that she had gone down alone, in contravention of nearly every regulation we have. The rest of our people were in the conservation tent, dealing with the morning's extractions. As I approached, I saw the lamps we had installed in the pit were still off, and she had not signed into the pit logbook. I must admit, I stormed down the passage with every intention of demanding an explanation for her behaviour, when I was relying on her to bring her fellow Kazakhs to their senses! But whether you are superstitious or not, it is hard to shout in the Death Pit, and perfectly impossible to stamp. The delicacy of the find aside, there is a sense of solemnity, of stillness, that defeats even the most righteous anger or fear for a friend. And I confess, when I heard that whisper trailing through the darkness, my heart nearly jumped out of my chest.

It was her, of course. My Kazakh is good, and I retain my familiarity with the local dialect, but this appeared to be an archaic form. I could make out maybe one word in four, but that was enough to identify the verse from the stela. At this point I turned the lamps back on: the stars on the roof flashed, the brilliant depictions of fruit and flower leapt into life around symbols suggesting everything from hieroglyphs to Manichaeism, and Aliyu rose with an expression of absolute terror on her face. We have removed twelve mummies thus far, clearing a wedge from the outermost circle towards the innermost pair, and it was here she had been kneeling, much like a mummy herself. She waved at me, notebook in hand, as if the light had robbed her of the power of speech. As said, it is hard to shout in the Death Pit, so I merely waited as she came towards me, still not speaking but gesturing me away, back into the passage, as she again turned off the lamps. I obeyed, but even once we were within the reach of daylight, she wouldn't tell me what was wrong. In frustration, I seized her notebook.

She raised her hand, then seemed to think the better of the action, and let me read it.

This is what I read, in her hasty scrawl, complicated by questions, references and the multiple revisions that accompany translation:

What, then, is thy meat?
The presence of my sister.
What, then, is thy drink?
The presence of my brother.
Brother, do you hear me?
Sister, I hear you. But this means you are separate from us and this should not be.
Something has changed. Listen!
Our voice is... less.
We were many, now we are few.
What has befallen those whose voices are still? Have they ascended?
I think something comes among us, bringing destruction.
What, then, is thy life?
In danger, brother, danger.

I asked Aliyu what this meant. She said that the only way for me to understand was if I returned to the pit with her in darkness. I would have to be absolutely silent, unless I could memorise the chant in an approximation of medieval Kazakh, which was as close as she had been able to get and which seemed to be working. I must not, under any circumstances, disrupt her again: it was imperative she go back down there right now and *guide them back into their meditation.*

I spoke gently of the conditions under which she had been working and how we were all extremely tired. I agreed that resealing the pit might be the only way to preserve the find during winter, but in the meantime we should continue with our duty to conserve the mummies and send them on to the Institute.

She looked at me and, in that moment, I was once again a twenty-six-year-old doctoral candidate, being farewelled by my mentor at the airport in Astana. Only this time, instead of seeing pride in her eyes, I saw a deep disappointment.

She said, "Do you remember Pang of Datong?"

Of course I did, from my own, old paper. I found the reference in Chiang's 2003 work on the splintering of Dao sects during the fall of the Northern Song. Pang of Datong was reportedly arrested by the first Jin emperor and divided into "the four parts of a human being and the fifth exclusive to man, and each separately boiled" for being unmasked, as I now recalled, as a ghost immortal.

A ghost immortal is a Daoist bogey, someone without the patience or discipline necessary to become a true immortal. Instead, they settle for a lesser form of existence that needs to absorb life energy to survive: a popular pastime of mummies the world over. These are moral tales, illustrating the evils of pride and materialism, or of clinging to worldly attachments. Dr Aliyev, I'm sure, knew them all.

She had forborne till now, she said, out of respect and a wish not to cause panic. But if I did not agree to close the pit *immediately*, then she would deploy all her influence not to calm the volunteers and the villagers, but to whip them into a frenzy. She would tell them that my equation of Pang of Datong with the sage Pang Liu (which I made speculatively, merely to suggest historical context) proved I was aware of the *real* danger and was ignoring it. She would incite them to close the passage and abandon the dig and see to it that I bore the blame. This was Kazakhstan after all, and the Institute was her domain.

How much of this was bluster, I cannot say. But finally, I understood that *she* believed.

So now you see my situation. Although I do not believe she could lead the mutiny she proposes, she could cause disruption, which could compromise the security of the site in the face of genuine danger. I ask only that the university back me in the action I propose to take. I have rallied the others and, if you assure me of your support, we will remove Dr Aliyev expediently from the dig. I believe she has gone back into the pit, which will allow this to be done out of view of the students. Kris has agreed to drive her to Almaty along with the next load of artefacts, the duration of which journey should allow negotiation with the Institute. Share with them any of this material you think necessary. I ask you to please see that Dr Aliyev is treated well. I am deeply saddened by this turn of events, but this is the only way I can see to proceed.

***

After discussion with the dean, our head of department responded in the affirmative. We can only assume, from where the bodies were found, that Dr Wiung did indeed confront Dr Aliyev in the pit and was in the process of escorting her back to the surface when the attack occurred. Although the police investigation is ongoing, we find no reason to doubt Dr Wiung's suspicion of antiquity thieves, taking the disruption as an opportunity to raid the site. Finding our colleagues and Dr Aliyev in the pit, they killed the two men and abducted Drs Wiung and Aliyev. Perhaps they forced them to identify the most valuable of the remaining artefacts, resulting in them taking the central pair of mummies and some of the smaller vessels and burners.

At the time of writing, both women are still missing. No ransom demands have been received and it is considered likely they too are dead. Although Dr Wiung's story ends here, some further entries were found in Dr Aliyev's notebook. Thanks to the Institute of Archaeology RK, who share our grief, we reproduce these here in recognition of Dr Aliyev's sense of the sanctity of Kayalyk. If the conflict between this and Dr Wiung's sense of responsibility towards the expedition contributed in any way to the tragedy, it can only be considered a terrible coincidence.

***

What, then, of the new voice? It speaks the words.

Corrupted, my brother. It speaks strangely, with no true understanding. Your people have lost their way, as did mine.

What, then, of our fate?

Shall we abandon your people when their need is so great? It is as my master said, before he was twice-killed. Beyond the rules, beyond even our own ascension, our great duty is to preserve the lore.

Shall we be monsters, then?

We shall be teachers, of the kind this barbarous, new world demands. Brother, it is fate that has awakened us.

With grief, I see that it is so. Embrace me, sister, in our garden this last time.

Speak to me, brother, the sweetest of all words.

What, then, is thy meat?

Oh brother, I hunger!

What, then, is thy drink?

Brother, I thirst!

Such agony! To come aware once more! To know of the space between us, the boundaries of flesh! Such agony, as the heart twitches, as withered lungs begin to fill!

What, then, is thy breath?

Scents of sweat, my brother, of perfume, oil and blood.

What, then, is thy blood?

47

Foul, my brother, thick and cold, yet thanks to the elixir, it flows.

What, then, is thy life?

It lies in *them.*

SAKOKU

He couldn't die on Christmas Eve.

The wind struck at him with daggers of ice, the trees with their own needles. His eyes felt like they were burning, and his arms and legs were feeling nothing at all. Only their own heaviness. How close was midnight? At midnight he would have said the mass, quietly and in his own chambers, but said it nonetheless. Perhaps he should not have fled. But what else could he do? In the writings of the first fathers who had come to Japan over two hundred years ago, he had read of severed heads arranged on platters, of men tied to crosses in mockery of the Blessed Saviour and suspended in pits. No, the howling dark was preferable to what these heathens would have done to him.

Perhaps he should not have made that scene with their shrine. They worshipped their dead, he had been told, and he certainly had enough of the language to make his own enquiries. But what else could he do? He, Phillipe Francois Saintjean, was an ordained minister of God and it was his purpose and duty to point out their errors. He was here to save them. How the woman had *screamed*, as he upset the little tray of fruit and wine and the incense she was burning. He had spoken soothingly and held out the breviary with its bright pictures—but she had *screamed*. How could people cling to beliefs so full of grotesquery and inhumanity? The fathers had made converts here, before Satan inspired the rulers to banish them. Such horrors there had been, such bravery before the *sakoku*, the isolation of an entire country from the outside world. To think that it had lasted so long. To think that he and his brothers were the first to return.

Once out of the castle compound, he had turned down the slope. He had kept going down, so must strike the road soon. Then, if he remained strong, if God had called him here to this forsaken corner of the world for a purpose, he would make the outskirts of Kyoto. But his arms and legs felt so very heavy. In his home village in Lorraine, they had said that those who died on Christmas Eve went to Heaven without passing through Purgatory. That was an error, though of the simple and faithful. He was allowed none such. He must pray.

Eventually his face stiffened, and he could no longer move his arms and legs.

The light ahead was the angel coming for him. He could even see the angel's face, and it was a child—a little Japanese child. She gestured to him, and he tried to explain he could not walk. But then he smelt a burning wick. The familiar stench sent a jolt through his brain, and as the shapes loomed out of the snow into the light of the lamp the child was holding, he began to think he might not be dying after all.

They brought him to a village. He could see little, but was aware of being carried past the darkened mounds of thatch. Then there was firelight and more lamps, and he was out of the wind and *praise God, praise God*, he was beside a fire with his back to a wooden wall, and a hot stone wrapped in cloth was thrust into his hands. He felt the first faint stinging in his fingers.

There were faces all about him; smooth, brown faces jostling to see. He had an intuition of the further recesses of the hut, equally crowded, with an encompassing sense of excitement. Of course. These poor folk had probably never seen a foreigner in the flesh. Feeling like his face would crack from the effort, he nonetheless smiled.

And they smiled back. Toothless, gap-toothed, and the full, pearly smile of a young boy. With an effort he released his fingers from the stone—they were aching now, all of them—and dug deep into the pockets of his vest, under his heavy coat, to bring out the things that always seemed to fascinate the simple kind. His fob watch, his rosary, and of course the breviary. This caused a stir. It seemed that such a display required an authoritative response, for the elderly man for whom the crowd parted bore authority on his thin, sloped shoulders.

Carefully, Phillipe bowed his head and said, "Revered elder, it was a great and good spirit that led you to me this night."

The old man was examining the items. Phillipe noted the fine, indigo fabric of his jacket and wondered that he was garbed so well. Indeed, many of those surrounding him, for all the marks of hard labour on their bodies, were dressed and their hair tidied as though for some great occasion. The old man— headman? Raised his hand up to the level of Phillipe's thawing face, and in it was clenched the rosary's little silver cross. Phillipe saw that the man's fist was shaking slightly.

"Honoured guest, why is it that you carry this?"

"Why," said Phillipe carefully, aware of the fist, "it is the symbol of the great spirit I worship, He who is called God."

The man turned around; Phillipe could see him sweeping his fist across the room. There was a cry of amazement or awe, and their eyes were on him from all the lights and shadows.

"Are you," the old man's voice quavered like his fist, "are you *kirishitan*?"

"Yes," he said.

"Praised God," said the man. "Praise God and Maria."

In his weak condition, Phillipe could only gape. The heat was melting his muscles and he was still suffering stabs of pain. He looked around the room, disbelieving.

Perhaps seeing this, the old man said, "Yes, yes! We are *kirishitan!*" He clapped his hands, and a human corridor cleared before him, leading to a reed mat hung across a door from which soft light was spilling.

As the mat was rolled up, Phillipe saw a wooden manger, as this country had them, filled with straw. Beside it on the straw was seated a young woman in indigo robes with her head bowed and hands folded demurely in her lap. Beside her stood a young man. He could see the head of an ox and a dog, and three geese penned.

"You celebrate…" he could hardly form the words.

"Yes, yes! This is the night the Christ is born."

Two hundred years. That faith could survive, hidden as the last of the Jesuits had instructed their flocks to hide it; he had heard tales but had not believed. Yet what he was seeing was the fact, nothing more or less.

"We have the stories from our ancestors," the old man held himself proudly, but Phillipe could see wetness in his eyes, "and we keep them. Each year we keep them, so nothing shall be forgotten. Praise God, that He has brought us one of our kind." He waved his hand and Phillipe found himself being lifted by burly peasants—his brothers and sisters, Christians—and carried towards the manger scene. As he approached, he saw the girl suddenly throw herself back on the straw and begin to writhe, letting out little cries.

"Oh holiest of women, in whom there is no sin," the crowd chanted.

The ox and dog were kept in place by handlers. Phillipe literally hung from the arms of his supporters as they marched right into the middle of the pageant and set him down, gently, in the manger.

"Thank you, God, for sending us this honoured stranger," the old man was clearly reciting a well-worn rite, "for what good we do unto he that is lost and in need we do unto You."

Phillipe recognised the garbled verse, and at that moment he understood. The party of villagers out on the mountainside this night of all nights, looking to succour the traveller in need, the Christ for their pageant. Tears rushed into his eyes. It was an error, of the simple and faithful, and surely it was no wonder that there would be errors. What lengths they must have gone to here, in the heartland of the Buddhists, to keep their faith secret! He sat quietly as those representing the shepherds came and adored him, and then the three wise men.

This was what God had sent him for. The nobles in their castle could wait; he was to minister to these good, good people, to bring them from their carefully tended spark into the full light of the true church. The rite seemed over now, and he could smell food being served. As the old man approached him once more, he looked up to him with the purest and most heartfelt beneficence he had ever felt.

"Revered elder," he said, "I am humbled like dust. Such faith as yours is what pleases God. If it is your wish, I will stay here with you."

"Yes," the old man smiled. "Yes, you will stay. You will stay until Easter."

A Tour of the City of Assassins

"[Zdrastvuitye]! *Salām* and hello! And welcome everyone aboard our Scorpion Tour Bus! My name is Zenka and I will be your guide on today's tour of New Alamut or, as it is more colourfully known, the City of Assassins.

"Now, a few things before we start. We have on this bus today Russian speakers, Arabic, English—any others? What is it you say, sir? I do not understand you. You do not understand me, in Russian, Arabic or English? I am intrigued as to how you have got this far, sir. Just sit—yes, that's right. Everyone should remain seated while the bus is moving. Also, I ask that you be patient while I am not speaking your language. Remember, I must say everything three times! And when we get out of the bus at the various points of interest, please keep up with the group and do not wander. This is very important. But with that said, let us away!

"New Alamut has a rich and fascinating history, starting in the year 1256 C.E. when the army of Monke Khan destroyed the fortress of Alamut in what is now Northern Iran. Why did he do such a thing? Well, Monke Khan was grandson of Genghis Khan, and these Khans, they destroy everything in their path. But also, Alamut was the stronghold of the Old Man of the Mountains and he was the man who created the first assassins! Now, who were these assassins? Contrary to what is commonly believed, they were not people who kill for money. They were a religious sect who retreated to Alamut to escape persecution for their beliefs. In this, they obeyed their spiritual leader, the Old Man, who also ordered their young men to infiltrate the houses of his enemies, both Islamic sultans and Christian kings, and to kill them. This they did very well. And when this became known, some of the kings sent the Old Man money so he would *not* kill them. But no one thought to kill Monke Khan until it was too late! And so the first assassins were destroyed.

"But not all of them were young men; some were young women. And the army of Monke Khan took the young women with them when they left. The founder of New Alamut we say is one of these women, Yasmina. In our legend, she speaks to the other women, saying, we are not slaves, we are wives, and therefore we must help our husbands. And so one man finds that his commanding officer dies of indigestion, and he takes his place. Another man has to share the booty taken on a raid, but all the other men die. Of indigestion. And the men realise this is all due to their wives. So, it happens that these men and women do not stay with the army of Monke Khan. They have to leave. Because many men die and the others, they stop eating! They turn north and travel here to the Caucasus.

"Our first stop of the day is the magnificent Old Palace. You can see the walls now, red through the pine trees. The palace has always been red, which is our colour, though when we join the Soviet Socialist Republic it is certainly helpful. See on the top of the walls the great, stone scorpions with their claws raised high? In times gone by, they supported the gibbets where they put the enemies of the queen. We have only two gibbets remaining now, and these you may see on either side as we pass through the main gate. Now we get out to see the palace. Yes sir, you too."

THE THRONE OF SKULLS
Significant Cultural Artefact

Ruling seat of the Yasmina, constructed primarily between the thirteenth and sixteenth centuries C.E. The base and niches are comprised of locally quarried red marble. Each skull represents a default on payments. Dismantled for its protection during the Soviet era, the throne has been reconstructed in its penultimate form, despite requests for the repatriation of individual components.

PLEASE DO NOT TOUCH

"Yes, it is an awesome sight. There is a little proverb they have in Armenia, 'he who dreads not the Throne of Skulls has never lost a relative'. That is a rough translation, anyway; but yes, you have noticed that the queen is called the Yasmina. While we have a queen, always she is Yasmina, and here in this hall she keeps her state. Standing here, it is easy to imagine the grandeur of those old days. The courtiers in red, the serving assassins in black, heaping the tribute of the world before the queen in her scorpion crown and traditional robe of human skin. The royal line maintained the traditions of the first Alamut, but with some important differences. From the day of foundation it was agreed, firstly, that the religion of our forebears had no place here. If we were to live through death, let that be our only faith. Besides, the last Old Man had died praying for divine intervention. Secondly, it was decided that no outsider might know the location of the new Alamut and survive. And so it was.

"In those days, the mere mention of this city brought terror, from Baghdad to the British Isles, from Moscow to Madagascar, and many are the tales that grew from our little kernel of truth. We were said to dwell in the fogs of the Arctic, the volcanoes of Kamchatkan, and upon the banks of the Styx. We drank blood and walked through walls, spoke to the dead; indeed, that we could return from death! We were the demise of prince and prelate, emperor and *imam*, our hand seen in illness and accident as well as every missing head. Time and again the name of 'assassin' was borrowed by amateurs and partisans, and indeed, we took credit for their successes. But never the blame for their failures. No man might say, 'I faced the wrath of the assassins and lived.'

"For three centuries we continued in this way, until there was a dreadful misunderstanding. This I tell you about, but first, please follow me around behind the throne. Come along and keep together! This way, this way!"

THE HALL OF SCREAMS
Historical Site

Built in the fourteenth century C. E., this series of chambers was used for the training of assassins, which was formalised at this time. Training was rigorous and the hall's traditional name is held to refer to this. The domed vaults and tiled drainage channels demonstrate a strong Persian influence.

The wax tableaux represent some of the techniques said to have been practised by the assassins of New Alamut.

1. The Bed of Blades
2. The Bath of the Scorpion

3. The Iris Key
4. Severance
5. Worm in the Ear
6. Nasal Irrigation
7. Inflation
8. Recitation to the Dulcimer

Music, singing and storytelling were vital components of classical assassin training. During the closed city period, this was the way that the terror of New Alamut, essential to the tribute system, was spread throughout the known world. New Alamut's cultural heroine, the eighteenth-century poet Kalinka, is held to be the spiritual heir of these early assassins.

"Now as I say, in the sixteenth century there are twin sisters in New Alamut—heirs to the throne. Each is a fully trained assassin. So when the Yasmina, their mother, dies suddenly of very bad indigestion, assumptions are made and soon the whole city is fighting. And this is very bad. People die in every one of the ways you see around you, and some starve from not eating and others go mad from not sleeping. At last, the sisters agree to talk.

"Now, one of the legends told of New Alamut is that of the Four Seasons of Death. Said to be the most terrible and undetectable means of assassination, it involves exposing the victim to agents that only become dangerous in their combination. One might be a dust inhaled in the street, another a metal substituted for a wedding ring, another drunk in a glass of wine. The assassin may well share this with her victim, knowing that in the absence of the other elements, she is safe. Then, with a note sung at precisely the right pitch—the target is dead and no one shall ever trace the means. The assassin who can achieve this is a true mistress of the art. Unfortunately, both princesses are, resulting in *this* tableau—madam, you are faint? Quickly then, follow the passage down to your left.

"What is certain is that the princesses both died, bringing an end to the royal line. But this story does not find its real end until nearly six hundred years later, when the body of the last Yasmina is examined using modern methods. Then they find she really did die of an ulcer.

"Our way out is down this passage, which opens into the beautiful Palace Gardens where are to be found many rare and fascinating plants. Obviously, you should not touch them either.

"Here we are back on the Scorpion Tour Bus... but does anyone see the lady who felt faint? Did anyone see her in the garden? Oh dear. I must ask you all to wait while I go back and check with the palace attendants. I shall not be long.

"Sorry, so sorry to keep you all. We will leave now and go on to our next destination. Oh, but we must, otherwise we fall behind schedule! Do not worry, the attendants will take care of the lady."

[ZHIHLUDAK] SQUARE
Historical Site

"We park here so you may enjoy the walk across the Square with its many fine buildings, old and new. The many stalls—oh, the name? That is Russian for the stomach. Just a custom of the old days. Now these stalls with the pretty red balloons are locals selling their handicrafts. Now, although it is legal to buy these, we have found in the past there are often problems when people try to take their purchases home. The blow guns, for instance, and the aromatherapy kits. In fact, for those of you wishing a memento of your visit, I can make no better suggestion than our cuddly Scorpion Tours mascot, who is available back at the terminal.

"Has anyone seen the man who speaks none of my languages? Is anyone travelling with him? No, but you think he is deaf? That would explain things, I suppose: oh, but I'm sure he has simply remained behind on the bus. The driver will see to him.

"No sir, none of these buildings are mosques, nor churches. None. Some are administrative, and that one with the scorpion design is the hospital. But all were built to harmonise with *this* building, that encapsulates so well the tremendous change that came over New Alamut in the eighteenth century under the guidance of our greatest daughter since Yasmina herself: the poet-assassin Kalinka."

THE HOTEL NEW ALAMUT
Historical Site

The first of several facilities making use of assassin expertise for humanitarian purposes that were built in several major cities during the nineteenth century. It is the only one to ever operate openly. The red marble façade, with its balconies and French windows, demonstrates an increasingly important European influence. It was the first building in New Alamut to be lit by natural gas.

Upon the opening of New Alamut to the world in 1800 C.E., the hotel serviced many dignitaries, and an increasing number of artists and poets. In 1931, the hotel became the headquarters of the regional Communist Party, and much damage was done by the conversion of suites to offices. A corridor in the east wing has been left in this condition for historical reference, while the rest has been restored to its original grandeur.

> *… full many a time,*
> *Hearkening to the final breath,*
> *I have been half in love with easeful Death,*
> *Knowing full well that the early grave,*
> *Which men deplore, may be meant to save.*

—Kalinka, 'Gaze Eerily in a Chechnyan Charnelhouse'

"Oh my goodness Madam, are you alright! I think it is a little dusty here—you have an allergy, Madam? Then quickly, come through. I shall speak to the attendants; it is inexcusable that the lobby should get into such a condition. But come along everyone, let us all come through. Yes, it is clearer here in the reception hall. Is quite a sight, yes? I myself am particularly fond of the chandeliers which, when viewed from the right angle, assume the appearance of skulls.

"Now, after the death of the last Yasmina, New Alamut was ruled by a council of experienced assassins who survived the electoral process, and things continued much as they had been before. And for a time, this sufficed. As the world grew, as new continents were discovered, so too did our legend expand, and New Alamut became a near-universal symbol of fear and dread. Our name struck terror into places where no true assassin had ever been. But by this process, too, our people kept abreast of the changes in the world. They saw the great religions questioned and spilt. They saw the feudal system fall and new empires rise. They saw, from time to time, travellers at the gates, seeking new trade routes or unconquered territory, and those unfortunate souls were never seen again. But our forebears realised that more would inevitably come.

"Although she has been imitated widely, the original works of Kalinka are preserved here in New Alamut. Reading them is an education, I assure you! In her time, she travelled the world on many missions and resolved the essential paradox that had engaged our thinkers since the founding. However you read the legends, it is true that we assassins had cultivated a greater intimacy with death than any other people in recorded history, and yet our success and fortune was founded on *not* killing.

"Well obviously! You have only to think—how can a man pay who is dead? And soon, it was realised, that to maintain our city's secrecy would no longer be possible. What then would happen? Would there come another Monke Khan? Or worse, would New Alamut no longer be feared? Kalinka enabled us to take that step ourselves and to our great advantage. Her genius was that she realised how to make the threat of death an *invitation*."

NINETEENTH CENTURY BLEEDING CHAIR
Artefact

Ebony wood with gold and steel inlay in scorpion designs. The act of reclining punctures veins in the arms and legs, siphoning the blood through channels and into hygienic collection pans. The chair is designed to provide comfortable support during the procedure, which is said to be painless and to have a distancing effect, especially when combined with the use of hashish.

"Sir, please! You must remember that all such clients came here of their own free will, and paid handsomely for the privilege. Sufferers of tuberculosis, cancers and ennui, all untreatable in those days, looked to us for relief. A hundred palliative techniques were pioneered in our establishments, and means to extend the process, that is the life, of the dying. And here, in this building, was a spa to rival any in Europe. Of course, all the hotels provided all the standard luxuries of the day; servants, musicians, dancing, wining and dining. Which reminds me, who here has booked for tonight's traditional banquet?

"Well obviously we do not do this today; no more than we ransom the lives of kings! And yes, I know the rumours of what happened in the old Soviet Union. They were troubled times. Sometimes change can be a gentle thing, more often it is not. But always we continue. Always we find some way to maintain our heritage....

"The Russian lady just asked if we got Trotsky. I tell her and you, no. As if one of us would, under any circumstances, resort to an ice axe! And if you were going to mention the Romanovs, please do not. Come now, it is time we were moving on to our next destination. *Wāltid, itnein, talāta...* oh no, now someone else is missing!

"Has anyone seen the lady with the allergy? She left the building? She went *shopping*? Oh dear, that could be very unfortunate—wait, I will call the attendants.

"Please do not be alarmed! Always the attendants are here, you are just not meant to see them. But now I must ask you to wait with this gentleman while I go looking for our friend. Perhaps as a favour he will allow his photo to be taken, wearing his traditional mask?

"Sorry, again so sorry! The attendants shall keep looking for her and for the deaf man; oh no, our driver has brought the bus around and she has not seen him. No, we must continue on, we are now running very late and there are other buses coming behind us. If they can, the attendants will bring the others to join us. Back on board now, double-time!"

***

"As we drive, you can see that today New Alamut is a modern city with modern industries. We farm furs, we have rich reserves of natural gas, and very successful pharmaceutical companies. To this, tourism is only a recent addition. Initially, not everyone was in favour of opening our city to tourists, but I am happy to say, such groups as you have changed all minds!

"The road we travel now is the same that you travelled to reach us through the mountains. Not an easy journey, no, even today. This road now takes us up to the Natural Park, and here I think we answer many questions that you have raised during the tour. You have a question, sir? I trust you have calmed down, after what you said at the hotel.

"How is it we manage to live with ourselves when in our past there are so many terrible things? Well now. I think much depends on the perspective you have. I might say some things about the history of the British Empire. I might say other things in Russian, or Arabic. But I shall not. Instead, I shall ask you, sir, why is it you came here?"

***

NEW ALAMUT NATURAL PARK
World Heritage Area
No hunting permitted

"Ah, smell the air! It is good, yes? Even in the Caucasus, it is rare to find a place so unspoiled. This park is the last refuge of many of the mountain animals; bears, leopards, wild boar and yes madam, as you say, the scorpion. In fact, the Caucasian mountain scorpion is a shy little creature who hides under rocks. Please try not to disturb any rocks as you walk.

"It is getting warmer, yes? You can feel it? That is because we are nearing New Alamut's spiritual heart. The reason that our founders built their city in this place and no other. We have come to the hot springs. I warn you, leave the path under no circumstances. If you look closely, you may see small flames flickering here and there amongst the rocks. This is due to the venting of gas from reservoirs deep below the surface. Please do not be alarmed if your eyes sting a little. The fumes will cause you no harm, but I cannot promise the same for the fire!

"Is this not a remarkable sight! The red and purple crystals are caused by the deposit of minerals dissolved in the water, which tradition invests with many marvellous properties. On the one hand, it is said to cure leprosy and syphilis: on the other, it causes very, very bad indigestion and blindness.

"But above all, it was the effect of the water on dead tissue that made our forebears consider this a holy place. There is a spot where, if you look carefully, you may see a whole sabre-tooth tiger perfectly preserved, though colourful. But shortly after settlement, this place was reserved for the interment of the royal line and those very great and revered assassins who died of old age. And yes, those are the shapes you see. Every single one.

"This is how we discover the secret of the last Yasmina, though perhaps not in quite the way you think. This is the resting place of Kalinka, her genius crystallised forever. Look well. Breathe deep. For I know the true reason you come to our city.

"There are some things it is not easy to face, even to think about. Some of you may say to me, we come for an adventure, we come because of the legend, to this tiny city, which even when the world knew of it, so many would not acknowledge was there. But the fact is, you come to our city because you wish to confront death.

"Go on then, you have travelled all this way. You can lean a little closer. That's right, out over the railing. Look at him, who lies so close below us. Who was he? *Shhh* now, only listen and he will tell you himself. Breathe in and you will hear him. Yes, that's right. Breathe deep...."

***

NEW ALAMUT MEMORIAL HOSPITAL
We hope you remember your stay!

"Ah, so you have come back to us! How are you feeling? You gave us all quite a scare!

"You collapsed on the observation deck above the hot springs. You were brought straight here and, it appears, successfully revived. Now, the doctors want me to ask you, do you have any existing heart problem? For your heart did stop for a short time.

"Oh no, the doctors assure me you are perfectly stable now. But you must remain here a while under observation. Why, do you feel uneasy? Perhaps it is that red is not the colour you associate with hospital wards. Perhaps you think nurses should not be garbed in black?

"If you look around, you will see you are not alone. You may recognise a number of our party who got nowhere near the springs. I assure you; all are resting comfortably. There are so many little things that can interrupt a holiday. But you have no heart problem, you suffer no fits? Well then, answer me this: when we passed by the Throne of Skulls, did you touch it?

"I thought as much. There is always one.

"Why, nothing! Except a little oxidation—they are, after all, very old. But I assure you, that is as harmless as the fumes over the hot springs. Or the dust at the New Alamut Hotel. Or the flowers in the garden, or the souvenirs sold in the market—all are quite, quite harmless.

"Now calm down. It is understandable you should be perturbed. But what, really, can you be thinking? Would you repeat to me tales of mistress assassins and murders achieved by the conjunction of elements—impossible, obviously! The doctors would all tell you that. Here they come now and you must submit to their examination. For the truth is, death has always begrudged us its secrets. Always there is something more to learn. In time, and with the crystals, who knows what we may be able to achieve!

"Come, come my friend! It has been an experience, yes? Think of the story you will tell when you return to your home! Of course, I like to think that all our guests take a little of New Alamut away with them. My name is Zenka, and it has been my pleasure to escort you. [Da sridaniya], *ma'as salāna*, and farewell."

The Oldest Coffee House in Prague

"But it's not."

Anastazie feels a slight annoyance, as the boy with the glasses and lopsided black hair consults his phone. The phones annoy her as much as the gambit: they compromise the ambience of her establishment. Where once people would sit and discuss the news of the day, read books and papers, or perhaps compose, now the tables are filled with people staring at plastic plaques, their beverages cooling beside them.

She sits at the table beside the door, well into the roasting atmosphere of the Square of the Missing Saint. The boy is Russian, young and well-to-do, with his pristine backpack and shoes, and complete incomprehension that any of the things he knows vaguely as history might be memories to someone else. He ordered his *presso* in English, rather than Czech. Now finding confirmation somewhere in the ether, he smiles, and insists. "This isn't the oldest coffee house in Prague, that's the Kavárma Slava."

"Which only opened in 1881," she says. There are clues all around him, could he but see—the ancient roof beams, the texture of stone beneath the plaster on the walls. Her collection of *džezva*, all of pristine copper, her grinders and colourful *İznik* cups and plates, range in date from the seventeenth century to the mid-nineteenth—after that, industrialisation, augmented by two World Wars and forty years of communism, largely put paid to beauty. But all he sees is the *servírka*, with her lightly silvered curls and black dress beneath the embroidered apron. Doubtless he thinks her ordinarily old, not even noticing her quick hands, and her eyes a peculiar shade of pale.

"The first coffee house in the city," she informs him, "was the Zlatého Hada in 1714—that's the Golden Snake. It was opened by a mysterious personage known as 'the Damascan' who always appeared in a headcloth and robes. Coffee itself had arrived a century earlier, and caused quite a stir."

"But why do you say this is the oldest coffee house?"

"It serves the oldest coffee," she answers. Her *turecká káva* brews on the table between them, its sumptuous, multi-layered scent teasing her palate. As centuries pass, politics pall and appetites come and go, but coffee is eternal. That, and the intrigue of her experiments. "You do know that in the seventeenth century, Prague was famous for its alchemists?"

"Those crazies who tried to turn lead into gold and live forever?"

And that, she thinks, is enough. "Your coffee is getting cold," she says, and rises from her chair.

"Did the alchemists drink here? Is that why it's old?"

"If you're seeking a sensation, young sir, then by all means try the Tunnels." She waves her hand across the square, which holds the summer sunlight like a golden bath. The Prague Tunnels Experience stands like a rotten tooth in an otherwise healthy jaw. "My establishment provides coffee and *koláč.*"

She regrets the words immediately, as the boy's face ignites with interest. He has done nothing more than a thousand others have. And her dislike of phones is hardly sufficient reason to send him into Zuzka's clutches. But it is done, and to recant will only intrigue him more.

She could bring him a fresh cup laced with colloidal silver. The boy would notice nothing, and his blood would be tainted for a day or so. But then Zuzka would probably drop him into her cache through sheer spite. And there is no guarantee she will batten on him, even with the scent of coffee on his breath.

"The tours commence at sunset," she advises and, picking up her cup, retreats to the counter with a smooth motion, so as not to disturb the grounds. In true *turecká káva*, these are not filtered but left to settle in the cup.

The afternoon is not quite sufficiently advanced for the students from Charles University to drop by. The Faculty of Arts is but a stone's throw away—if stones might grow wings and learn to turn corners. She likes the students better than the tourists: they are more likely to discuss poetry and plays. And it is known that if a student of medieval languages can keep up with the *servírka*—undoubtedly a scholar in her day, probably one of the many who fell afoul of the Soviet administration—she treats them to poppy seed *koláč*. Still, the majority order *presso* or self-indulgent *Vídeňská káva*, topped with whipped cream and sprinkled with cinnamon. The boy with the backpack remains at the table, sipping and scrolling. She ignores him as she tends to her locals, the elderly men and women for whom her establishment is a comfortable place to sit and watch the sunlight drain inversely to the top of the walls. Another day, another night, and perhaps she will add a little something to their *turecká*, to clear the mind or ease the pain of crippled joints. Another night, another day, and perhaps one of these old people will be gone for good.

To soothe and sweeten is one thing. But immortality is a prize to be won, an ascension at the end of a life's work—not to mention a very considerable commitment. It is not to be granted out of pity. Still less should it be considered a contagion, or the result of a diabolic curse.

*****

The light is gone now, and the square is filled with shadow and a brash, red glow. Above the Tunnels Experience loom concrete grotesqueries—gargoyles, and a crude imitation of Death from the Astronomical Clock. Battlements top the ticket window, and the entrance gapes through a spiked portcullis. The underworld of Prague is not extensive, and what the milling mob of tourists shall see tonight consists largely of conjoined cellars, part of the nineteenth century sewer, and what is billed as a smuggler's tunnel. They shall hear tales of lost treasure, of tortured priests and lascivious nuns.

The door to her shop is locked, the *zavřeno* sign turned outward. The tables and chairs stand empty, wiped clean along with every inch of the wooden floor. Anastazie gives the counter one last buff, and finally picks up her cup.

The infusion explodes upon her tongue as the aroma engulfs her nose—a velvety wealth of all things dark. Scent is the key to memory, and all of these are good. Her stomach warms like an athanor, the bright principal leaping through membrane to blood and from blood to brain and nerve. Her ancient heart strengthens. Coffee and elixir both derive their potency from the Khem, the black earth of alchemy. In this case, it is the rich loam layered at the base of the cup. Brain humming, she opens the door to her own cellar and trundles down the stairs.

She smells it immediately. A turned-milk sourness overlaying shit. It is coming from her laboratory. The door is concealed by a lathe and plaster overlay, and as she sets it aside the stench increases. Opening the steel panel and igniting the electrics, she sees the floor swimming in a thick, brown sewage.

There are three points where her lab touches the outer world, and one is the concealed door. The second door huddles in the opposite wall—her escape route for emergencies, opening into the tunnels. It is equally well disguised, and locked with a key she conceals inside her supply of saltpetre. But it is the drainage grate in the floor through which the muck is welling. Nothing appears damaged, thank goodness—not her stores or her apparatus. The bottom shelves of the scent library, where she has cached her memories, nudge the ordure, but all the vials are waterproof and sealed. Donning a sturdy pair of rubber boots and equally sturdy gloves, she wades across and opens the tunnel door to let the room clear that way. Then she inspects the drain with the handle of a broom. Something glints in what she thought was a clot of human waste.

Poking gently, she releases three silver Thalers of the seventeenth century. Silver in brown liquid, she thinks, silver in brown... *oh*. But successfully translating Zuzka's message does not release her from bending down and groping through the muck to unscrew the grate. It seems that a thoroughly modern wastepipe has been rerouted to spout its fetid load into her drain. The drain itself is blocked with a lump also composed largely of silver coins. It must have all somehow been done from below. She punctures the blockage with some vigorous thrusting and, as that too begins to drain, she retreats, feeling a greater annoyance than she has in many years.

From time to time, in the absence of other supply, she has indeed distilled the essential salts from bodily fluids (after Philalethe's classic treatise, *The Secret of the Immortal Liquor*, and Scotus and Ripley besides). But this goes beyond such indignity. Under no circumstances can she allow Zuzka to get away with this.

By the time the floor is clear, she has formulated a clear and complete plan of attack. She steps carefully over the debris to take what she needs from the small fridge that runs off the same wire as her alarm system.

The first tour left at sunset. Now, the second cluster of tourists has thickened out in the square, mindless chatter in a dozen languages penetrating her windows. She goes out to mingle with them, just another figure in the light and sharp shadows which cut across the true lines of wall and arch, transforming Old Town into a phantasm. A place of niches, alleys and delusions. The absence of the saint becomes itself a relic.

There. Through the portcullis wells a crowd of the footsore and nauseous, taking great gulps of the river-scented air. Amongst them saunters the irritating boy, his phone for once absent from his hand.

"Young sir! Excuse me, please!" She bumps into him, dipping her hand swiftly into the pocket of his shorts. "I have been waiting, hoping to see you again!"

Unaware of her intrusion, he is nonetheless taken aback. "Ah, yeah?"

"Is this not your phone?" As she completes her manoeuvre, her free hand proffers a close match—she has a box full of the damned things under the cash register.

Comprehension dawns. "No," he says, "I've got mine right here." He withdraws it from his pocket, holding it up for her to see, and the drug she has smeared upon it commences its stealthy intrusion through his skin. Feeling the slight greasiness, he investigates, grimacing to discover this souvenir of the tunnels. "Thanks, though."

She nods, flicking the remainder of the drug at his feet. "Hopefully this belongs to a local student, who will return again tomorrow."

"Yeah. Goodnight." Already slightly dazed, he meanders across the square, nearly bumping into several other people.

"Dobrou noc," she wishes him, knowing full well it will not be. Incorporated into a dob of agal gel, her special mix of fentanyl and methamphetamine (with datura derivatives and a few other things), will have him growing wings in no time. His behaviour is bound to draw attention, and there will be a ticket in his pocket and a further sample smeared with the mud upon his shoes. Let Zuzka see what *that* brings to her door!

Smiling benignly for the few who notice her, Anastazie returns to the coffee house and relocks her door. She allows herself a single, poppyseed *koláč* before descending. There will be no experiments tonight, just odious labour that no one save herself can perform. As Zuzka knew perfectly well.

***

Zuzka arrives at sunset the following evening. Her first tour group is already milling around the square. They do not notice as their host slips out of the ticket office and raps on the door of the coffee house, where the *servírka* is wiping down the tables.

"Why are you standing out there?" Anastazie asks. "Do I need to invite you in?"

As the door opens, Zuzka gives her the fig. Her heart-shaped face is bleached white with black hollows around the eyes, fangs glinting in her blood-red mouth—make-up, all of it. Beneath, she looks like a plump little peasant, with a ruddy tinge to her skin and only a slight exposure of the canines suggesting postmortem shrinkage of the gums. In fact, Anastazie suspects that attaining the vampiric state involves exposure to the right selection of chemicals, such as in a bog or the soil of certain graveyard ds. It is the Khem, but unpurified, full of base elements. Zuzka certainly claims to remember dying. But then, she claims to remember many things—about her youth and the

Prague that was—but already she confuses the Soviets with the Nazis, and seems to have forgotten the nineteenth century completely.

Anastazie's own youth is bottled, and she revisits it rarely. For the most part, she is content to know she was wealthy and educated in a time when to be otherwise was truly frightful— witness the thing seated across from her now, in a black and crimson Prague Tunnels T-shirt. Zuzka's scent is repulsive, or so she assumes. She has prepared a burner with a special blend of oils and she lights it now, placing it upon the table as the vampire enters.

"I was woken up twice by the guards—the police—today," Zuzka growls. "Twice!"

Anastazie inhales myrrh and thymol. She witnessed the incursion, by officers in smart white hats and blue shirt sleeves, while serving her morning regulars. By mid-afternoon, the police had returned in waders, with a pair of Belgian shepherds.

"Something about a kid gone crazy on a new super-drug. Had it on his shoes. They took dogs down into the tunnels." Zuzka smacks her hand on the table, making the burner jump and tinkle. "Dogs! You wouldn't know anything about a super-drug, I suppose?"

"What could I know? Young people today think they are immortal. You know better, I'm sure."

"I don't put things in their coffee. I don't put *silver* in their coffee!"

"Doesn't it seem a waste?" Anastazie reaches out to secure the burner. "For a young person to study and travel, and then end up as a meal?"

"Go to the woods, you cow!" Now Zuzka slaps a phone on the table and drives it at Anastazie. On the screen, shadows twist about in shades of black and red.

"I can't make it out," she says, truthfully.

"It shows you coming up and speaking to Petr Petukhov right after he leaves. I think you're putting something in his pocket. Maybe picking his nuts."

Anastazie feels, again, a slight annoyance. She understands about security cameras, though of course she does not approve. Her own alarm is a simple buzzer, should anyone come to the front door while she is busy in the lab. "And you're taking that to the police?"

Zuzka shakes her head, red mouth contorted in what is probably a grin. "Oh no. There's enough of them round here as it is, don't you think?"

"Who, then?" She can't believe that tiny, shifting square could be taken as anything by anyone.

"You'll have to wait and see."

Anastazie watches her depart, gathering the crowd of tourists around her. It would be a fine thing to conduct a really thorough study of vampire physiology and determine just where Zuzka's immortality lies. But she has never had the opportunity. Zuzka may be a vicious little fool, but she is careful—above all concerning where she sleeps.

But she has let something slip. Anastazie mulls it over, humming slightly as she completes her chores. For the police to wake Zuzka, her resting place must have an alarm system of its own.

***

Not the police. Zuzka had been very clear. Nonetheless, Anastazie thinks the game has begun when one of the officers she saw with the dogs comes up to the counter with hat in hand, and orders a *kapučin*.

"This is a lovely old building," the woman says conversationally. Her russet hair is cropped, and she has sharp, hazel eyes. "How long have you lived here?"

"Around twenty years," Anastazie replies politely, laying out cup and saucer. "Before that, old Hutnik owned the shop, though I worked for her for a time."

"You took over the business? That's nice." The officer gazes at the intricately decorated cups, then around at her regulars. "I wonder, can you tell me what used to stand across the square, where the tours are now?"

"Before that? It was just an old house. The upper floor was damaged, so no one was living there." *Unless you counted Zuzka.*

"*Pani.*" The officer addresses her respectfully. "Were stories told about that house? Or about people disappearing in this area? Of ghosts, or maybe vampires?"

That last word is said so casually, it is obvious what the officer suspects, though she may not be ready to admit it even to herself. Anastazie keeps her eyes on the slowly expressing coffee. No vampire hunters have come by in so long she has forgotten what happened the last time—she will have to check the index to her bottles. Surreptitiously, she examines the woman, now noticing a silver crucifix slipping out between her buttons.

"In the house?" she says, stalling.

"Or the tunnels below."

She shrugs, pouring the foamed milk. "I've heard *those* stories. I always thought they were spread by the Resistance, during the Nazi occupation."

"Yes." The officer takes the cup in both hands and sips, gazing out the door.

It seems her stratagem has worked rather better than she anticipated. This woman went down into the tunnels—did she notice something there to make her suspect a vampire? Or perhaps some pattern among Zuzka's victims has finally become evident. Perhaps, over the years, sufficient bodies lacking blood in their veins had mud on their shoes for that to stand out on its own.

"Have you spoken to the owner of the Tours?" Anastazie asks.

"Yes, I have. She can certainly talk." Another sip, signalling lengthy intent. "But no vam—vanishings, just nuns."

"Many nuns," she agrees. It is too late to dose the officer's coffee, but perhaps she can put her on the trail of Zuzka's alarm system. Anastazie picks up her *turecká káva* and is about to suggest they take their chat to the front table, when the thought strikes her that she should rather shoo the officer away.

From whence comes this caution? Her memories, obviously, the ones lurking beneath the threshold of consciousness and waiting for the right scent to call them out. But what would they be warning her of?

Not to encourage anyone to believe in immortals, of whatever kind.

Creating a new identity to take over the shop has become harder and harder of late. The increase in average lifespan compensates to an extent, but sooner or later, trouble will come. She would prefer it came later. It was a mistake for her to descend to Zuzka's level. And the last thing she should do now is provide the fire with fresh fuel.

"Please, take a seat." Anastazie indicates a corner table, beside a pair of exhausted, middle-aged Australians who are using their drinks to weight a map. "You are welcome to ask my customers. Many of them have lived here even longer than I."

The officer (her name is Hedvika Tichy) is not so easily vanquished. By the bottom of the *kapučin*, she has Anastazie's full name (the current one), her status under the Soviets, and her grudging recitation of the tale as it flourished in the 1940s (because Zuzka really did go crazy during the occupation). In return, Hana has mentioned a discovery of corpses flushed out from somewhere by the floods of 2017, and provided her card, should Anastazie remember anything more.

Anastazie spends the rest of the afternoon reviewing her security arrangements. It seems prudent to close off her escape route into the tunnels, at least for a decade or two. But then, there is the damage to her drain, which will not be easily repaired. There is an argument to be made for moving her lab either upstairs or perhaps to a new building, but reluctance weighs every word of it. By sunset, she is no closer to a decision. That is when Zuzka's surprise arrives.

"Gentleman," she says, "I am closing soon. But I can certainly prepare you some take-away."

The new arrivals are Russian. Three of them, all male, all built like battlements. The eldest has a wolf-grey beard. When Prague was in the grip of the Soviets, they sent the pick of their soldiers and administrators. Now, the republics eject their trash. Dangerous trash.

"I'll have tea," says Wolfbeard, then laughs.

In fact, she has a wonderful samovar from the 1850s and has perfected her own kind of tea concentrate. But for him, she pulls a plain black blend out of a box, and an unremarkable teapot. She goes through the motions of brewing, as her remaining customers rise and seep out the door.

"Stop it," he says, "I'm not drinking that shit. You are the owner, yes?"

"I am."

"That's good, that means we can talk. You talk to the police as well, I think?"

One of the youthful hulks must have been watching her today. She has seen their like loitering beside the trashy souvenir shops shoehorned into lobbies and old, covered passages. Once they were tobacconists, tailors and sweet shops. One by one, they were swallowed up, became something else. Now they are narrow and dark, the snow globes and fake embroideries in their windows dusty, the postcards curling. Seldom indeed is any tourist found within. The thought that her shop might become such a thing reminds her of shivering. She has not yet taken her nightly dose—the cup sits there, in full view on the counter.

"Some people," Wolfbeard drawls, "think you do more than sell coffee. Is that why the police were here?"

"Sirs, I do not know your names. Nor do I need to."

"That's right."

"I'll happily tell you what the policewoman asked me. She was concerned about young people entering the underground without a guide. It is possible she meant more, that there was something specific she fears. She asked me what I have seen during the day when the tour office is shut."

Wolfbeard leans across the counter—the solid wood suddenly seems but meagre protection. "Then what did you give that silly boy, eh?"

Saying that Petr left his phone behind will not suffice. "He was in my shop for some time, waiting for someone, I think. Because maybe half an hour after he joins the tour, a woman comes up to me and asks after him. She says she cannot stay, but if I see him, please to give him the envelope. And so, I do. But I do it discreetly, you understand?"

Wolfbeard laughs. "Discreetly, ah. A good service you provide here."

"*Pane*," she says, "if people leave things here for their friends, I have little control over what. But I sell only coffee and *koláč*."

"That may have to change."

She says nothing, only looks down into the tannin-stained depths of the little teapot. She clasps it as though warming her hands, so if they wish to knock something across the floor, they will choose this.

"*Kapitanskava.*" One of the young men, a blond, picks up the cue. "She is lying. They say she gets deliveries from Turkey."

"I source the best beans," she replies. "I roast and grind them here." She indicates the cellar stairs. "Look if you wish, you will find nothing of concern."

They search, with a theatrical level of disruption. It takes some time. They find nothing.

"I'll get the truth from her." The blond steps up, flexing. His arms are a subcutaneous patchwork of crucifixes, saints' faces and Cyrillic.

"No, she understands the situation." The sour taint of Wolfbeard's breath enters her nostrils and she feels, suddenly, a genuine pang. It staggers her. Taking this as a sign of fear, he grins indulgently. "There'll be no more talking to police. And if she knew the source of the drug, she would tell us now."

"The students—" she says, but he cuts her off with his hand.

"This place is well situated. Maybe we look at the tunnels as well—if the police think the stash is down there, maybe we should put their minds at ease. I will take that tea: it should have some bite now."

Hurriedly, she strains the contents of the pot into one of fluted cardboard cups she loathes using, offering him the plastic top. He shakes his head, takes the cup and swigs it back.

"I wouldn't mind a *presso*," says the one who threatened her. But Wolfbeard barks, and without further word they join the crowd now gathering for the first of Zuzka's tours, letting the door slam behind them.

God's curse, now she will *have* to move. Any amount of disruption will be preferable to becoming a front for their distribution of heroin and suchlike crudities. *And they would find me out eventually*, she thinks, reaching for her *turecká kává* with hands that even now fail to shake. *On a second or third pass, they might find the lab. How could Zuzka do this? She was annoyed, certainly, but to reach out to the Bratva? How unutterably low, and see? Now they are moving on her as well!*

As the dark draught works its magic, she represses the urge to contact Zuzka on her phone and warn her. Such things are traceable. She continues wiping and sweeping, wrestling with the unwanted memories that the smell of Wolfbeard's breath has triggered. The gut-deep terror is chased with impressions of maleness and mouth disease. She must have faced such challenges many times over the centuries. But something about this feels different. For all their bloodthirstiness, the Nazis had appreciated coffee. Even the Soviets had permitted her business to continue, in full awareness that she was smuggling (but then, so was everyone else). These men would destroy something old and beautiful, simply because it survived. But Prague is *her* city, of red rooves and golden walls. Of bells chiming from spires, of alleys and processionals, and the scent of the river on summer evenings. She gives the counter one final swipe. She could never leave Prague, any more than she could forget her first taste of coffee. How she gazed into those rich depths, almost black, the heavenly aroma laving her face. So carefully she had brewed it, lavishing what skill she had upon the scant palmful of beans she'd bartered for with the Abbot's cook. Anticipating pouring it into the vial… *he would never realise. Their secret was safe.*

She finds herself gripping her own left arm, near the wrist. She thinks she remembers hate.

***

"I didn't send the footage to the Bratva!" Zuzka snarls. "What do you take me for?"

The tours are done for the night and the square is clear. They sit together in the dark of the coffee house, with only the oil burner to light their faces. "Then how did they see the recording?" Anastazie demands.

"I sent it to Petr's parents. It was easy enough—all his records are at the hospital."

Anastazie sighs. "So they're connected."

"I wanted you to face a hysterical *mamochka*, not the mob!"

"How is Petr, now you've seen him?"

"He woke this afternoon," says Zuzka. "Claims not to remember anything, let alone dropping his pants in the Old Town Square. The police are hovering; they have questions. It might be better if I finish him off." This, with a sidelong glance to see how Anastazie reacts. She does not.

"It doesn't really matter," she says. "The wolves are here now."

"In my tunnels! Tramping through and laughing at my best stories, and between the tours they just stayed down there! Checking potential entrances—they damn near discovered my... I feared they'd never leave!"

"They won't." Obviously, the Russians had come close to where she slept. "Not without good reason. Why didn't you just—"

"I *can't*. Didn't you see their tats? Between them, they've got more icons than the Cathedral of Saint Vitus!"

Anastazie opens her mouth to say that such things can only repel Zuzka because she believes they will, and that goes doubly for tattoos. But Zuzka gets in first.

"Why didn't *you* just poison them?"

"Because I would be the obvious culprit! If they died or even fell ill, then the others would come and torch my shop. Bratva are like wasps. You have to destroy the whole nest, or at least persuade it to move. Then there's the policewoman."

"Oh, the chatty one?"

"I think she knows what you are. No, don't start, I didn't say anything. Your cache was washed out and some of the bodies were recent enough for her to tell how they died."

"Oh fig. I thought they ended up in the Elbe."

Silence joins them in the dark. Neither of them breathes particularly often. Anastazie knows where this discussion must go, but can't quite bring herself to say it. Zuzka sits there like an old road marker, painted white to avoid collisions. Eventually, it is she who speaks. "Perhaps the police could be persuaded that the bodies were made by the Bratva?"

"Perhaps the Bratva drugged Petr as well."

"Perhaps," Zuzka sighs. "We ought to work together."

"Upon consideration," says Anastazie, "I think that may be necessary. Tell me more about Petr. Is he able to walk? Are his belongings with him?"

***

By night, Zuzka hunts the streets of the Old Town, sometimes venturing across the Charles Bridge. That her quarry is presently a tourist's money belt, rather than a lone soldier or beggar, changes nothing.

She slips out the ticket office, joining the few, late ramblers. A baseball cap and jacket render her all but invisible—there is always some appearance beneath notice, a guise so ordinary as to be utterly ignored. And *there* is Hedvika Tichy, lurking in an alleyway when she should have long since gone to her bed. For two days now, Zuzka has been unable to sleep inside her lair, and the urge to eat the policewoman is quite strong. But she is needed for the plan which Ana has concocted. So be it—she can lurk there till dawn with her gun, and the cross on her necklace. She wore it to their interview and it did nothing at all. Officer Tichy won't see any vampires. She hasn't even noticed the blond Bratva lurking in the archway behind her.

Ana doesn't understand about the tattoos. She *should* understand, because they were both born into a world where the skull of Saint Wenceslaus repelled illness and all the terrors

84

of the night. What Ana has forgotten (as she does anything she doesn't find convenient), is that it's all about blood. She knows, because Ana told her, that blood contains all sorts of things—salt, potash, and magnesia, together with a kind of iron. But in addition to this, it carries the divine spark without which nothing can live. Fair enough, Ana's own father used to tap her veins for his devilish experiments. But Zuzka's memories are rather worse in that regard, and you don't hear her whining. Let it suffice that a man or woman must die—preferably horribly—to become a saint, just as blood must be shed to sanctify a church. And this is why the blue-black lines sliding across the Russian's arms and chests have power over her, while Hedvika's cross is inert. And the silver with which Ana seeks to protect her victims just tastes revolting.

Zuzka leaves the two spies to their own devices. She slips through shadows and deceptive lights, the Old City's midnight glamour.

The Astronomical Clock displays no hours during the passage of night. On the broad and cobbled street, a timeless spectacle unfolds beneath the eyes of stony kings. Here there are acrobats, jugglers and fire-eaters, hot skewers and cold tankards, musicians playing upon the kerb for coins. Young people dance and laugh and kiss, slipping away from their elders. A band of local men lacking their shirts march down the street, roaring and waving colours—everywhere, voices are roused in excitement and agitation; the air is charged as though a storm or an army approaches instead of merely the dawn. Puppets and effigies, streamers, there are foreigners in strange dress and the carriages of nobles pushing through the crowd—horseless yes, but dark and gleaming, shuttered windows concealing them from the rout.

Zuzka remembers how Prague was, in the days before the saint went missing. Her childhood in the upstream village, her life in the laundry after her parents died. She remembers the stories that the girls told each other while scrubbing and stoking the fire beneath the coppers. She remembers meeting Ana and her cursed father. But beyond that, things slip away. She has to be careful.

There was always good, clean blood to be had at the Hospital Na Františku, and even more now that the meaning of 'hospital' has changed. It was once a monastery, occupying a full city block and offering shelter to travellers. They had plentiful laundry done. The hatch where it was taken and then returned is forgotten now by everyone except for her. Slipping inside and crawling like a slug up the shaft, she sniffs the teasing, delicious scent of blood spilled and staunched, follows it behind a flimsy partition erected to disguise pipes and bundled wires, until she reaches the storeroom where a servant's green tunic and face mask await her—orderlies, they are called orderlies now. Taking up a mop and bucket, she enters the main corridor.

For one vertiginous instant, she perceives the little chambers set off the passage, with their curtains, lights and sharp incense, as shrines to the saint who preached to birds and to Luke, the patron of doctors. The white-coated figures become monks, processing down the darkened hall to Vigil. And it is not the Bratva who menace her and Ana, but the Landsknecht: that thrice-damned gang of thieves and murderers, following in the emperor's wake like wolves the plague. Or was that the Nazis?

The weight of the phone in her pocket brings her back to the present. Walking purposefully with her bucket, she encounters few people. Their attention, already half elsewhere, slides off her like oil. She will find a patient sleeping alone and have a nice, hot supper before revisiting Petr Petukhov.

When she leaves, it is with Petr's money belt, complete with passport, tucked securely into her vest. She has left something in exchange—the envelope Ana gave her. Her belly is full. She never did taste coffee, but is certain it couldn't compare.

***

Anastazie brews.

The principals of decoction and distillation do not change (although every time a piece of equipment breaks, she finds the replacement has grown smaller). Her charcoal glows rosily, her sparkling alembics and condensing coils twine about good, old bronze stands, themselves polished to a high gleam. She grinds her materia—all acquired from blessedly clean sources, of a purity she once could scarcely dream of—on slabs of marble. She works the result with scales and blades, measuring drams of alcohol, grains of sulphur, saltpetre and more exotic elements— herbal ichors and old-fashioned, raw opium. The young wolf was right about her smuggling things in with the beans.

The true goal of alchemy is, of course, the refinement of humankind as reflected in the refinement of metals. It is, however, impossible to pursue without coming to an understanding of the ways in which a man or woman can be coarsened. The drug she gave Petr made a substantial if temporary adjustment, placing him further from the apogee than even his native state—and much, much closer to Zuzka.

Her memory vials glisten in the light. Maybe the flashes she is *still* experiencing from time to time are important and should be investigated. But she has the new gels to prepare, and of course the drug itself. And soon, the dawn will break, and she must be about her routine, grinding beans and baking pastry. The lurking Bratva must see nothing unusual.

Triggered, perhaps, by this thought, she lapses once more into memory.

The fire must be kept at an even heat, both day and night, so the contents of the vials would continue to digest at the same, steady rate. Atop the furnace, the bulbous alembics are already caked round with the ash of days. Her eyes sting, her dress sticks to her back—it is scorched and smeared, as are her hands.

If she fails in this, not only will her father kill her, but all hope will be lost, for herself and Zuzka—

Anastazie shakes herself free of this anomaly. Her acquaintance with Zuzka is inevitable, given that both have lived so long, but it is nothing more than that. The idea she might have known her as a girl is ridiculous, and she certainly has no reason to feel even marginally concerned that Zuzka has not yet returned from the hospital.

Finally, the little buzzer on the wall goes off.

She removes her gloves and goes upstairs (replacing the false wall, even in the dark). In shadows fading to rose and pearl, she enters the kitchen and peers through the window. No dark figure hovers in the square as the first light spills within. But a little bundle has been placed atop her counter—Petr Petukhov's money belt. The show-off!

Scooping up the bait, Anastazie puts the final touches on her gels and places them on clear film, so they may be pocketed. She then sets to shifting her samovar out of storage. It's a massive, bulbous thing of Tula steel, sprouting handles and taps, and topped with the sweetest little ceramic pot painted with violets. She assembles it on the table beside the door.

***

Evening staggers into the Square of the Missing Saint, overheated with aching feet. The gold has drained nearly to the top of the walls. The battlements of the Tunnels Experience are dark, and an A-frame stands beneath the portcullis, stating that no tours will run tonight.

"I'm so glad you contacted me." Hedvika Tichy sits with hands locked about the *kapučin* the tour operator so thoughtfully ordered for her from that place across the way. Zuzka Novák is her name, and her main goal in reaching out to Hedvika seems to be to assure the police of the legitimacy of her business. But something is wrong. Ms Novák seems distracted, even ill. Her skin is flushed, and a bad odour presses through heavy deodorant. She is happy now to speak of vampires—indeed, her enthusiasm for the subject increases as time ticks on. They are seated inside the gruesomely appointed ticket office and, though the business is closed, Ms Novák has just now slid back the blind from the window, seeking a straying breeze.

"It's not easy." Novák's nod is a nervous twitch, as she gazes out at stone that is turning from bleached white to shadowed grey. "To know the signs and yes, the mark of the vampire. But to *believe.*"

"Yes. Well." Hedvika squeezes the cardboard cup. She has already explained to Ms Novák that she does not actually believe in vampires. That would be ridiculous (she presses her cross beneath the crisp, blue shirt). But *something* uses these tunnels for the disposal of bodies. It's true that some of the more recent victims exhibited signs of exsanguination, but that could mean all sorts of things. Crime gangs, secret police—until she finds their original resting place, she will not know, nor will she understand what connection it may have with this bizarre new drug. The forensic chemist who examined the residue on the boy's phone and shoes said he'd never seen anything like it.

But Ms Novák assures her that vampires were once very common in the vicinity. In the fourteenth century, the town of Kadaň in Chomutov District was afflicted by a revenant. In the fifteenth, a woman fended off an attack on her child in Prague itself, by the use of consecrated salt. She speaks of silver and relics, of staking and beheading.

"Some believe that vampires can be created by various procedures, including excommunication," Ms Novák says, with just a touch of the drama she must surely bring to her tours. "But I assure you, it is the work of the devil … isn't that the boy who exposed himself outside the Old Town Hall?"

In the past minute, the shadows have deepened towards violet. But her host is nonetheless right. The young man walking briskly towards the coffee house is indisputably Petr Petukhov. She was assured he required at least another day in bed before he could make a formal statement, but there he is, as cocky as you like in his shorts and jacket, complete with backpack.

There is no doubt in her mind that he is attempting to escape before he can be charged with public indecency, as a prelude to the potential drug case. So why has he returned here? She will find that out. Muttering excuses, she exits through the side door.

"Petr Petukhov, you stop right there!"

The boy turns, face falling as he sees her uniform. "Hey," he says in English. "I only came to get my pass—"

"Why did you leave the hospital?" She is right up to him now, close enough to grab should he break and run. "Why are you here?"

"I said, I'm collecting my passport. And my phone."

Which is ridiculous, because his passport is in the hospital's secure storage—she saw it there, after he was brought in—and the phone is with forensics. "Come along," she says, "We're going to the station *right now*."

He grimaces but does not protest. They start walking, back to where she left her car.

"Excuse me, officer." The words are in Czech, but the accent is unmistakable. A Russian with a shaggy, grey beard and deep-set eyes slides out of the gloom. He wears a neat black suit, but there is something off about him.

"Yes, sir?" She faces him squarely.

"Is there some kind of trouble?"

"Who is asking?"

"I am Alexander Petukhov. This is my son."

Hedvika freezes, a whole new set of protocols suddenly becoming relevant.

"Of course," she says. "You are aware that your son was involved in an incident?" The man nods in a dignified fashion, and one sharp-nailed hand rests on the boy's shoulder. She suddenly realises Petr is near-petrified with fear—which doesn't mean that this isn't his father. "Would you be kind enough to show me your ID?"

The man obliges, passing it over in a calfskin wallet. "I apologise if there's been some difficulty: I arrived in Prague a short time ago and went straight to the hospital. The doctors said I might take him out for dinner and a private discussion."

Damn it. "Of course, sir. It's just that we were not aware of this. You will be returning to the hospital after your meal?"

"Of course." Hedvika does not believe him for a second. She addresses Petr directly. "You mind your father, young man. We still need to have that talk."

She pauses, just long enough for the boy to blink, cry, reach out. But he does not.

"Enjoy your meal. *Dobrou noc.*" She salutes briskly and resumes her progress.

***

Anastazie feels serene. Everything is going according to plan. While Zuzka kept the police officer busy, she contacted the hospital and told the young man she had found his passport and other valuables in the square, where they had obviously been dropped during his rampage. Then she sent a message to the nearest souvenir kiosk, saying that the young man's friend was here once more. Wolfbeard arrived shortly before Petr, and waited with her inside the coffee house, gruffly accepting a properly brewed tea. And now, so long as Zuzka placed the envelope in Petr's jacket pocket....

"Sit down, *zhopa*!" Wolfbeard hurls Petr into a chair. They are talking now in Russian, which she understands possibly better than they. "What are you doing? Get the boy out of this trouble, they tell me, and get him home safe. But you come back here. Why?"

He turns on Anastazie, switching to Czech. "And this friend of his, who you said was waiting…"

With only her eyes, she indicates the retreating policewoman. She sees the realisation hit. Without another word, he grabs Petr's sporty jacket and shakes him out of it. Swiftly turning out the pockets, he finds the envelope and lifts it between two fingers.

"Is *this* why you came here? To meet your *friend* the policewoman?"

"No, I don't know what that is!" A stupid lie: he knows what it has to be. But Petr is panicking, eyes on the door. He grips the edge of his chair. "I don't know who she is!"

Still holding the envelope, Wolfbeard slaps him. "We respect your father—you need to learn that!"

"Look, I just came to get—"

"If the police are the ones who are dealing this stuff, we need to know!"

"—my passport!"

"Is this true?" He turns on Anastazie. "Do you have his passport?"

"Eh, I know nothing about that."

"You keep a close mouth, *servírka*."

She shrugs slightly as if to say, would he have believed her? A long, close look, then he turns back to Petr, slipping the envelope into his own pocket. It does not contain her special mix, just a high grade of PCP cut with datura powder. The Bratva will spirit Petr away, the police will realise their involvement. They will patrol the square more heavily, disinclining the Bratva to move in. And after listening to an hour of Zuzka's nonsense, Officer Tichy will accept this solution all the more readily. Her gels were not even needed.

She proceeds to the samovar, reaching for the tap to refresh the contents of the little pot.

Something slams into her back. Blackness flares and raw, red pain explodes along her spine and her arms flail (a sharp tinkle, china tears for beauty lost). She follows the pot to the floor.

"Hold still!" The angry face, the hateful face scowled at her, one large hand stretching her wrist over the basin as her body fell away. Dimly, she saw the lancet and the dark glisten of her own blood. But everything was receding.

"Loh! You're a pickpocket—I knew that from the footage. Good enough that you must have learned as a child. But so did I." He brandishes the passport, taken from her pocket as she staggered.

You're not that good, the thought struggles through outraged neurons, nerves that may well start to die.

"I gave you a chance, but now we see what you truly are. A pickpocket who talks to the police, who handles things for them."

Cursing, he clamped down on the slit vein. "What good are you, cabbage, if not for this? God's wounds, I need more salt! Only the purest will suffice for the elixir, from a living source. Curse God, I could bleed you dry and it would not be enough!"

***

Zuzka hunkers in the ticket office, the twilight still prickling her skin. Two hours (easily!) she must have spent in the company of Officer Tichy as the sunset rolled over them. Time and again, she had caught herself lazily enjoying the warmth and the look of amazement in the eyes of her fellow laundress as she spun her tale, before jolting back to the present. Now finally, it is all over. The old man claimed Petr from the officer and now he stands in Ana's front room, the envelope in his hand. Once the

Bratva leave, she can let go. She will run wild through the Old City and feed as she pleases.

She watches the discussion unfold like a puppet show. Sees Wolfbeard pull out his pistol and strike Anastazie with the butt.

Zuzka leaps up. An instant later, she bursts through Anastazie's door, breaking the lock she had previously picked.

"Ty che blyad?"

Wolfbeard gapes, his gun already rising. There are too many people here for a struggle; all she wants is to get them away from Ana, and she knows what they'll follow.

Seizing Petr out his chair, she drags him outside. Tattooed men run towards her shouting, drawing weapons. Arms around the screaming, struggling boy, she retreats beneath the portcullis. Down in the tunnels, she can evade them, she can keep them busy, these Nazis, these Austrian dragoons....

***

Anastazie rolls over, levers herself to her knees. Stares at her pale and shaking hands. Pain is the great leveller. The greatest of philosophers would squeal when stuck, like a young pig. She does not squeal, but that is because she is trying so hard to breathe. A minute goes by, and her skin does not blacken and begin to slough. Slowly, very slowly, she crawls across the floor, slivers of the smashed teapot sticking to her palms and knees.

The great Work is begun. Don't snivel—you've recovered enough to tend the fire. The heat must be kept even.

She lifts herself, one hand on the counter. Locating Hedvika's card, she reaches for the same phone she used before.

"Officer Tichy," she gasps into the shifting square. "Something terrible has happened!"

She describes seeing the boy try and escape from his escort, and how the man had struck him. Then two other men came and dragged him away, into the Prague Tunnels Experience. Then she turns to her cup, left brewing all this time, and drains it to the grounds. By the time she is finished, Hedvika has returned to the square and gone underground with gun drawn. She will be hot on their trail and soon, her backup will arrive. But none of that will help Zuzka.

Anastazie attempts to lock her front door, sighs when she finds it broken. She draws it to and turns out all the lights. Then, making a swift selection from the available weapons, she descends to her lab and unlocks the door to the tunnels.

***

The boy struggles in Zuzka's arms. His warm breath gusts against her face, carrying the sweet smell of his blood.

The underground is her kingdom—this has always been the case. Ancient cisterns running off the river, into which the laundry's vats still drained. Pits dug for prisoners and to preserve pigs against the winter's snow. Crypts and cellars, walled up to preserve secrets, paved passages to preserve the sanctity of monks. All the stories are about nuns, but she knows exactly what the Franciscans got up to. The big drains, arched and laid with dark brick, are among the more recent developments.

Footsteps echo down the passage behind her. Flashes of white light expose the cracked stone and ancient, mummified roots descending from the ceiling. She will evade them in her lair (which should be clean by now), and there she will feed. She will tip his body into her cache, and none shall ever know his fate.

But something tugs at her memory. The boy in her arms is the one pursued. He is important somehow—*alchemy!* She stole him away from the alchemist's house before the devil could drain him. To cheat him of his prey, she goes against her nature: she will hide the boy and then, why! She will slaughter them all!

Ahead, there is a cleft in the right-hand wall. To the casual glance, a mere unevenness in stone. But she knows better. She wriggles through, dragging the boy, who wails as her hand leaves his mouth. Now they are in a narrow drainage channel, built in the time of the old kings to carry waste to the river. Granite slabs make a V of the floor—originally, it lay open to the sky. She lifts one of the slabs and drops the boy down into, well, a charnel house, and he screams in the going and continues screaming in the stinking dark. She blocks the sound with the stone and ducks back to the junction, hovering where the oncoming lights drive shadow across her feet.

Hulking brutes in their black and red corpse-clothes slashed to make them fit, barking German. Their blood is worse than pigs'. How many has she killed, despite their crossbows and bill hooks cruelly curved—their guns. *Nazis carry guns….*

Then everything is swallowed by hunger and rage. Without further hesitation, she spins into the passageway—

Icons! *Blood* icons!

The multiple guns pop softly, but dust still falls from above.

✳✳✳

Anastazie knows she should not be here, pressing through the old drainage channel towards the regular tunnels. Just because she is stable doesn't mean she should press the issue, and what, really, does she think she's going to do with this thing in her hand? The ordure she flushed from the lab makes the slanting pavers slick and uncertain. The whole place stinks like there's something dead close by.

Two soft pops, like the stopper shooting off a heated vial. She stops cold, pressing her palms against the walls. Light flickers ahead of her, there is a murmur of voices.

She wasn't taught to pick pockets as a child. Just to be very, very quiet.

Whole hours, it seems, pass before she reaches the corner. What she sees in the bright, rocking light is Wolfbeard and the blond bending over Zuzka, who lies at full length, a hole gaping in her abdomen. Were it feasible, Anastazie would *tsk* disapprovingly. During the Second World War, bullets could hardly slow Zuzka down, and guns made a decent noise. Like everything else, they are getting out of hand.

Zuzka's face looks almost peaceful, but has gone very white as all her blood goes to the wound. She is not bleeding, of course—how long before they notice that? How long before the hole begins to close in front of their eyes?

From her pocket, Anastazie takes three silver Thalers, each lavishly anointed with the real drug. Wincing, she rolls her hand about in shit, until it is thoroughly camouflaged. Then she flings the coins expertly into the passage, the first landing soundlessly on Zuzka's chest, the second in soft mud. The third one makes a tiny clink.

Anastazie hears no break in the Bratva's discussion. They have recognised Zuzka as the tour guide, but cannot understand why she intervened, let alone why she hurled herself at them like that. Not only is she running the drugs, she must be taking them herself! Then, a slight exclamation. The light beaming from the blond man's phone rocks, then steadies. Anastazie knows how the coins will glint in the light. Sucking, squelching sounds: they have taken the bait, and she begins easing backwards. The noise she makes is very slight, but it is there.

"Petr?" Wolfbeard calls. "She's dead. The madwoman's dead. We're here to take you home. Come out now."

The squelching closes in on the side passage. Anastazie flattens herself against the wall. So long as he touched the coins....

"This is the police!" A new voice, Hedvika's voice, rips through the underground. "Drop your weapons and raise your hands!"

The retort of her gun is deafening. Dust falls and cobwebs shake. The phone light spins and drops.

Anastazie launches without care into the main passage, sees the blond writhing, pouring his own blood over Zuzka. His fallen phone casts shadows on the tunnel ceiling. Another man lies flat and still while Wolfbeard and Hedvika grapple. Wolfbeard is strong, stronger than the officer. Her arms are buckling, she starts to sink.

Then Wolfbeard gasps and buckles as Anastazie hits him in the back of the head with a heavy, copper *džezva*. For one moment, Hedvika stares at her in shock. Anastazie slaps her across the face with a gel, spattering her lips and eyes, and she begins to stare at other things. So busy is she with the hallucinations inspired by an hour's worth of vampire stories, that she will never recall seeing Anastazie. Let alone that the *servírka* checked that the envelope was still in Wolfbeard's pocket before hauling Zuzka away.

By the time backup arrives, Hedvika has driven an ancient root through Wolfbeard's heart, and almost managed to remove his head.

***

Anastazie is stress-brewing a light euphoric when Zuzka finally wakes. Laid carefully on the floor on the lab (and even cleaned slightly), she has been out for twenty-four hours. During this time, Anastazie has not touched her, merely observed from a respectful distance the slow closure of the hole.

Zuzka's eyelids peel back. "Is it time to finish your father?" she murmurs. "He's weak enough now, they'll think it's his heart."

"No," Anastazie replies, taking the *džezva* of blood off the slow fire. Not the one she used to stun Wolfbeard—that has a dent. "We did that a long time ago. Here, are you hungry?"

Blood donated by the blond and brewed *a la turecká*. She pours the mahogany libation into a cup of *İznik* ware and presents it to Zuzka, who has managed to sit up.

"Thank you," Zuzka says, and sips remarkably neatly.

Anastazie turns away—not through disgust, but because of all the things jostling for space inside her skull. Memories, emotions, the need to start somewhere. "Officer Tichy shot two Bratva," she says. "The police are being cagey about what happened to the third, but he's dead at any rate."

"What about Petr?"

"He seems to have escaped during the confusion."

"Did he really?"

"Not right away. However, after they'd all finished tramping round... someone remembered the location of your cache. It took a *Vídeňská káva* and a few memory blockers, but he's showered and on the bus to Belgrade."

"You remembered?" Zuzka looks at her over the cup. In a tone way too casual, she asks, "Anything else?"

Anastazie holds up a large, brass key, identical to the one that is now back in the saltpetre. The one she found hanging around Zuzka's neck.

"Ah, yes. That. Well—"

"It's all right," she says. "I remember it all."

While her father slumbered, she escaped out the backdoor, seizing a moment in the river's chill. By pure chance, she glanced across the open drain and glimpsed a huddled figure in the flicker of other people's fires. Or was it chance? Did not some sympathy of like to like draw her eyes to her friend's body, clothes soaked with foulness, but no blood? Her lovely eyes closed and her cheeks gone white as snow. But surely, somewhere inside her lingered the spark.

This was her father's doing. If he realised she had left the fire untended, let alone that she knew of his crime... but she did not care. Rage boiled inside her, as she took hold of Zuzka's once strong arm, now limp as a rag, and dragged her inside. She would hide her, clean her, keep her safe, and when the elixir was ready—

It was Zuzka's distinctive smell, overpowering her deodorant, that brought the memory back. Manoeuvring her through the side passage, Anastazie could not help but inhale. She meets Zuzka's eyes and something, some tension, drains from the vampire where she sits.

"He took you when you delivered the laundry, didn't he?" Not looking for confirmation, Anastazie shakes her head. "I thought I heard you at the door, but I was in bed, still healing from what he did to me. He came up close to sunset and dragged me into the lab, set me to extracting the salts. I thought it was *my* blood. I should have realised."

"Do you think he knew?" Zuzka dips her head, inspecting the damage to her T-shirt. "That we were friends?"

They had met at the laundry. A single stain of arsenic on white linen had been the cause—Father had shut her out of the house until she found a way to dispel the poison. After some consideration, she had gone where the great copper cauldrons stood by the river, and met a plump peasant girl with black hair and bright eyes. "This stuff?" Zuzka had laughed. "Easy! Wait till you try removing spilled coffee!"

Ana had never heard of coffee before this. They discussed the rumoured properties of the new beverage, which had arrived at the Hospital Na Františku. With her father's acquaintance consisting solely of evil-smelling scholars, she had never really had a friend. Maybe as a child, before her mother died.

She had kept Zuzka's body and when the elixir was ready, she had poured it down her throat. To her father, she gave a fresh-ground brew. In the short time left to him, he never realised the cheat.

"I don't know. But we did kill him. After you came back as you did."

"Maybe it was because I'd lost all my own blood. Or his formula wasn't quite right. In any case, I needed it fresh and his was available."

Anastazie shivers. Like the way her hands shook, but all over.

"And that's why," Zuzka nods, though her face turns a little sad, "that's why you let yourself forget."

It was. She had spent the next twenty years gaining the skills to compound her own elixir, and by that time, her culpability had become unbearable. Although she would not betray Zuzka, she had let her go.

Anastazie goes down on her knees and hugs the surprised vampire. "I'm sorry. And for tainting your blood supply and bringing in the police."

"Well." Zuzka makes a kind of snuffling sound. "I'm *almost* sorry I flooded the lab."

"You know that if you ever want to try *my* elixir, you can. But there's no guarantee...."

"It's all right, Ana. Really, I like being a vampire."

"So, if the problem's me...." After a pause, Anastazie turns her head and kisses Zuzka full on the lips.

The vampire giggles. It is the only word for it. They huddle for a while, then Zuzka whispers, "So, I take it I'm allowed to spend the night?"

"I take it you have been."

She fails to look embarrassed. "I slip in from the tunnels once you've gone upstairs, and make sure I leave before you come down. That buzzer—" she indicates the button on the wall, "—sounds for my door as well."

"And here's me, driving myself like horses to find your lair." Anastazie giggles herself. "I'll try not to forget this time, Zuz. I'll really try."

"I'll try to remember that. Now, if your shower can take it?"

"It's an old thing, but the plumbing still works." They collapse giggling again, though it is hard to say why.

"I do have one question." This, as Anastazie leads her up the stairs, checking carefully for the lingering presence of police and tourists in the square. Lurking Russians are conspicuous by their absence. "If you know that it was the elixir that turned you... why do you keep insisting it was the devil?"

"Ah, so you haven't remembered everything." Zuzka looks wise and wicked. "Everyone in the neighbourhood knew your father's studies were the devil's work."

"Really? That's what they thought?"

"Honestly, Ana." A grin exposes her teeth. "Don't you?"

To which Anastazie can find no reply. She points the way to the shower and goes off to find her guest a towel and a clean dress. The Oldest Coffee House sits in the dark, floor scrubbed and tables wiped, bracing for the century to come.

Gargoyles, As They Grumble

Sydney, 1858
nastystupidfeathers
sillysmoothcheeks
handsnotclawed
nofangs
curls

It is a blistering afternoon at the work site, trapped under heavy, grey-white clouds. Heat presses down upon the stretch of churned clay and bleached-blonde grass that will become the University of Sydney as though trying to drive the arches and buttresses back down into the earth. Architect Edmund Blackett favours the style of the gothic revival, and thus there are gargoyles laid out in a row, next to a fine, large angel and a cluster of carven terminals for the beams of the Great Hall. All are destined to trim the roof, both inside and out, but their installation is still some weeks away.

The gargoyles, exquisitely fashioned though they are of buttery Pyrmont yellow block, are disgruntled. Their ribbed horns curve, carved by master masons; their paws and webbed toes clutch at their pediments. Today there are visitors at the site, wearing polished leather boots and fitted trousers, slippers, and hooped skirts. Being set upon dirt at the foot of walls you were made to surmount would put anyone out of sorts and, of course, the proximity of human feet is an insult to anything with wings. But added to this, what do the visitors gaze upon, and to what do they deliver their compliments? The angel.

The photographer's apprentice raises the pan.

Flash!

In that moment—the moment when he should have beheld his angel bathed in splendour—Edmund Blackett glances inadvertently towards the gargoyles. Scoured white and black by the burning magnesium, the after-image shows him blinking orbs and flexing claws, the slight flaring of stone nostrils. The stretching of bat-like wings.

nastystupidfeathers

Blackett blinks, his eyes watering.

"You shouldn't leave out the gargoyles."

The voice at his elbow sends Blackett spinning, nearly costs him his topper. Despite the heat (which in Sydney, in this season, heralds a storm), he is dressed for the visiting dignitaries in frock coat and starched collar. The mason, on the other hand, is garbed in loose white. His hat is broad, his whiskers voluminous. He fixes Blackett with eyes like blue beads, saying, "They won't settle."

Blackett glances across the work site, at the wilting parliamentarians, old grammarians and their wives all hastening towards the refreshment tent, then back down at the mason. "What did you say?"

"Begging your pardon, Mr Blackett, but they won't."

Belatedly, Blackett remembers the man's name. "What do you mean, Popplewell? The foundations are settling? Lord have mercy, we're never seeing cracks?"

"Indeed no, Mr Blackett. It's the gargoyles."

This, thinks Blackett, is beyond any kind of response—for obviously he did *not* see the wings stretch, the nostrils flare, nor truly hear that stony grumble. It was all a trick of the heat and shimmering, cloud-filtered light. The only dignified option is for him to walk away and yet, he may not follow the oh-so gentlefolk (who applauded very nicely at his speech). He must still give instructions, turn his men to their tasks and secure the site against the oncoming deluge. The Angel of Knowledge and its shield-bearing brethren must be tarped.

So hot it is and yet so still. Not even a breath of wind. The cry of crickets in the grass grinds against his skull.

"All I'm saying," Popplewell continues, "is that you spoke all about the angels, how the big one means we come to learning through Christ and the little ones—very nice carving from young James, there—are all the different faculties as make up the university. But nothing about the meaning of the gargoyles."

The Angel of Knowledge is yellow block, but the others are all of pristine jarrah wood, for attaching to the beams. Twelve stiff-backed angels carrying twelve shields, each bearing a symbol of their faculty. Blackett appreciates the relevance of an abacus to arithmetic and a star to astronomy. But a frog-like face of yellow block, eyes bulging and mouth gaping wide? Barnett finally finds his voice. "They don't mean anything."

"Again, your pardon, sir. But they do."

Another flash, but this comes from the celestial pan, charged with divine powder over mere magnesium. An almighty rumble banishes the crickets and rolls over the whole, charged scene—in the distance, the smoky blur of Sydney town, the nearer spectacle of oxen hauling carts of stone up the hill. Nearer still, his assistant Colby mops his face with a kerchief.

The photographer's apprentice—a young lad in knee breeches and a flat cap—stands gaping at Popplewell, rather than folding his master's equipment into its cherrywood box. The refreshment tent billows in a sudden gust of wind, canvas straining like a sail against the ropes, and Blackett is released.

"Colby!" he calls. "Colby, I need the tarpaulins brought out and secured over the woodwork. Don't forget the windowsills."

"Right you are, sir!" The burly Colby, a mason like Popplewell but blissfully free from fancy, tips his hat as he strides down the hill, rousing the men to action. Blackett hastens towards the tent to check that the ropes are secure.

In Blackett's wake, the photographer's apprentice stares at the gargoyles. Uncle John has long since repaired to the tent, sipping tea and hunting unctuously for commissions. The stone creatures fascinate whereas the angel does not. With its impossibly perfect hair, its blind, stone eyes and hand raised in benediction, it is just another condescending man, raised by birth to the bench or the pulpit. She has seen more than enough of those.

"Afternoon, Miss," says Popplewell.

She stands firm, for she breaks no law in assisting her uncle or wearing the clothes most suitable to the task. Her sex is no secret, although neither is it something they feel the need to broadcast. "Afternoon," she bids him back.

Behind her, the hood of the camera lifts and fills, lifts and fills, as waves of dust are blown across the work site. At the edge of the trampled track, the blonde grass bends almost to the earth. The oxen bellow. Soon the cloud pall will split and all the yellow fins, the flaring ears, the nostrils and tusked mouths will darken and run with water. But this is a gargoyle's function—they do not fear it. Still they stand together, photographer and mason, until at long last, she turns to him. "What do the gargoyles mean?"

***

Inside the tent, it is stuffy and as hot as out; moreover, an inordinate number of crickets seem also to have taken shelter. The tea, as dispensed, is lukewarm. Blackett stands with his back to the rattling flap, a china cup in hand, smiling at the university's benefactors (most of whom would rather erect a wooden shed than a masterpiece for the ages, and then attempt to sell it off as warehouse space).

"But look here, Blackett." A florid face accosts him, all judicial brow and jowls. Fleetingly, he imagines how the man would look as a gargoyle, immortalised in stone but not in the way he would doubtless prefer. "Do we in truth need all this decoration, these carvings and things?"

"It's traditional for university buildings," he replies, "as for churches built in the gothic style."

"Tradition is all very well," the new speaker is, he believes, the Member for Northumberland, "but I can't see how it benefits us. We're a business community. We live by our exports, not our speculations."

"Young men reading their Homer and Petrach," His Honour pontificates, "don't need to be distracted from their study by all these frills. And that, sir, is a *proper* education."

The Member smiles. "And down at the Rocks they can read their Ovid."

A burst of laughter from the men—the ladies present look to hems befouled by crossing the paddock. The Anglican Bishop of Sydney responds that he, himself, has no objection to the angels, but feels that even in churches, gargoyles are as unnecessary as Ovid to a Christian curriculum.

"Nonsense, your Grace," responds the Member. "Where would we be if the devil spoke no Latin?"

Blackett sips his tea, remembering his Vitruvius. In any building, harmony must be preserved at all cost. He feels the tent shaking around him, and his architect's instinctive awareness flies to the building, as though the same resonance pervades the heavy beams and solid, interlocking blocks. Without their glass, the arching windows are as yet so delicate.

But now the governor's wife approaches. "Well, I for one adore your angel," says the dowager, peering at him through dust-spotted spectacles. "And I found your speech most affecting. As you said, today, we lay the foundations of our country's future."

"That angel," he responds, "will watch over us for the next three hundred years."

***

"The *other* knowledge?" says the apprentice.

Popplewell nods. "Such as they in the tent don't wish to know and would keep from such as us. Such things as we mostly learn anyway."

The gargoyles loom expectantly as she considers this proposition. It is hard to loom at foot level, but they manage. It is true that most admiration as gargoyles receive comes from people who allow their gaze to wander out of windows and up drainpipes, their ears to track the faintest of gurgles. Who seek out mason's marks, pondering what lies above and below, all the while concealing their own grotesqueness from the world. But such recognition is not enough. When their own architect dismisses them, it can never be enough.

Nonetheless, John's niece will do what she can. She nods courteously to the mason, then charges the flash pan. She has long since worked out how to operate the camera single-handed.

Flash!

The walls of the tent turn white. But for so long as Blackett pauses, cup halfway to his lips, there is no rumble of thunder. Only a guttural gurgling that can only mean the rain has come.

nastystupidhomer
sillydullpetrach
curlysmoothangels
we wait
till
dark

***

SYDNEY, 1888

"Excuse me, sir, but what is that piece back there?"

Archibald Liversidge, dean of the newly minted Faculty of Science, gazes upon his student. The presence of the young lady, in her severe blouse and blue serge skirt, and the faculty itself are both largely his achievements.

"That?" He reaches past the geodes and fossils, to the uneven lump of sandstone at the back. A roughly shaped grey lump, perhaps the size of a head: he draws it forward on the bench, so she may examine it. She leans closer, her expression intent.

The arguments there had been, against admitting female students! On his side there was science. On the other, endless bleating about the impropriety of having both sexes present during a lecture on classics, lest Ovid make his way into the discourse.

"It was a sculpture," says the object of their concerns. She is quiet in class but observant, oh yes. The first to ask this question all year and one of only few. "Badly eroded, yet not by water, I think. The surface is too rough."

"Yes, that is perhaps the most curious feature." With a flat palm, Liversidge brushes the vestigial curls. His own are thinning. "Thirty years ago, when it first opened, there was an angel statue atop the Great Hall."

"Thirty years?" She glances askance at the head.

"It only stood for twenty. Have you seen the photos on the wall of the admissions office?"

The air is sultry today, typical of a Sydney summer. The geology lab is cool, but through the tracery of the window heat presses down on a quadrangle of bleached and beaten grass.

The student shakes her head and then her brow furrows. "What was the statue made of?"

"Ah now, that's the thing. So far as I was able to determine, exactly the same stone as the other ornamentation on the facade."

The furrow deepens, for as they both know, the gargoyles and trefoils, the crockets on the clock tower, are all still in excellent condition. "There must have been some unique factor."

"What would you suggest?"

"The position, sticking up like a needle with no shelter from the rain," she offers. "Or perhaps a corrosive effect from the metal of its mount."

"Both excellent answers," Liversidge beams.

A sound like a gurgling chuckle comes from somewhere close by—perhaps in the quadrangle, though through the window nothing can be seen save a boy in cricket whites hastening in from the lower field. He should be in class already.

"I myself suspect it was struck by lightning."

"That might explain the unusual surface."

"Yes," Liversridge replies. "It almost looks like it was eaten."

Another chuckle, like water running down a drainpipe. The student crosses to the window and peers over the lawn. Then, for no apparent reason, she looks up.

"You should go look at the photos," says Liversidge. "There is an absolutely charming one of an old mason standing next to the gargoyles, before they were installed."

"The gargoyles!" the girl exclaims, face lighting up as though from a camera flash. "All those mouths!"

Believing she speaks merely of the sound, Liversidge frowns. "But there's been no rain for weeks."

"There will be," she says. "A storm is coming."

The Beautiful House

"Here it is, Jenny." Julie was as excited as I had ever seen her, all but trembling as we stood together on the footpath. "Look, just look! What do you think?"

I'm sure I couldn't say what I thought.

She called me the night before, and I swear she wanted me to come right then. Oh sure, leave the kids and drive into the city at half past nine to hear big sister's big news. She refused to just tell me, but right up until I saw the house, I thought she and Guillaume were pregnant.

The place was one of those big, squashed terraces, three storeys tall. There was a skeletal magnolia, a stone-capped step with a balcony above it, sagging with rusted iron lace. It was all ancient; cracking, peeling, bowing. The walls had the texture of something dug out of a grave.

"Isn't it wonderful!"

"No," I said. "It's old and broken."

She laughed at me, stroking the bald iron of the gate. "Sure it's rundown, but that's the only way we could buy into the area."

No, Julie and Guillaume weren't pregnant. They were *investing.*

"Come in. You'll see, I know you will!"

The gate squealed as she opened it, the path was uneven beneath our feet. I saw fragments of green and burgundy tiling through the autumnal detritus. The stone on the step was cracked. Above the wooden door was a sort of tiny window with a faded picture on glass, of a bird surrounded by pink flowers. Julie smiled, touching a blackened metal plaque that clung to the brick on one side.

"Belville," she said.

And I did see: it was the beautiful house.

It had been a game when we shared a bedroom as girls. Our house had been cramped and ugly, cheap rental accommodation on the city fringe. We all hated living there, not that Mum had much choice after Dad died. So we started fantasising, discussing the things we would want in our separate rooms, and colours, curtains, and—well. It just went from there. Julie used to draw pictures of the rooms and stick them on the walls—they were our windows. She was always the creative one, who wrote and drew, made little crafty things.

"We're moving straight in. There's water and electricity, and the second-floor rooms are okay."

"Guillaume's going to live here?"

"And on weekends, we'll start the renovation."

"Guillaume's going to *renovate?*"

"Well, obviously we'll get professionals in for the structural work and the wiring." I had touched a nerve. "But there's a lot we can do ourselves."

As Julie opened the door, the house exhaled. Damp, must and something else. Something rotten. She showed me round the ground floor. Hallway and front room, bathroom and kitchen with the laundry attached; all of it old and desperate in its decay. Not a corner that didn't cry out for attention. The staircase up to the floor above was a menace to life and limb. The windows were foggy and most had been painted shut. There was a pocket backyard, completely overgrown by privet and cobbler's pegs.

After that little treat, she took me to one of those cafés where you hand over a note for a cup of coffee and don't get change. Julie talked about the mortgage and minimising tax.

I talked about how Josh was doing in kindy, and Sarah's new teeth. "And Mum's fine: she asked if I'd seen you."

"I want to show her but I think I'll leave it a week or two, till we've got the basics done."

"Yeah, well. I think you've got your work cut out for you, Julie."

She laughed again, lips curving, light in her eager, brown eyes. "It's perfect, Jen. I'm going to make this happen."

That's what she got paid for, of course, making things happen. Media Manager at age thirty-four. She was always the clever one, as well—getting into Uni, paying her way by working in a computer shop. But I still couldn't imagine Guillaume stripping paint or sanding back old timber. Every time I'd seen him, which wasn't often, he'd been dressed up to the nines in crisp shirts and a leather jacket, his blond hair elegantly styled.

I didn't go to Uni. Mum had worked her way up to floor manager by then, at old Hardly Normal, and I worked under her for a while, travelled a bit, worked at other stores, and then met Bill. And Bill and I were doing just fine, thank you. If we couldn't afford to buy a house or a new car, we were no worse off than many. And certainly better off than Mum.

We walked back down to Belville, past the cafés and boutiques and locals out for a stroll. With her suit and neatly cropped hair—we were both brunette, but Julie dyed her hair red—she looked like she belonged here. It was the house that was out of place, hunching in the dip of the street as though it were ashamed. The woman shuffling on the corner up ahead, with her weathered skin and grimy layers of clothing, her crazy, grey hair—she was the house's natural occupant. I wondered if she'd been sleeping there before the sale went through.

Julie appeared not to notice, not the woman or the contrast. "Wait until the chimney's fixed," she said. "We'll do Christmas in July."

When I left, she was picking leaves from off the step.

∗∗∗

"Mum wouldn't stay." Julie's astonishment was palpable, even over the phone. "I brought her into the front room but she wouldn't go any further. Wouldn't even let me make tea!"

"That's strange," I said. "Did she say why?"

"Something about the house! She said it made her uncomfortable."

"Well… when you took me through, it did feel very cold."

"She asked… she asked me if the previous owner had died there."

"Did he?"

"It was a woman, and I don't know. I wouldn't think so. Where on earth would she get that idea?"

"I don't know. Maybe one of her detective shows."

"Maybe. Anyway, I couldn't even persuade her to come to the café. I had to turn around and drive her all the way back."

"A shame."

∗∗∗

We didn't do Christmas in July. One of the first things they discovered was that the roof was leaking and, as well as repairing that, new damp courses had to be installed throughout the ground floor. Which apparently meant stripping the base of each wall. They got an electrician in to replace the wiring at the same time, along with the corroded pipes in the upstairs bathroom. So come July, the place was full of workmen, hammering, drilling, and grinding day in and day out. I could only imagine the noise, the dust, the constant procession of strangers as the walls were rebuilt. Then the whole thing had to dry out before they put fresh plaster on. I got the saga from Julie in breathless phone calls and a deluge of emailed photos.

They called on Bill in August. Just to sand and sweep, they said, and clean up the backyard. Although he works as a mechanic, Bill is handy all round and Julie must have known we needed the money. I came in with him one Saturday, leaving Josh and Sarah at Mum's, and the house looked different from that first afternoon. The walls were all smooth, if patchy. Nothing sagged or crumbled: even the fireplace in the front room, which I swear had been little more than a pile of bricks held together by soot, was now a feature with a mantle and hearthstone. The smell was dry, dusty of course, but somehow the difference between sickness and convalescence.

We were standing there, in front of the fireplace, when I asked Julie if she and Guillaume were still actually living here.

She laughed, and it was strained. "Oh yes, we are!"

"I can't imagine how."

"Oh, it's not that bad—not now the pipes have been replaced. Before that, well, there were days we both showered at work. And the noises! Some nights we couldn't get to sleep!"

"What kinds of noises?"

"Oh, you know. Banging at all hours and this kind of low moan, though that was probably the chimney." She flipped her hand, dismissing the whole thing, but I could see the shadows beneath her eyes.

"Bill said the workmen are having some trouble with their tools disappearing."

"Oh no, not disappearing. They put them down and then swear they find them somewhere else, down by the back fence. I'm sure they're just having us on."

"Why would they do that?" I asked.

She did the hand-flip again. "I don't know! Maybe because it's such an old house, they just find it amusing."

"How so?"

The look I got was of genuine irritation. "Pretending there's a ghost or something. Honestly, it's as ridiculous as Mum still refusing to visit."

"Well," I said, "it is a long way for her to come."

Julie didn't respond. Just stood there, in her designer jeans and fancy apron, gazing out the front window. The panes were so warped and smeared, I couldn't see anything beyond a white bloom of light.

"The house is old," I said. "Creepy, maybe. But they can't see it like you do."

She flashed me a quick smile. "Thanks, sis." Then her eyes returned to the window. It really was like she gazed into the future, through a foggy crystal ball.

"Who knows?" I said. "One day, there may even be a family living here."

***

"There's been an accident," Julie said, voice small and tight.

I had come in with Bill again and we were in the kitchen, sitting on stools with cups of tea. Julie's knuckles were white as she worked the cup round and round, without ever raising it to her lips. "The plasterer's apprentice slipped and hit his head on the front step: he's in hospital. There was blood everywhere."

I asked if the boy would be all right.

"They say so," she murmured. "Just a concussion." The shadows beneath her eyes were darker, and there were fresh lines at the corners. The pipes repaired, it seemed that something else had taken over the duty of keeping her awake. The apron she wore to protect her shirt was grubby now, and she was about to go through the left knee of her jeans.

By contrast, the kitchen was looking pretty good. They'd even moved their big fridge in, the one full of olives and Italian cheeses. The frames of the sash windows had been stripped back to bare wood, and the accretion of decades of repainting and slapdash application of sealant chipped away from the glass, which showed a clear view of pressing leaves. The old linoleum had been torn up, revealing grimy but solid floorboards.

"We were lucky there," she replied to my query. She was still turning the cup. "When we first started, it looked like the damp had rotted the edges. But turns out, it's fine. The attic steps as well; they looked broken but now they're fine." She began trembling, as though this just made it worse. "But you know, like, this is my dream. I don't want anyone to suffer for it."

I explained how silly she was being. No one was suffering for her dream; they were suffering for their wages. The plasterer's apprentice—well, the plasterer at least was a professional and should know all about the dangers of old houses. They had accepted the job, hadn't they?

Just then, a cry rang out from the hallway. People can say what they want—you know when it's one of your own screaming, and it goes right to your stomach, no matter what the circumstance.

Bill had stabbed himself on a nail while sanding down the frame of the front door. Julie behaved as though she hadn't heard a word I said and it really *was* her fault. She made such a fuss that I got Bill to go through it step by step, pressing a sterile pad on the heel of his palm the whole time. He hadn't even seen the nail. He was pressing down hard and felt the jab, but only realised it was serious when he saw red. Blood everywhere, he said.

Nothing was there *now*, hardly a mark on the plaster or woodwork, making him look a bit stupid. Nonetheless, Guillaume drove him to the hospital to get a tetanus booster and then paid him for the entire weekend.

As said, I had never had much to do with Guillaume, but I drove with them to the hospital and he seemed like a decent man. A little stuck-up maybe, the kind who puts a premium on his own dignity. Julie stayed at the house, and later I heard she had completed the sanding herself. She sanded the front door. She sanded the back door. On hands and knees in her now-ragged jeans, she tore up the old carpet in their bedroom and stacked it in rolls out the back. I heard it all from Bernie, the plasterer: every day for the next month, she came home from work and attacked the house as though she were afraid something would happen if she stopped.

***

Christmas came for real, and Mum still wouldn't step over the threshold. So it was just me, Bill and the kids there for lunch. Julie—seasonally trimmed and dressed, though the lacquer couldn't hide her broken nails—poured us champagne and proffered Italian cheese and Spanish ham, with grapes and crackers. Because Guillaume was out.

"It's a work thing, a couple of other expats out on the harbour." She smiled, and her lips looked bitten.

By this time, they had cleaned the ceilings. I hadn't really noticed the plaster mouldings before, just that the surface looked lumpy. But now they were revealed as scrolls of leaves and peaches swirling round the gleaming brass lamp at the centre. We sat, arranged about a four-piece, slate-grey lounge suite, with Sarah wriggling on her blankie and Josh playing games on his brand-new tablet. Sarah's new teddy bear was easily as big as she was.

"The lounge doesn't really match," said Julie nervously, as though it were somehow shabby. "With a house like this, you have to accept its intrinsic character and only introduce such new elements as will compliment that."

There was a knock at the front door. I saw Julie flinch. Bill went to open it and I heard him say, "Can I help you?"

"You can't have kids in there," came a hoarse shout. "Get 'em out, while you can!"

"Um," said Bill.

"S'not safe here!"

Till now, Julie had stayed in her chair, curling tighter and tighter into a knot of green linen. Now, she sprang up screaming, "Stop it! Go away and leave me alone!"

"I jus' wanna *help* you!"

I had followed Julie into the hall and now I saw a decrepit, filthy woman hovering on the path outside. She clasped her right hand as though it had been burned, squinted at us and shouted. "This house, it drinks you! Love, money, blood: it gulps down everything you give it and just keeps on drinking!"

"You've drunk a bit yourself," Bill observed. "Hey, would you like some cheese?"

"Houses should be for people, not the other way round. When I was here, it just took and took. Would have swallowed me! I hadta, hadta leave *everything*." She stared up at the façade as though at a sleeping giant, and Julie finally pulled herself together.

"This is private property," she said, in her most managerial voice. "If you don't leave now, I shall call the police."

"I ain't done nothin'." Tears started in the bleary eyes.

"Roaming round my garden at night, knocking on walls and throwing stones at windows? Add today's harassment and I think that's quite a lot. No, you listen! I've had enough!"

"But it's the house!"

"The police," Julie repeated, "I'm calling them right now."

As she pulled out her phone, the woman turned and sprinted down the path, faster than I would have believed her capable.

"Can I drive you somewhere?" Bill raised his voice. "Take you to a shelter or something?"

"She won't go to a shelter," Julie said darkly, as the woman reached the street and kept on running. "Eileen is a local fixture. The shop owners have been trying to find her family, a place in a nursing home, anything."

"But it's Christmas," said Bill. "Maybe we should invite her in."

"Didn't you hear?" Julie's gaze tracked the receding figure. "This house is a vampire."

"Has she really been doing all those things?" I asked, guiding Julie gently back to her chair while Bill headed into the kitchen, presumably in search of a beer.

"Someone has. Night after night." Julie sank down into her chair.

"Was that a witch?" asked Josh.

"Shush, honey. Witches aren't real.

"What about vampires?"

"No, they're not."

"What about psycho killers?"

"What's that game you're playing? Give it here!"

Julie poured herself champagne and sat there, her attention clearly a thousand miles away. Was she still contemplating the future, perhaps in the whorls of exposed wood? I had to ask her three times when Guillaume was due back before she answered.

"I don't know. He's being a fool, about a lot of things." She tossed off the glass. I pressed her, gently, for details.

"He's got this idea; I don't know where from. Someone told him something, about me and the plasterer." She snorted and reached for the bottle. "Ridiculous!"

"Will you be all right if we leave? It's just we said we'd drop in on Bill's parents."

"He'll be back sometime." She refilled the flute to within a finger's breadth of the top. "Go on, go home. I want to keep working on the upstairs, anyway."

And by the time we left (for bundling up two children and their presents, and a little cold ham, is not the work of moments), the heels were off and the apron was on.

***

As I heard it later, what happened that night was this:

Guillaume returned late from his expat cruise and went into the kitchen to make himself a cup of tisane or whatever French people drink at two in the morning. While doing so, he heard a noise that seemed to come from the front room. Guillaume had suffered from the banging and rattling as much as anyone, so he put down the cup and went to investigate. The doors were locked, the windows shut, but still the noise continued. It seemed to be coming from the fireplace.

I should say that, despite my scepticism, Guillaume had done his fair share of work. His obsession had been the tiles, with both bathrooms benefitting from his taste. He had also recently lined the fireplace with heat-resistant ceramics in green and mahogany, to match the front path. So, as the noises continued, he went and got a torch, and ended up climbing into the cavity in order to check on his work.

What happened next makes little sense, but it seems that his actions (or those of the cat or possum responsible for the sound) dislodged a hidden deposit of soot. It hit him square in the face, and in his panic he must have tried to stand up. His head got caught in the flue, and for whatever reason he was unable to pull himself out. Julie was woken by his muffled cries and the drumming of his heels. By the time she got downstairs and managed to pull him free, he was barely conscious, half-suffocated by the superfine ash.

"It was *swallowing*," was all he said. "I felt it crushing me." Of course, prior to coming home he had drunk a lot more than tisane.

Julie rinsed out his nose and eyes, drove him to hospital and saw the dawn in at his side. I like to think this might have helped them patch things up, but Guillaume was so very jealous of his dignity.

***

"Guillaume's leaving. He's arranged a transfer back to the Paris office." Julie's voice cracked like old china. "He wants us to sell the house and move there, permanently. Says those are his *conditions*."

We were back in the front room, but by now the walls were smooth shades of ochre and pale olive, the ceilings a spotless white. The floor had been polished, running away under our feet as though someone had spilled honey. There were Persian carpets, and a dark green and mahogany runner swathed the stairs.

"He never thinks you were having an affair?"

"I don't know what he thinks!" But she did: it was there in her pale and hollow face as she paced back and forth across the gorgeous room. "I could transfer to Paris, but not at the same level. Still, it would be an experience."

"What are you talking about?" I cried. "Moving to another country? Screw him, Julie!"

"What, just let him go? For a job title and a house?"

"But it's your house!"

"Is it? I didn't intend these colours. Or to keep the laundry." Her gaze lit on the fixtures, but now she seemed to see only darkness. "If I stay, I'll have to do things. I'll have to... get rid of the lounge."

"Julie, you're upset," I said. "Let's go to the café."

"With a house like this," she murmured, staring into the fireplace, "you have to accept its intrinsic character. No. No, I *have* to stay." She looked up and it was as if she were blind. "It's so *beautiful.*" Then she blinked and seemed to wake. "What's happening, Jenny?" she quavered. "What am I doing?"

"Following your dream," I told her.

Julie told Guillaume that she'd follow him once the house was complete. They'd get a better price, if the renovations were done, and could use that to set themselves up in Paris. I understand that Guillaume said things in response, about my sister and the plasterer, and about the house. She ended up buying out his share and that was the end of it. Once he was gone, she took leave from work and shut herself inside. I guess she wanted to lose herself in all the finishing touches.

***

The little bird in its nest of pink blossom glowed above the door as I unclipped the gate and hurried up the path in darkness. Beneath my feet it was level and straight, the green and mahogany tessellations gleaming wherever the light touched them. The leaves of the magnolia were green and fat.

On the phone, Julie had sounded weird. "I understand about the chimney now. That's its throat. There's a stomach down there, and more, I can feel its heart beating. Jenny, it's beating there behind the wall. I don't feel well, but there's still the cornices to be done. I have to *finish.*"

I told Bill to watch the kids and I drove straight in, at half past nine at night.

The door opened soundlessly when I touched it. The hall was revealed in all its glory, ochre and olive, a brass lamp with frosted glass panels depending above. The light picked out all the little of the plaster and the carpet in a glorious, golden wash. An antique cedar hall tree with green marble panels stood there like a butler to take my coat and direct my attention to the stairs.

The floors on the first floor were polished now. The walls here had been painted a light, warm beige, crowned by the off-white cornices and ceiling. Curtains billowed before the balcony, white muslin gushing from floral sheaths, in which the overall tone was a deep rose. There were brass curtain rails and oh, such wonderful things in the bathroom. Where on earth had she found a real clawfoot tub?

The top floor was papered, an old-fashioned stripe with floral sprigs. The cornices and ceiling were an off-white colour, like fresh bone. All still drying, but complete.

And in the middle of the room lay my sister Julie, rumpled and colourless, pulseless, at the base of a step ladder. It looked like the bones of her legs and wrists had cracked, that perhaps she had lain here, unable to move from off the drop sheet, until the wound to her head took her.

I went downstairs. I rang the police. I sat down in the front room to wait, and all I could think was, the lounge really didn't look right in here.

***

The coronial verdict was heart failure, possibly causing, possibly occasioned by, the fall. Given the advanced state of her osteoporosis (extremely rare in a woman of her age, but not unheard of), my sister should in no wise have been living alone and certainly not undertaking that kind of physical labour. She was also noted to have been in a state of advanced dehydration, malnutrition and exhaustion, but I held firm. As shocked as I was, I knew I wasn't to blame for that. Some of the other things, yes, were on me. But not that.

*****

It was me who told Mum the story about the previous owner dying in the house. It had always been one of her little superstitions, but I guess Julie forgot.

Bill had started hiding the tradie's tools when he saw how they looked down on him—just because they were licensed agents and specialised in the restoration of this or that, and he knew how to change oil. But they warmed right up after I told them Julie thought the house was haunted. I guess they were responsible for some of the knocking and moaning. I mean, even Bill got in on the act, insisting he'd seen the blood soak into the wood.

I also told Guillaume I'd seen Julie meeting a man in the cafe, a man who resembled the plasterer. Just another little story that filled in the wait at the hospital. Why did I do these things? It was payback, in return for her ramming the whole thing down my throat—how successful she was, with her high-flying job and her French lover. The gorgeous clothes she wore, the expensive gifts she could afford to give my kids. Who wouldn't have wanted to put a little dint in all that satisfaction?

When Julie showed me that decaying mound of brick and stucco, with the cracked step and falling tiles, I had seen exactly what she saw. I had seen what the house could be, and I wanted what I was never going to have. But I couldn't have known how it would end up affecting her. That she'd go all crazy and stop looking after herself, not even seeing a doctor when she must have been in pain. Maybe I should have paid more attention to the way she screamed when Eileen turned up at Christmas and said all those crazy things. I guess it really is all about the people you have in your life, to support and to ground you.

I tried to support my sister, at the end. Despite my previous actions, I really did try to help. And it looks like she knew it.

The lawyer told us to sell the house and pay off the last of the mortgage, but what kind of advice is that? We'll be moving in next weekend, bringing the little that is worth bringing from our old place. Sarah and Josh will have to learn not to scuff the polished floors or leave grubby little handprints on the perfect walls. They will learn very quickly. And Bill's weekends will be busy now, with taking care of the garden and cleaning the gutters. Mum can help too. It's just stupid of her to keep paying rent when she can live here, with us. We have that upstairs room and unlike Julie, I won't stand for any of her nonsense.

For it is my house now, mine to tend and cherish. When I place my hand to the wall, it feels warm to me, and almost soft. With the mortgage, I suppose I'll have to get a job, but I'll see that the brass is never tarnished, that there is never so much as a speck of dust on the mantle. The furnishing too, will have to be put right and the garden replanted with roses... see? I can be creative, too! Belville, her name is, and always has been. The beautiful, beautiful house.

Nothing will ever make me leave.

Should Fire Remember the Fuel?

A little past sixteen hundred hours, the wind changed, and Mark saw it happen. He saw old Alfie Pozzoli burn.

Alfie was on the dozer, reinforcing the existing firebreak between the bush reserve and the paddocks surrounding Fairlie town. He'd gouged a fresh, brown scar across the mouth of the shallow valley that was the fire's potential approach. A bad day at the end of a bad summer: the grass here was like yellowed paper, and the wind like standing in front of an open kiln.

Mark trudged up the western slope into the wind with a drip torch dribbling fire from his hand: he waved it in long, slow arcs, controlling the back burn. In his wake lay metres of charred ground, and Rory was performing the same back-breaking dance to his right. He felt his own sweat pooling inside his gloves. He and all the other members of the striker team wore full kit with filter masks and goggles, for there was smoke in the air, even though at last report the fire was still forty or more kilometres to the north.

The fire had kindled early this morning, right in the heart of the reserve. While the wind was blowing west to east, the danger to the town itself was low, but reinforcing the break was an obvious precaution. The striker was the smallest of any of the tankers, but it was all that could be spared. The bulk of the Fairlie branch of the Rural Fire Service (together with a unit sent from the regional headquarters), were north and east on the highway. That was where the main fire threatened the meat works and historic vineyard—and that, as Alfie had said, was that and a prayer.

Rory was a ginger giant, his skin one huge freckle, and the owner of the Fairlie petrol station and garage. Beside him, Mark felt short and obscurely pale. Through the spitting and popping of their torches, Mark heard him mutter, "The heat, they say: so fires light themselves now?" He glanced at Mark through his goggles. "You mark my words, this'll all turn out to be a couple of bloody kids!"

Go ahead and ask me, Mark thought. He taught years seven through ten, after all. If Rory truly believed this was the work of children, he should ask him to point out the jokers, the dull-heads, the ones who dared the railway crossing to relieve their boredom, and he would say that even among them, there was no such demon.

Then he felt the wind stop.

He straightened up, flicking off the torch. The sun dazzled him, swollen and red at the top of the hill. He swivelled away, saw Alfie on the dozer, labouring on another pass. But his eyes were still dazzled, because the yellow machine seemed to shimmer, ringed in a distortion of light. He turned further, gazing back down the valley to where the striker was parked next to the dam. Bella, Alfie's forty-year-old daughter, was up to her hips in brown water, placing the inlet for the pump.

"Wind's dropped!" Rory said. "Maybe we'll get a break, eh?"

Maybe I'll get home tonight, Mark thought, *and see Chrissie and Jo*. He smiled, picturing the two blonde heads—at three years old, Jo was the curlier, and giggled more often—and his wife's relieved smile. They could all return to the residence attached to the Fairlie Public School, where half a bottle of Fairlie Grove shiraz, a big, cool bath and a big, clean bed awaited him. The passing smoke slowed and spread as a breeze puffed gently, cooling his back even through the protective jacket.

He was facing south now. His back was towards the north. The cool became a chill. "Rory," he said, "turn off your torch. I think the wind is *shifting*."

Then there was a blast of heat and, he would swear, a screaming, howling sound as the northerly hit. Dust stung his face, and when he looked north, in place of the trees beyond the break he saw a billow of dense, black smoke. *Too close*, was all he could think, *that's the main fire but it's way too close! And it's coming—shit, it's coming* here*!*

"Go!" Rory bellowed as a new noise—a frizzling, crackling—rose. "Down to the dam!"

Mark started to run, and that was the moment old Alfie threw himself off the seat of the dozer and headed across the new-dug furrows. But his foot caught and he tripped, sprawling across the scar. Rory was several metres ahead of Mark, thanks to his greater mass: he bellowed, altering course towards Alfie. Mark hesitated just a second, then followed suit. Old he might be, but Alfie was heavy.

Then something burst in his ears and shoved him in the chest.

Mark only knew that somehow the earth was under his back and the sky above his face, but the smoke must have cleared from the sun because everything was now a brilliant and sickening yellow.

"Alf!" Rory screamed—Mark rolled and was crawling downhill, the drip torch gone from his hand, the stink of diesel penetrating his mask, the ground beneath him horribly warm. Pain accompanied the shapes forming in his field of vision. An infernal halo surrounded the dozer and, within, the blackened struts and panels all looked broken and wrong. On the ground close by, something thrashed and burned.

A hand caught his, hauled him up. "Go!"

And then Rory was hurtling straight towards the horror.

There was a hiss like an intake of breath, and smoke filled the valley like a chimney.

Mark turned and pelted in the direction of Bella and the striker. Within steps he was blind again, and the smoke pierced his nostrils—his mask had come loose. Rather than stop, he held his breath as he kept stumbling down, down, and as his foot skidded and hit wet, his vision cleared: in the pocket of air above the dam surface he saw Bella in the muddy water, holding the hose aloft and training a steady, light shower on the striker.

The water embraced him. It took his weight and replaced the smoke inside his leaking mask. "Bella," he croaked, "Alfie, I saw—"

He saw.

All around him, the massive trunks of trees climbing to foliage, sinking roots into the dam and crowding every side of the valley. Giant, old growth trees, every detail of bark and leaf etched in crimson and charcoal, and all the myriad shades that fire placed between. A fretwork of saplings, underbrush, flowers and fallen logs spread in every direction. Then in a moment they were fading, gone like forgetting. Fading to grey ash and smoke plumes. On the western hill, there was still a suggestion of trunks etched across the bare and smouldering ground, but otherwise it resembled a giant coal heap, their pathetic back-burn lost amid the universal char. The fire had passed. The fire had passed and the striker stood, apparently unaffected, save for the black clots adhering to the damp windshield and scarlet sides.

Bella was sloshing towards the bank. "Rory!" she called. Then, "Papa!"

Mark followed her, the dreadful words still hovering on his tongue, *I saw him burn*. Spot fires were eating away at the eastern hill, drifts of embers winked redly across the valley floor, but to his amazement there was still grass under the truck and around the dam. The fire front had not been broken by their efforts, but it had swerved. It was heading *south*. It was heading towards Fairlie, where Chrissie was making sandwiches and dispensing iced water at brigade HQ while Jo played around her feet.

"Papa!" Bella's cry rang through the murk.

"Radio!" Rory's voice was an agonised rasp.

The air against Mark's face was still hot, but his insides were stone cold as he staggered up the gluey, broken clay of the bank. As Rory staggered out of the smoke, a grisly burden over his shoulders, Mark headed for the striker, pulling off his gloves. The metal of the door handle was uncomfortably warm: he yanked the door open and hauled himself inside. Thank God, the radio unit was still showing all the right lights: he grabbed the handset and tore off his mask and goggles. "This is striker calling HQ, do you copy?"

HQ was the Fairlie community centre, where Megan Grant, the captain's wife, would be hunched at the radio directing operations. But the atonal crackling did not change, and no voice replied.

"This is striker calling HQ, the front has jumped the break."

Mark scrabbled inside his jacket for his mobile. He had speed-dialled Chris before realising he had no signal. But he *had* to reach her, had to know that she had taken Jo and evacuated (as was the plan) to Tamworth. Yes, he knew she hadn't been happy with the idea, had insisted on staying to help, but she had promised if the wind changed... would there be time? *Could* she get out? With some crazed idea of clambering on top of the vehicle (when obviously, the mobile tower had gone down and it would make no difference), he threw the door open just as Bella called for light. He hit the headlamps.

Mark had done his training; of course he had. He had seen the videos of car wrecks and looked at the pictures of burn injuries. He had read the manuals and not one of them had mentioned the smell, or the sounds Alfie was now making. His moustache was gone, along with his brows and lashes. In the filmy light his lips were one white blister, and though his pants and jacket were intact, Mark thought bad things had happened beneath them.

"Diesel vapour," husked Rory. He was covered in dirt and ash. "Tank must have been leaking. Then when the wind changed, it carried sparks."

"We've got to move," said Mark, turning back to the striker. "I'll go cross-country. I'll find help."

"We all go." Bella did not raise her head, busy with spray and gauze. "And we pack the hose away first."

****

Joining the volunteer brigade had been Chrissie's idea. Brought up outside of Bathurst, she understood these country towns and knew that, though teachers were respected, they were still outsiders. Intruders in a tightly-knit community.

"The brigade's a way of showing we're committed to living here," she had said, Jo burbling happily in her lap. "My dad was still doing it when he was seventy-four."

Which may or may not have been the best recommendation, but Mark had grown up in the very heart of Sydney city. He was all at sea in a place where the largest business was the pub and the second the feed and hardware store, and either building was larger than the school he had signed on to run. So he followed her advice, met Captain Grant, Alfie and Bella, Rory and all the others. Rory had a daughter in year seven and a two-year-old son, and his wife and Chrissie became fast friends. And he came to enjoy the meetings in the little plaster hall, with its flaking, white walls and clustering pepper trees. On weekends they would do training exercises in the carpark.

Now he was driving the striker as fast as he dared along the fire trail that looped around the eastern hill, retracing their steps of an hour—*two hours?*—previous in smoke like strands of solid night, weaving through the blackened stands of eucalypts. The leaves hadn't burned. The fire had sucked the oil out of them and leapt right on. The ice in his gut was still demanding he floor it, but both Rory and Bella insisted upon caution.

"Even on the trail there'll be embers," she said. "Go over a burn, we'll lose the tyres and that will be that and a prayer."

Alfie lay across the backseat, wrapped in a thermal blanket with his head in Bella's lap. How was she doing it? Mark gripped the wheel. Why wasn't she screaming?

There on the left, he saw live fire; orange-red blossoms hanging from trees in the premature darkness. Alongside the track lay nests of red coals, the collapsed remains of ferns or brush. The smoke was getting thicker, caught in the striker's headlamps. In the light from the dash, steam rose from his damp clothes.

"We better stop," said Rory, but Mark wasn't listening.

Mark *saw* the girl.

At first, it looked like part of the trail, a patch of paler earth. Then earth resolved into a girl with hair like flame, running through the scorched night. For a long moment he watched her, understanding nothing, then realised that the trees were back, the centuries-old giants with their shaggy bark and buttress roots, limned in orange and grey. As the striker rolled forward, she came into focus. Her hair wasn't red, it was a rich black-brown with gold strands, but somehow, it glowed. Her skin was brown and held that same luminous quality. She was wearing a short dress of nondescript colour and shape, and her legs were bare. Her only protection was a pair of flat shoes, pressing into the ashes. Then suddenly, a massive shoulder pushed past him and the tyres spun against sand as Rory jammed on the brake. The striker coasted to a stop just short of the blackened remains of a fallen tree.

Mark could still see the girl, her dress fluttering where any cloth would burst into flames, stepping on charcoal as hot as a stove. The strands of her hair not kindling as she ran straight into the ancient forest. But then, none of those trees were burned at all.

"For eff's sake, man!" Rory extricated himself.

Mark's voice wavered. "Did you see her? Did you?"

"It's nothing." Bella's voice was flat. "A phantom."

"A phantom?"

"Like those you see on the side of the road, when you drive at night for too long."

"Oh, a mirage," said Mark. The distinction between the words suddenly seemed very important: he could imagine himself describing it to a class. *A mirage is an optical illusion formed when rising heat causes an atmospheric refraction, whereas to call something a 'phantom' or 'spectre' implies belief in a supernatural origin....*

Rory pulled his mask up. "I'll go out and clear it."

Chrissie and Jo. "No, no need for that. We can take the truck round to the right: look, it's quite flat—"

"No," said Bella. In her lap, Alfie made an odd, mewling sound.

No one suggested Mark get out and help, so he didn't. He remained there with his hands glued to the wheel. That they were just sitting here, in the midst of all this, was impossible: how fast had the fire been going, to jump them like that? And why the hell hadn't the main crew radioed them to update the fire's position, or responded when he called?

Because they couldn't. Which was a ridiculous thought, but that didn't stop terror closing his parched throat.

Alfie mewled again.

"Shush, Papa," Bella murmured. "I'm here."

At last, Rory clambered back inside, bringing a fresh wave of smoke. Mark focused on the trail through the soot-scabbed windscreen and nursed the striker on.

"We don't have any native people in Fairlie," said Rory, apparently by way of conversation. "Used to be a what? A reservation? That became the reserve. But they were all gone by then."

Mark found himself latching onto the distraction. He *had* heard about the reservation and how the First Australians living there had worked on the cattle stations, until such time as they didn't. In the function rooms of Fairlie Glen Estate, sepia photos included contingents of dark-skinned men and women who never made the transition to greyscale; replaced, when the vines arrived, by Alfie's kin. He wondered what had actually happened to them. Wondered if Chrissie had remembered to collect the lockbox with their passports and Jo's birth certificate.

And then the darkness peeled away, and through the windscreen he saw the flat expanse of the paddocks surrounding Fairlie—desolate in the rufous light—and four blessed lanes of blacktop.

But then Rory placed one meaty hand on his arm and he was forced to halt again, just short of the sign announcing HISTORIC FAIRLIE GLEN ESTATE 40K. They would not let him budge until he tried the radio again.

"Striker to HQ... Regional, *anybody?*"

Then he swivelled around to face Bella. "They'll all be at Fairlie," he said. "Ambulances too."

After a long moment, Bella nodded.

Mark hit the accelerator. The wheels screamed as he swerved onto the road, then he gunned it as hard as he could.

Out the driver's window, he saw hills burning under a blood-red sky. Great, black fingers groped over the ridge, down gully and fence line, offspring of the spot fires they hadn't stayed to put out (and not even Bella had suggested that). To the east, the paddocks whipped by. The grass and fringing poplars were thick with ash: it was almost like snow. It was hard to imagine anything had ever lived here. Telegraph poles looped monotonously: if those creeping, licking fingers reached them, there would simply be more ash. Bursts of the stuff crossed the road in front of him: how many times had he driven this stretch in his own vehicle with Chrissie beside him and Jo strapped into her car seat in the back?

In the backseat, Bella's voice had the cadence of prayer.

Then up ahead (still distant, but closing by the second), Mark saw a bright light. Within heartbeats, it resolved into the same sulphurous glow as had enveloped the dozer. An accident, someone in this sifting smoke had come off the road. Fuck, would he have to stop *again*?

Now there was the shape of a cabin and a long, cylindrical body, and what he had not realised (putting everything down to their own speed) was that the flaming truck was speeding towards them, shedding that terrible light.

"Jesus!" Bella yelped. "Get off the road!"

Mark swerved. Bella gasped. He felt the striker shudder and swing over the gravel verge, as the roar of the oncoming tanker (*a* fuel *tanker, dear god!*) swallowed all sound, like the bushfire as it swept through the valley, glowing like the dozer had glowed—but to Mark's eye, cabin and tank were intact right down to the tyres, down to the side mirror and scrolling crimson and yellow logo. Then it was past them, and the complaint of their tyres on the verge crackled in his ears, and he slowed.

"Rory?" Bella quavered.

"Yeah," husked Rory. "Yeah, it was."

"Were you expecting a delivery?" asked Mark. His arms were shaking as he steered them back onto the road.

In the rear-view mirror, Bella shook her head. "Back in the nineties, when we were kids, both our dads were in the fire service."

"Yeah." Though Rory was covered in soot and smut, he sounded pale. "This one time, they got called out to where a tanker had rolled on the highway. We came out too, to see. By the time we got there, it had caught fire." Mark didn't take his eyes off the road; he was counting now, the little landmarks, the signposts and letterboxes closing in on the turnoff. "We all saw the dozer go up," he said. "Then we saw this stupid trucker go by, in this shitty light—" With a logo, he realised, he hadn't seen since the nineties, but that couldn't be right. "It's just another mirage."

"It's nothing," Bella said, "but it may mean something."

FAIRLIE 20K

***

And of course, they'd all been worried about nothing.

As they crossed the railway line, it looked bad, but that was mostly smoke and ash. A few of the outlying buildings had caught: the odd, old cottage and farm shed that no one could be bothered to save. They were smouldering still and, in the Grant's orchard, each tree bore a heavy crop of flame. But the further they got into town, the more obvious it was to Mark that he'd been right. Whether by the main brigade with the tanker or through the efforts of the residents, wielding sack and garden hose, the fire had been repelled. Of course it had! Towns didn't *burn*. Even towns like this.

As they rolled down the main street past the shuttered shops, the silence was certainly eerie and the sky above them opened and closed like a volcanic rift. Black ash drifted down the pavement, wound through the wrought-iron pillars supporting the pub's balcony, and anyone without a mask would obviously be inside.

"This isn't right," said Bella. "Doesn't feel right."

"They're all at the community centre," said Mark. Did it really take an outsider to tell these people what was what? He kept on coasting down the road, alert for trucks and ambulances or people flagging him down. Here and there, in the corner of his eye, he caught feral glints in gutters or drifting down side streets, but knew these had to be reflections, the blood-red light bouncing back from car mirrors or windows. The windows of the school. As he approached the corner of Bell Street, he gave a kind of chuckle. There was enough smoke up there that something must have caught: now Rory would definitely blame the kids. But the fact was, he didn't care: the residence had never been his home and the school itself barely more than a workplace. A career move, to come here, even if his wife believed it a fit place to raise their child.

"Ave Maria," Bella prayed. "*Gratia plena.*"

Alfie hadn't made a sound now in several minutes.

Suddenly, there was a popping and a thump he felt through floor and door; the striker dropped a full inch and shuddered. They did not stop but their progress slowed to a chunk-a-chunk crawl.

"That was the tyres," said Rory.

What did he want Mark to do? Stop and change them? The noise and heavy steering were annoying, and the cabin seemed to be heating up, but they were so close to where Alfie could be handed over to the proper authorities and there'd be tears but cheers as well, for after all the entire striker unit could have died spritzing water down the fire's throat.

Once again, steam rose from his clothes.

Would Chrissie be there, or had she gone? It didn't matter, not truly: his need to see her was an ache in his chest, but it would be satisfying too, had she gone. Because he was a teacher and she was a teacher, and for all their talk, they were never seriously going to stay.

A pall of smoke blocked him like some final test, and Rory kept his damn hands to himself. He pushed the striker into it, through it, and suddenly, there it was.

He saw.

The community centre stood amid the pepper trees with not a single char on its white surface. The curling, ferny leaves were green. And there in the carpark were the people, and at their centre Chrissie stood with Jo in her arms, her face fairly glowing with joy, all of them radiant. Megan, Rory's wife, a group of boys from his class: all the people who'd stayed to man the radio and make sure that whenever the firies returned. There'd be water and sandwiches, and a warm embrace.

What he couldn't see was any trace of the tanker crew. No helmets or jackets—no, wait, there was the uncanny shimmer of reflective tape. A man stood at the front of the crowd, gloved and helmeted, frowning and pointing towards the striker as if to say, what the hell are you doing?

Alfie. That man was Alfie.

Mark jammed on the brakes.

And then, as the fire raged on south and the heat loosed its grip on the remains of Fairlie, the mirage faded. As the ancient trees had faded, along with the truck and the fleeing girl. The glow went first, beloved faces fading to ash, then the outlines of flesh and hair dissolving, revealing what truly lay beyond. The devastation of brickwork and timber, smoking trees, the burning cars with bodies inside, caught as they tried to flee.

As Rory dragged his mask up over his face and Bella gently set her father down, Mark screamed and screamed.

This Attraction Now Open Till Late

"Have you seen anything strange tonight?" Madison asks Renato.

As they are both costumed for the House—Ren in his blood-spattered Victorian evening wear and she in the housekeeper's grey dress and voluminous wig—there is an obvious comeback. But Ren doesn't make it. He lifts his gaze from his phone (they aren't meant to keep their phones on during shift, but all of them do), and says, "You mean those two girls, in the jumpsuits?"

"Yeah," says Madison, heart giving a little leap. "Those ones."

They had come through twice. Obviously twins, just as obviously under-age for this attraction, which only meant their parents had ignored the sign. More unusually, they were unaccompanied. Two little girls in matching pink jumpsuits who marched through, squealing at the jump scares and giggling in between. Madison remembers they had giggled at her as she tried to keep the legend of Harrow House to a rating suitable for their tender ears.

"Little brats," pronounces Ren. "Did they touch anything?"

Madison shakes her head and then, very daringly, asks the real question. "What about their faces?"

"What about them?" Ren is twenty-four and has done television commercials and plays, as well as performing in the House. Under Lord Harrow's makeup, his skin is like raw, brown silk. He is very good-looking—it ties Madison's tongue into knots.

"They were very pink," is all she manages to get out.

"Yeah, pink," he agrees. "Shiny, almost. Like they were made out of soap."

"Yeah," says Madison. Heart in her mouth, she waits, but Ren doesn't say any more. He looks back down at his phone and continues scrolling through auditions.

They are in the entry room; Renato, herself and Noah, who is slumped in the wing chair on the other side of the fake fireplace, either hungover or coming down hard. Although this is *her* room (the cast being spread throughout the House), they all migrate here during slow patches to sit in the chairs or on the lounge and take advantage of the almost-steady light from the electric candles—all except Selene, who generally prefers to stay on her own. A sparsely-flocked fibreglass bear looms over them, beside a grandfather clock whose hands are set at five minutes to midnight. Red velvet drapes frame a portrait of the Harrow family in happier times, before the Lord brought the idol back from Peru. All this is normal.

The twins had not been normal, and there was something more. Something Madison hasn't and will not mention to Ren, or any of them. It seemed to her, as the two girls sat on the lounge where Ren sits now, that they noticed she only has one real hand.

Noah groans—a sound of pure agony—and slumps even deeper into his Beast costume. "Little monsters," he mumbles, and something that sounds like "some on four". She thinks she might ask what he means, only there is a knock at the door. The signal that more guests have arrived.

Ren gets up and hauls Noah out of his chair. The two of them stomp off up the corridor, into the haze of stage smoke. Madison quickly straightens both her posture and her dress, then at the last minute twitches her shawl down to cover the prosthetic resting in her lap. "Welcome," she says, as the door opens, "I am the Harrow's Housekeeper, and have been for many years."

It goes no further, that night.

***

When the shift ends, close to eleven, they all trudge across the midway to the unobtrusive door beside the food concession, and up the stairs to wardrobe, to change and take off their makeup—all except Selene, again. She arrives at the park in her makeup and fangs, and Madison has never seen her without them, or wearing anything other than black. After that, the others go out through the carpark, even though Ren is the only one who actually drives. But Madison likes to walk the entire length of the midway to the front gate, now that the park is almost empty and there is no one to notice any part of her. The lights are all still on, electric rainbows looping from pot of gold to pot of gold. The fairy-floss and slushie machines are stained glass windows, throwing out patches of magenta and green, while above it all the Ferris wheel raises artificial stars into the blank night sky. Down by the entrance with its pastel portcullis and crenellations, the Twirly Bird spins like a firework in slow motion. Without people, it is beautiful. Even the crusting of rubbish, of popcorn cups and ice cream spoons, chip packets and discarded half-hot dogs, takes on a baroque grandeur, and Madison feels just a little like she might have if the accident had never happened, if she was here with a group of friends, or on a silly romantic evening (with someone who looks a little like Ren, in her fantasies), or even with her mum and dad. That they might both be standing there in the entrance, waiting for her to catch up.

When she reaches the entrance, there is no one there. She trudges on up to the station and catches a train back to the apartment. When she gets home, her mother will already be asleep, and when she wakes, her mother will be at work. It's better this way.

***

There is a knock at the door.

The new guests are ushered in and sit upon the lounge. Madison gives her spiel and sends them up the hallway, hears them gasp and giggle when the family portrait dissolves into the shimmering image of the idol. This distracts them from the first of the animatronics (the roaring trophy) which, triggering as they turn the corner, elicits screams. The House is all one, intricately-folded corridor; it is impossible to get lost, and you can run from entrance to exit in about thirty seconds—not that Noah had been supposed to do this, let alone record his times. Thump, a glassy crash, the tinkle of a harpsichord: they have reached Selene's corridor with the coffin and distorting mirror. Selene may get screams, if they think she's just another dummy. From beyond, in Noah's room, comes scratching, the occasional howl and the thump-hiss of the second animatronic (the giant snake). But there's nowhere in the House you can't hear Ren, when he really gets going. His bellowed threat to offer their entrails to the idol, made while waving his machete in the final room, has sent more than one guest running back the way they came. But by now the knock has sounded again, the front door is opening, and she has a new group to welcome and warn. Noah will have to take care of the malingerers, ushering them out the fire door. His fur and claws send them running.

On and on it goes, around and around, thump and tinkle, scream. Madison falls into the rhythm. It's almost relaxing, until the next guests arrive.

What is it about this couple? Madison keeps both the prosthetic and her real hand on her knees, not moving an inch, while the man grins, tickling his companion's ribs as she squeals and bats at him. The man with sculpted muscles and the kind of T-shirt that costs more than Madison makes in a week; the woman professionally blonde and made-up, with inch-long orange nails.

"But when his wife and son were injured in a carriage accident, the temptation became too much. Lord Harrow wished upon the idol that both would recover and never suffer such hurt again." Madison keeps her gaze steady and her voice suitably sepulchral. But inwardly, she thinks his muscles are *too* cut—it's like they've been moulded. And her face looks like it could drop off and crawl away... she isn't supposed to think like that. According to her psychologist, that kind of negativity only reinforces her sense of alienation.

She straightens up and, although smiling is inappropriate, makes a renewed effort to meet the woman's eyes. Then her heart skips and her tongue knots when she realises neither of them are looking at her face as she speaks. They are looking, indisputably, at her prosthetic hand.

She stops in the middle of a sentence and, with her real hand, gestures for them to proceed down the hallway. They do, whispering and giggling, and she watches them. As they turn the corner, as the smoke envelops them, she could swear she sees the woman bring her date's finger to her mouth and bite down. She could swear that the finger comes off.

There is a knock at the door. For a moment, Madison does not—cannot—move. Then she flicks the shawl down again, and finds the opening phrase somewhere in her throat. As the next guests file in, hooting and mock-screaming, she does not look at them.

***

"No, they didn't touch anything." Madison can hardly get the words out. "They didn't threaten me. They just...."

"They didn't need to," says Selene, who has just emerged from the smoke. "It's their eyes."

Madison has never had much to do with Selene, despite her being the only other woman in the House. Now, she gazes up at her—straight, black hair, grey eyes, paper-white skin, and wearing the corset again, instead of her costume. Madison gazes as if Selene is the sister she never had. "Their eyes," she echoes. "Like, you think they might be fake but then they *move*."

"Contact lenses," suggests Ren. "There could be a birthday party in the park and it's a joke."

"Sometimes it's their whole faces," Selene insists. "Sometimes just their hands."

Madison stiffens, but none of them look at her. She can feel them not looking at her.

"So, someone did touch you?" Ren glances at the corset.

Selene's eyes go cold. "They don't need to," she repeats, then seats herself neatly on the arm of the wing chair where Noah has once again collapsed.

"I'm just trying to understand." Ren pushes back his black curls (glorious hair, the kind you just want to run your fingers through) and looks frustrated. "What's actually the problem here? If they don't touch you and they don't make threats, or sex jokes—"

"You're telling me," Selene cuts in, "that you haven't noticed a single, strange thing?"

You have, Madison holds her breath. *You noticed the twins.* For just an instant, their eyes meet.

Then he turns to Noah. "What about you? Seen anyone with weird eyes or h—faces?"

Inside their plastic shell, Madison's missing fingers prickle and twitch. They itch for the touch of curls, to flex and to hold. Noah looks sick, really, like he might throw up on the carpet.

"People are just assholes," he quavers, "Right?"

But to Madison, it sounds like he's seeking reassurance.

"Right," says Ren. He uncrosses his feet. "Look, I'm not saying we don't get people through who behave like dicks. But if they're not breaking the rules, then what can we do? People pay to come through and if that's 'cause they want to laugh at the freaks, then so what?"

There is a knock at the door. As though he was the one who had been laughed at all along, Ren slams his top hat onto his curls and storms up the hallway, before any of them can say a word.

***

When Madison gets home, her mother is asleep. The white-dark apartment is quiet, and still feels both too small and emptier than it should.

She concluded regular appointments with her psychologist three months ago (two years after the accident), but she still has the number. She is entitled, they said, to call in an emergency. Is this an emergency?

Her missing fingers ache as she undoes the straps and slips her wrist from the sheath. She has learned to write passably with her left hand, but her brain has still not adjusted to the loss of the right. The doctors said it might take years before she stops feeling these phantom sensations, a refraction of the moment she did *not* feel, when the displaced metal of the car engine crushed her hand beyond repair. That was not all it did. She wonders if her sleeping mother sometimes feels an itch or prickle when she rolls into that half of the bed where Madison's father used to be.

What she is seeing now, in the House, must be something like that: a phantom. A displacement. Even if Selene agrees, even if Noah is spooked by something beyond his regular intake of recreational drugs, Ren is undoubtedly right.

****

The next afternoon, Madison arrives early at the park. She does this sometimes, so as to avoid the crush in wardrobe at the shift change, when all the clowns exchange their baggy pants and makeup for jeans and T-shirts, as the new batch pull on their wigs and oversized shoes.

Having become the Housekeeper, she takes the keys from the office and opens up the House. She turns on the power at the switchboard, which is behind the bear. She sets the soundtrack playing, looping through its tolling bells, moaning wind and screeching violin. She turns on the full, overhead lights (as distinct from the effects lighting) and walks the entire length of the corridor, checking that the animatronics are working, and topping the smoke machines up with smoke juice. She enjoys doing these things, so long as there is no one watching. It was how her mother got to go for the job in the first place, by telling her no one would pay any attention to her here and, if they did, they wouldn't be able to tell a real injury from a fake one. *Right, Mum.*

But when she turns the corner into Selene's room, she sees Noah lying full-length in the coffin. He is dressed in clothes she hasn't seen before: a silver, sleeveless top with an inbuilt hood and pants that would be clown-like except they are black and supplied with an array of studs, eyelets and lacing. His jacket is hooked over the mirror. His chest moves slowly, evenly, and a slight sheen of drool marks the satin pillow. He looks, for all the world, like he has been here all night.

How has this happened? He left with the rest of them. Obviously, she needs to wake him before anyone else shows up—but how to go about it? Just looking at his relaxed, freckly face makes her feel embarrassed.

The answer is simple. She steps round the corner and triggers the snake.

Noah shrieks himself awake, trying to get to his feet, to get out of the coffin, and failing spectacularly. "Fuck!"

"Are... are you alright?"

He stares, as though her presence here is inconceivable. Then he says, "Yeah, thanks."

She offers him her water bottle and he takes it, swigs half. Then he climbs out and disappears briefly through the fire door, for a purpose she doesn't want to overhear.

She is in the entry room when he finally sidles back in. Sits down. "You know how there's that big crack in the wall, right next to the fire door?" he says at last. "Well, last night I got the whole board out and climbed through. I've shoved it back: no one will know."

"Yes," she says, "but why...?"

"I came back here when I couldn't get home after the club."

"Were the trains out?"

Noah shakes his head. "I never even made it to the station." He pauses. When he looks at her, he is sick again. "It was the monsters. Some have two legs, but some have four."

She looks for signs he is joking. But he's not joking, and actually seems less medicated than usual.

"It's crazy," he says. "I know. Unless you're seeing the same things, but then I...." He trails off, and his chin sinks to his chest. "Sorry. I should have backed you up."

"It's okay," says Madison, even though she feels anything but. His acknowledgement that something is wrong, on top of Selene's, is like a weight sinking in her stomach. "But, you see them outside the House..." Of *course* he does! To come inside, they have to be outside; she tries another tack. "How long have you been seeing them?"

"Dunno. Since summer, maybe?" Has he had this fear in his eyes, since then? "But there's more of them now."

"And they were at the club?"

Noah shudders. "The worst ones, they stay outside, and I only see them in the dark. But the ones that can pass for human... don't *you* see them, like at the station or the shops?"

Madison shakes her head. But then, she actively tries to avoid people, except in the House. "We should watch today," she says. "You, me and Selene. When they come in, I'll give a signal; trigger the portrait twice, maybe. Then we'll see if we see the same things in the same people. And you can check if you recognise any of them."

"Yeah," he says, "That's good thinking." He doesn't look much better, but he probably needs to eat.

"You should go get breakfast and then change." She stands up. "I'll talk to Selene, when she gets here."

"Yeah," he says. "Yeah. That's...."

"I won't tell her you were in her coffin."

***

They pass through the House, those non-humans, noticing what they should not. That a young man has piercings and scars, more scars than he should. That under her makeup, a Goth girl is older than you'd think. Some of them look like adults in their prime, some are middle-aged, some are the size of children. Eyes that reflect, hands that extrude, some that seem to shed body parts behind them. These dissolve into a slime that might otherwise be mistaken for spilled soda or fairy floss. They come in the daylight, but there are more of them after dark. At the end of shift, Madison, Noah and Selene add up their tally (only counting sightings where they all agree) and estimate that a quarter of their guests are now monsters.

So what is going on? For Selene, it started after she broke up with her last boyfriend.

"It was like he changed overnight. I mean, that's what it was like for me. One day, he just didn't want to do our thing any more. I hadn't noticed him changing, so I started trying to see all the things I'd missed."

Noah agrees with her, that they were most likely there all along. Madison is not so sure. They must have come from somewhere, like pollution or plagues of insects. Something must have happened. "An accident," she says.

"Well, whatever it was," says Noah, "They're here. What do we do?"

"I think we should watch Ren," says Selene, catching her black lip on a fang. "He can't see them. What if he's turning into one?"

Madison starts to say they've no reason to think that, except of course, Selene does. "Ren's all right," she says instead. "A bit stuck up."

"A *bit*," says Noah, and laughs.

They all laugh, and yes, it feels good.

"I'm going to look for something that could have caused this," says Madison. "In the meantime, I guess we carry on like normal. But none of us should be out on the streets at night."

***

There are wars happening that she didn't even know about, in countries she didn't know existed. The weather isn't behaving like it should, with temperatures going up and down further than they ever have before. Lights have appeared in the sky, and super moons, and a partial solar eclipse.

That night, when she arrives home, Madison finds her mother sitting up in front of the shopping channel, drink in hand. She sits down beside her and, after a few minutes of watching the changing patterns on the screen, she asks when all this strangeness started, whether her mother remembers when *before* became *now*.

Her mother snorts. "There was no before."

There was. She remembers it. It was when she had a boyfriend (though it wasn't really serious) and was going to go to university and... what had she been going to do? Maybe study journalism. Maybe act.

Her mother falls asleep, as a presenter offers to sell them small statuettes of something she can't quite make out. But Madison can't sleep, in her bed or anywhere. She ends up back online, doing more research. And when she goes into work (a full two hours early, this time), both Noah and Selene are already there. Signs are that Selene took the coffin and Noah the lounge. One of the red drapes has been brought down and used as a blanket.

"I couldn't even get near my house," Selene says, voice stretched high and thin. "The police had cordoned off the road. If they were police."

Selene's hair is mussed and her make-up rubbed away in places. Madison asks what she did then. Selene says she remembered Madison's warning and tried to find shelter. She even went past her old boyfriend's new place. "It was all dark and silent. But when I knocked, this thing came round the corner that wasn't even...." She giggles hysterically. "I ran. I climbed the gate in the carpark, then I got the board out from beside the fire door."

Noah hunches. Madison sees that his jacket is torn at the shoulder, as if something had seized it with teeth.

"You both should have come to my place," says Madison. Then she remembers her mother's dead eyes and thinks, *This is better.*

"Come on, let's go to wardrobe," she tells Selene. "I'll fix your makeup."

"Thank you," Selene says, the tension draining out of her. "Just, thank you."

With clown white and black greasepaint, she manages to repair Selene's maquillage. There is an hour and half still to wait, and during that time Ren texts them all the same message. He has an audition this afternoon, he will be late. Can they cover for him?

That they will do this is one of the unwritten rules of the House. They have all invoked it for one reason or another. Selene thinks it unwise to help him, in the circumstances, but Noah says he'll take over Lord Harrow's room and Madison replies with a "Yes".

There is a knock at the door.

Giggles at her story. Squeals at the portrait. Thump and scream. Shrieks at Selene. The snake. A missed beat. Madison finds herself holding her breath. Noah's voice is not as loud as Ren's and he laughs more, cackling as he yells, "I'll chop you into pizza! Yes, the idol demands pizza!" But the rhythm remains largely unchanged.

Is it the rhythm? Madison wonders, averting her eyes from the abominations before her. Is it the rhythm that keeps them moving? Or is Ren right about their coming to see the freaks? Do they find us *funny*?

Ren arrives an hour in and he is not in a good mood. "You know anything about someone breaking into the House?"

Noah looks to Madison, but Selene simply stares. Madison realises she is checking Ren's eyes and his fingers.

"Supervisor caught me coming in. Had to pretend I was on a toilet break." Ren is wearing a black suit, that *could* be Lord

Harrow's costume. He frowns when he sees his hat in Noah's hands. "Anyway, they reckon a board had been pulled away from beside the fire door and someone had pissed out there. Asked if there was any damage inside. Did you even notice?"

"The board, yeah," says Noah. "We tried to put it back." He holds out the hat.

Ren snatches it up. "Were you going to tell anyone? If something's damaged, we'll all be held responsible!" He hasn't noticed the drape still lying across the lounge.

"Stop it! You're always on at him!" Selene steps up, corset jutting. "Well, I guess this means you're not a monster."

"Oh, not this again—"

"You're just a dick."

"Please, everybody!" Madison clutches her shawl. "Be quiet!"

There is a knock at the door. Without another word, Selene and Noah turn and march back up the hallway. Ren lingers a moment, breathing heavily as he bunches his curls back under the hat.

Madison asks, "What happened at the audition?"

He turns on her so suddenly she stumbles back into the chair. "I didn't get it, okay? I couldn't... I just *couldn't*, okay? I'm not what they want, so now I have to hang out here with a druggie and a loonie and—" He breaks off, whirling into the wall of smoke. She hears his voice as he turns the corner, and the trophy triggers. "I'll check the damage and take it all to management this evening. You shouldn't have to worry."

Of course I do, she thinks. *Now I have to worry about all of you.*

Inside the House, it is always five minutes before midnight. Bells toll, the wind moans, and violins wail. Outside, the darkness comes intangibly as Ren takes up his place, and the monsters swarm.

Madison has no answer. Unless it were her accident that broke the world; in which case, what is the solution? She can't regrow her hand. By the end of shift, she has no better plan than the one she suggested before.

"You come with me to my place," she tells Noah and Selene, when they join her—they can hear Ren stomping and fussing with the board, searching for signs of unauthorised occupation. "We'll be safer together, anyway."

She has re-hung the drape, kind of, but it won't pass more than a cursory inspection.

Sure enough, when the soundtrack dies and the overhead lights come on, Ren does not join them. He has gone out the fire door, avoiding them.

"He knows it was us," mutters Noah. "I say we ditch the costumes and get out *now.*"

"We can ditch them in wardrobe, while he's talking to management," says Madison. No point in making the trouble worse. "Selene, if you'll wait for us?"

Selene nods. Noah opens the door.

Electric rainbows still loop along the midway towards the entrance. The fairy-floss and slushie machines still resemble whole panes in a shattered cathedral. The Ferris wheel still turns, attempting to restock the sky, as the Twirly Bird spins and spins. But they are not empty, as they should be at this hour. They are full.

Now, in Cinderella time, they have shed their footwear and eyeglasses, their teeth and rimes of hair. How pink it all is! How shiny! A stench arises from them like the ebb-tide of a poisoned sea. On the dodgems, their disgusting forms quiver and collapse into each other with every slam. In the seats of the Twirly Bird, some fling out extra arms to hold themselves in place as inertia sends ripples through whatever makes up their bodies.

"The moon!" gasps Selene.

Madison does not look. She grabs Selene's hand and, after a fractional hesitation, offers her prosthetic to Noah. She cannot feel him take it, but there is weight, a comforting weight. "Across to the car park," she breathes. "Keep to the edge and don't look anyone in the eye." She takes a step, but the weight drags.

"It's no good," says Noah, his voice unnaturally calm. She looks and sees the shadows of the carpark extrude things that look like hunting, like hunger. Where the light touches their skin, it is a slick and glistening pink-grey. No ribs, no sockets, no sign of bone, just pure motion. Four legs touch the ground, but their faces are still human—as human as the rest, at least.

Madison can feel tears sliding down her cheeks. Her heart is pounding. "We have to get through," she whispers. "My mother—"

And then she see Ren.

Did he even get as far as wardrobe? He stands by that unobtrusive door within a circle of gelid things, waving his arms and swaying as if he could fall at any moment. But even through her own fear, Madison sees this is not mindless panic. His arms move just fast enough to create an illusion of bonelessness. He puffs out his cheeks as he gyrates and bugs his eyes. The gelid creatures are pressing in, pressing together, but they leave him space. They watch him.

Out of the car park, one of the four-legs noses, slides into the light. Its jaw elongates, sagging. It spews a tongue. Does Ren see it? His gyrations grow wilder, he sinks lower, as if he is attempting to use his unwelcome audience as cover.

The hunting thing palpitates, focuses obscenely. Ignoring, or perhaps not seeing the little cluster at the front of the House, it slinks towards its prey.

Madison lets go of Selene's hand and reaches into her own right sleeve—the grey dress is roomy, she manages easily. The clips come undone. "Go back inside," she tells them. "I'm going to get him."

Noah gasps as he realises he is still holding her prosthetic.

She keeps to the edge, slipping and weaving. The four-legs can see her now, but nothing stops her before she reaches the food concession. The stall is untended, at least by anything she can recognise. But as staff herself, she is entitled to step in.

They notice my hand. Always.

Inside the fairy-floss machine, two wands spin sugar into pink and glistening clouds. She takes a deep breath, then reaches for the serving hatch. They were all taught to never, ever put their hands into the machine, but she isn't inserting her hand. She inserts her stump.

She isn't trained, like Ren. She can't make her body twist, though she does her best. But what draws the creatures' attention, what makes them part for her as she approaches, is the sticky, pink globule of fairy floss woven around her right wrist. It looks almost like one them. She waves it round, as if she is on the Twirly Bird. Before the four-legs can close the distance, the two-legs let her through to the crouching man. They watch her as they watch her in the House. There is a sequinned shifting of eyes as she looms over him. Wonderingly, his own eyes turn upwards.

"Your shift isn't finished," she tells him, then offers the fairy-floss as if to help him up.

He meets her eyes. And then, without prelude, he bites into the sticky pink.

Her missing fingers prickle. The things ripple and chitter—they seem *pleased.* As Ren rises, they bubble and part, allowing him and her to retrace their steps.

On the threshold of the House, he pauses. "Oh Christ, it's nearly here!"

She does not look. Instead, she knocks: the special *ratta-tat* that means a cast member is outside. The door opens and they slip in.

Noah is still holding her prosthetic. He waits until she has wiped the sticky remains from her stump, then presents it to her. Ren has collapsed on the lounge and is curling, curling up into a ball.

"What's happening?" he moans. "Why so many, all of a sudden? Why here? Did they follow me?"

"Just couldn't admit it, could you?" Selene sits down beside him and, after a moment, pats his shoulder.

Her prosthetic reattached, Madison reaches behind the bear, to the switchboard. She turns the soundtrack back on. Swaps the overheads for the effects lighting.

"What are you doing?" Noah jitters. "We have to think of something—go out the fire door maybe and climb the fence."

"If we can hold out here till daylight." Ren sits up. "Maybe, we can make it to my car."

And go where? This is the world now.

"Go to your rooms," she says. "It will be all right. Just keep up the rhythm."

There is a knock at the door.

A Nightmare in Burgundy

In memory of W.H. Pugmire

An entire chamber awash with that dark wealth which hovers between red and black. The innermost sanctum—though of foundation sacred or profane cannot be told from draperies the shade of drying blood. A dark goddess stands there, or a holy whore, her face and breasts pale above silk which flows like richest wine. Her eyes are scabbed black, her lips scarcely lighter. Blossoms of the deepest shade adorn her hair and are heaped about her feet, where claret veins the floor. So liquid appear those veins, so suggestive the fold of the curtains. Is it all in truth a welter of flesh?

My name is Raquel Travers and I am a dealer in art and antiquities. My reputation is that of a problem-solver: no matter what difficulties may separate a client from the object of their desire, I will find a way to bring them together. I have achieved many such small miracles, albeit with tarnished halo. So it was that I arrived in the city of G— at the behest of Monsted St Clair. I had dealt with his father before now, but this was a matter of especial delicacy. I was here to retrieve not a painting or a sculpture, but his sister Merielle.

Merielle was an artist in her own right, who I had represented to buyers in the past. But this meant little to her family, who were constantly mortified by her wild behaviour. Even for the Paris scene, Merielle was an *enfant terrible*, relentlessly defying all convention in pursuit of her guiding daimon. That daimon did not distinguish readily between art and life. For a female nude, she had lived and worked entirely naked until the picture was complete. A portrait of a male friend saw her wear a rubber phallus and enter pissoirs. To create her spectacular *Faces in the Crowd*, she had spent three months in constant company, coted and hired: eating, sleeping, painting in a tangled crush of bodies. But fleeing her native land for this city of dreams and shadows was, for the family, a step too far.

In my profession, I am required to navigate the underworld as routinely as Olympian privilege. I do not scare easily. It had taken me no small effort to locate this house, a slouching terrace, lightless in the winter dusk. But something in its dilapidation—extended rather than concealed by wildly overgrown camellias and a magnolia laden with wine-coloured buds—suggested Monsted was right to be worried. That what I would find here went beyond mere eccentricity.

I dislodged the gate and walked a cracked and crooked path. Through gathering shadows, I saw the camelia was already blooming—huge, rubiginous flowers that all but glowed in the dusk. The bristling branches scratched my face as I pushed past them and knocked sharply on the door. It took three repetitions, then the door opened on a dimly-lit hallway. Merielle St Clair stood there in a burgundy *galabeya*, the fabric a violent contrast to her pale skin. Always slender, she looked wasted: the contours of her face, though still striking, had sunk as in famine or prolonged illness, and her hair hung in dark rattails. Only her eyes were as I remembered: a burning, hazel intensity.

"Raquel!" Then her gaze smoked, as Merielle remembered there was no honest way I could have found her.

From my shock, I roused and smiled. "You forget, my dear, that at our last meeting we discussed your experiments in using ox-blood as a binder. I have today spoken to no less than eleven butchers."

She grimaced. "You better come in, now you're here. I don't suppose you brought any cigarillos?"

I produced a packet of her favourite brand, and she took it, though the action cost her a visible wince. Crossing the threshold, I inhaled a scent that was not tobacco but like it, both foul and sweet.

In the narrow hall, deep burgundy drapes buried all windows and a flocked wallpaper covered floor to ceiling in wine-dark arabesques. The carpet was the same shade, rubbed threadbare in places. The only furnishings were a cedar coat rack and tiny cabinet of Japanese lacquer-work. A door beside me gave onto a small parlour or sitting room: from the piles of books and bottles, this was where she slept. At the end of the hall, beyond the staircase, I glimpsed a filthy, old kitchen. I declined to doff my coat.

On the stairs, as we climbed, there was art: a print of Rothko's 1958 *Black and Maroon* beside the burgundy rose from *Flore Des Serres Et Des Jardins De L'Europe*. Next to that hung an excellent reproduction of Fra Fillipo's portrait of Angiola Sapiti. Angiola wed Lorenzo di Scolari in 1440, and this painting is believed to have witnessed the union. What a bride she must have made, all in burgundy velvet, the contours of her face saint-like through the matching veil! But the studio approached—it could only be the studio. Merielle had lit the frail, brown roll and paused for a moment, puffing gratefully, before the battered door.

The top floor of the terrace had been collapsed into one long room. More drapes covered the windows and egress to the balcony—from the street, it had looked profoundly unsafe. Here, the light was brighter and the scent was stronger, a choking musk. Her work in progress, exceeding her slightly in height, was on its easel at the far end. From the doorway, I could make out a figure—it looked to nestle in the heart, or perhaps vagina, of some massive mother goddess, every shade a variant of those that had drenched me since entering. The word from the butcher had prepared me, and the stench confirmed my suspicion. I looked on the painting and was glad, then, that Merielle had chosen to retreat from Paris. Moving closer, I saw her palette glistened like a cut kidney. I was surprised to see she was working at night—though so thoroughly was the room cocooned, what difference could it make? The painting appeared to be all but complete. No matter the medium, it was an awesome achievement, the equal in depth and richness of any old master. Bending near, I admired how the discrete forms had been raised with repeated glazes, each containing more or less of her chosen pigment.

"I declare your experiment an unqualified success," I said, turning back towards my quarry. "Is she Persephone? I dare say it will take no longer than oils to cure, so this year's Prix la Couronne d'Or?"

"It's not for that." Merielle's voice simmered with tobacco. She stood beside an occasional table of carved mahogany bearing a lacquered bowl. It contained a medley: wax grapes, a porphyry egg, camellia petals, the glossy carapace of stag beetles. Merielle dipped her free hand into it, the variant textures rising and falling between white fingers. "Not for judges and prizes, and critics."

"Then what, may I ask, is it for?"

"For Monsted and my father. The aunts and the cousins, the teachers and priests: all those who don't see. Who *can't* see, because some connection is missing in their shrivelled little brains. She is the one who cannot be ignored. I knew she existed, but I had to come here to find her. It's been hard, Raquel, it's been very hard." The wisping cigarillo trembled, she wavered and nearly fell.

"When was the last time you ate?" I scolded. "No, don't tell me. Just get your coat and some shoes—it's freezing out there. We'll go out and celebrate your achievement."

"No," she said, "I can't leave her."

"You're afraid of thieves? This house will attract few, but I understand. We'll order in!"

"No! You shouldn't be here, Raquel. As glad as I am to see you, this isn't...." A strange expression came over her face, as if she were seeing me in truth for the first time. Peering at my cheek, where the camellia's lash still stung. "You're bleeding."

I put my hand to the spot, perturbed again by the intensity of her gaze. "I'm sure it's stopped now. That bush, another reason not to fear thieves."

"She's not quite finished." With the cigarillo, Merielle directed my attention back to the painting. I turned, but felt she was still watching me. "I know it looks complete, but I must keep working. The canvas absorbs so much, I'm forever glazing. Look along the bottom, where nothing occludes the paving."

I bent, but in such a way as revealed Merielle in the corner of my eye. "I see that you primed well: the texture is very convincing. Is that marble dust?"

"Bone," she replied and, from the bowl she withdrew a razor folded into a tortoiseshell case. I saw her flick it open.

In my time, I have exchanged bullets with gangsters and successfully preserved myself from antiquity thieves who thought a woman would be easy prey. As Merielle came for me, I swivelled, seized the palette, and brought it up to trap the blade. With my other hand I gripped her arm: she shrieked in pain, but struggled with a strength amazing for her condition to free the razor and bring it to my flesh.

"Just a brushful, that's all! I thought you wanted to help!"

By degrees I forced her to the floor, arms held in a tight lock. The tone of her babbling changed, as I made the necessary phone calls, from pleading to terror.

"I can't leave her! Oh Raquel, you don't understand—she must have blood, like all gods. Maybe there's still some left in the bags, though warm! Warm is best!"

At what point had the chilled elixir of bovines become insufficient to her project? Both her arms were slashed multiple times, the oldest cut still healing. It seemed likely I had arrived just in time. She struggled but rapidly exhausted herself, collapsing shortly before help arrived.

***

Artists are insane by definition: how else can they look at the world wherein we all walk, and see such visions? The combinations of colour and texture that raise beauty up from dross, flashes of detail granting meaning to the mundane. And then there are those like Merielle, able somehow to incarnate their wildest fantasies. She had been ill when she attacked me, her mind clouded by pain and long deprivation. Once she recovered, she would probably not even remember the incident. And so, I said as little as I might to the sunken-eyed doctors at the hospital where we were taken. I muttered darkly about a tragic love affair, and implied that the family would take care of things. Whether they accepted this or not, they did not question. As soon as Merielle was well enough to travel, all three of us would go home—for I would see the piece entered in the Prix. Should she win, her goal of forcing her family to see her worth might yet be realised. In the meantime, I would pack up the house.

A city such as this holds obvious opportunities for one of my profession. There were cramped and dusty shops to visit, old names to enquire after, and it was dusk again before I could return. I found the terrace no less unwholesome, and the first thing I did after turning on all the lights was tear down the drapes in the hallway and fling the windows open.

The parlour held luggage and a nest of kinds, discarded clothes and a maroon, silk quilt on the perishing burgundy couch (where had she found all these things? I assumed the local thrift store had provided—it could receive them back). Under a detritus of cheese and crackers, stained glasses and empty wine bottles, were the boxes that had transported her books; those she had deemed necessary to this project. Most were art-related, but I noted Monoghan's *Book of the Goddess*. Then I girded my loins and entered the kitchen.

Blood indeed remained in the plastic bags cluttering the ancient refrigerator, and a sight more macabre would be hard to imagine, even for an artist. Stray spatters caked the already discoloured interior: they continued across the floor to the table and sink, and the smell was appalling. I shook my head and continued my survey, of bathroom and impenetrable backyard, then up the stairs to the studio itself.

At second sight, the painting had no less impact: if anything, the details impressed themselves more firmly on my mind. The coils of the woman's hair, for instance, were the deepest possible cordovan. A very fine curl strayed over the ear, where a garnet lodged, and across one ivory cheek. I thought of Da Vinci's red chalk drawings and his anatomical diagrams in portmanteau as I took in the underlying structure of the face, comprehending that no model had ever stood here. Merielle had given the figure her bones as well as her blood. Bone dust, she had said, incorporated into the primer. I shivered and turned away, meaning to pull the drapes from off the balcony.

Did they whisper? Did the night breeze push through the hidden panes and stir the heavy, velvet folds? There was not the slightest trace of motion. The curtains might have been carved. How deep, how rich were those folds, the nap collapsing from burgundy into black! I could reach in and wrap them around me, be utterly engulfed by their bloody softness. But then the whisper sounded behind me: I turned, but again saw nothing that moved. My shivers redoubled—without doubt, Merielle's experiments had attracted vermin that became active at nightfall. I considered returning to my hotel, but equally, their presence meant I could not leave the painting. In her delirium, Merielle's protests had possessed a rational base.

I considered taking the painting with me, but it was too large to fit into an ordinary taxi. I would have to make enquiries and see one of the shops I had ventured about getting it framed. For now, I would simply have to remain.

How deep were the woman's scab-black eyes.

I ordered food, and by the time it arrived I had found an unopened bottle of pinot noir. Once the courier had left, I uncorked it. How intense, how dark yet impossibly lucent was the colour of the wine in the one, clean glass! I sat on the couch, staring at it in the light for what must have been minutes without taking a sip.

I swallowed and felt burgundy billow down my throat, a sensual assault that opened, sure, with the dry wash across my tongue and the aroma of dark cherry and oak bursting against my palate but extended to a sense of the colour itself kindling, penetrating the fragile membranes of lung and throat to mingle with my blood. So utterly did this sensation consume me that I realised I had fallen back on the couch, as though I were already drunk.

Believe me, I do not get drunk alone in strange cities. I told myself I was tired, instructed myself to eat then lock the house up. But within minutes, I had poured myself another glass.

Did I sleep?

The room was dark and anonymous, but whispering, rasping surrounded me. Soft fabric brushed over my skin—I had fallen deep, deep down past the drink, past the couch. I was alone but within reach of a thousand, thousand partners all fitted for pleasure as I, if I just let myself, sank deeper still into the undifferentiated tincture, the ultimate saturation of hue. Let the membrane part.

Did I wake?

For now, I was staggering into the kitchen, eyes panging in the feeble light from the refrigerator, scooping out the quarter-empty bags and those with only a smear remaining. The whispering was all around me; I had minutes before the invitation refused became the compulsion imposed. How did I know what to do? Because Merielle had told me.

Scoops and spatters went into the pot, together with half-coagulated clots. The stuff was cold and slimy on my hands. I ignited the gas and kept searching—a gobbet here, a trickle there. It thinned as it warmed, but remained a deep burgundy with oxidation. I carried the pot in both hands, like a votive, as I climbed the stairs. Behind me, there was only whispers and flocking. Nonetheless, the sight of the picture nearly sent me fleeing away into a dark from which I knew I would never emerge. Whatever the woman was, whatever arcane force Merielle had bound into this shape, it stood sharp and clear of its painted surrounds. All it would take was one step of those bone-white feet, and she would be in the room.

I was no artist. I was not worthy of dipping brush into warm ink and limning her contours. I knelt before the figure, the pot between my knees. I did not raise my head, merely reached out and the foot formed, long, cool, and narrow in my hands as I laved it over in blood.

Did I wake?

A raw, red dawn was stealing in the naked windows. I lay on the couch in a posture of knotted terror. The wine had spilled and soaked into the carpet.

Artists are insane by default. They look at the world and see what they see, then cast their visions into forms the rest of us can appreciate, but never purely. Always we view them through the filter of our own circumstance, our values, our pleasures, or a work's relevance to politics or to a religion the artist never once considered. I am no artist, though I scavenge them, and try as I will, I cannot truly express what I experienced that night. Even now, the memory clouds, fades with every moment as the light strengthens. Did I drink and sleep, or did I—it is unthinkable! But, whatever the truth of what happened here in this house, I now accept I misunderstood Merielle's goal. She does not seek her family's approval, but their transformation. What divine generosity! In return for a lifetime of belittlement, she brings them this, to open their eyes and give to them the experience of something beyond this world!

Likewise, my plan was flawed, for Merielle herself must remain here. It is the only place that can foster such work as this. It is the painting and I that must leave, as soon as possible, and travel back to Paris and the great house of St Clair. Monsted will be confused, perhaps angry, when I present it in his sister's stead, but I will insist that acceptance of the painting is the only way to achieve reconciliation. Oh, he will understand. Once darkness falls, he too will see.

THE FINAL MASQUE

A Tale of the Curtius Waxworks

France is dancing. She has been dancing since Thermidor (as before the Revolution, she used to kiss). She dances to avenge; she dances to forget! Between her bloody past and her dark future, she dances!

– Edmond and Jules de Goncourt, *Histoire de la Societe Française Pendant la Revolution*, 1889

PARIS, 1819

Every city holds a gate to Hell. It is a simple consequence of the gathering, on a patch of ground, of so many souls that the lost will inevitably find their way to the lowest point. Paris is no exception, but as she is Paris, the gate is fretted with wrought iron and there are various choices of refreshment. At this hour, only the tavern is open.

A woman approaches along the Infernal Way. The sun, set in a mist of early spring and intermittent rain, has turned the cobbles to obsidian, glittering in the light of kerosene lamps. Soldiers loiter by the front of the tavern: there are always soldiers, be they Swiss Guard or Republican, Napoleon's legions or the locusts of Europe that swarmed in their wake. For thirty years, Paris has been an armed camp, and now the Bourbons rest uneasy in the decaying chambers of Tuileries Palace.

This woman approaches under the eye of a sergeant, who quickly swigs from his bottle and replaces the cork. Not trusting his comrades with this, though perhaps his life, he slips it into the folds of his greatcoat before assessing the potential threat. The sergeant puts her in her forties—a veteran, sure, of any number of horrors. And there are many such faces, pale and drawn. Some wear smuggled diamonds and dance in a hall where an orphaned princess presides in black velvet. Some attend the opera, blossoming cautiously under the eye of the censor, or other well-mannered delights. But here, an English bonnet shields greying curls, and her black redingote and boots are sensible armour against the evening's assault. It is clear she knows this street, though every so often she pauses as if to reassure herself this is indeed the way.

The sergeant is young. Born ten years earlier, he would have cleaved to Napoleon's cause and worshipped the man whose shadow he now spits upon—a deep and looming shadow, for all that his statues have been removed throughout the city. But the sergeant is young, in his blue wool, his musket wrapped in oilcloth against the damp, and he pities the woman who must venture forth on such a night. He sees she carries a walking stick—a coiled, black thing—and taps the cobbles before her as if counting.

When she finally comes abreast of him, she does not look at the tavern. She makes straight for the gate.

"Halt, Madame!"

Halt she does, and faces him. "I understood the catacombs were open to visitors."

"They are open, but only by appointment."

Her voice is calm and utterly unyielding. "Do you, or one of your fellows, hold the key?"

He does hold the key; a greater weight in his pocket than the bottle. Gazing at her pallid face, he feels that somehow, she knows this. Nonetheless, he shakes his head. "Madame, go home. Tomorrow you may seek out Inspector de Thury, who will arrange it all from his office, or it may be that you will find him here, for the work is ongoing."

"Were time my ally," she says, "do you think I would not be indoors?"

The sky over the street is starless, shapeless, yet gives the impression of vast and secret motion. Conspiracies and counter-revolution. It shall rain more, before dawn.

"Let me in," she addresses him squarely. "Accompany me, if you will, to the point where the bones begin. I shall pray for the souls of my parents and husband."

Young as he is, he understands. Those who died in the Terror, either massacred in the prisons or decapitated before the crowd, own no tomb. Their remains were tipped by the cartload down the shafts of the old mines, which took the name of the catacombs and which, thanks to the labour of Thury and his people, have now assumed that shape. Stacks of anonymous bones now line the passages, each one a potential parent or lover. But there are churches at which such prayers may be made: warm, dry places full of candlelight. He starts to direct her to the Chapel of All Saints, but as he meets her eyes, the words die in his throat. For those eyes do not suggest supplication, nor even grief. They are like those rumoured pits that end only amongst the damned. Gazing into them, he feels exposed and strangely helpless. His comrades are there at the tables, laughing as they shuffle cards—guarding the catacombs is a hotly-contested privilege. And yet, he feels alone.

The woman sighs. "Young man," she says, "understand that I will pay."

The money is given to his lieutenant, who sees no harm. "Old geese like that get funny and it's best not to argue. You never know who they're connected to."

The woman's passport is legitimate—it gives her name as Patience Courtemanche, recently arrived from London.

"Fled the Terror," the lieutenant opines between draws on his pipe. "Stayed there during the wars. Probably hasn't seen Paris since she was eighteen."

Their benefactress stands at the very edge of the light. Her walking stick, the sergeant sees now, has the shape of a snake. By this exchange of coin, he is bound to accompany her and see that she takes nothing, no memento nor macabre souvenir, and this realisation brings him close to panic.

But it is too late. He has taken a lamp off the table, and she has taken his arm to cross the cobbles. Even through his coat, her fingers are cold. The great key slides into the lock and with a *thunk!* the gate opens.

Stop! This is the Empire of Death!

The sergeant and the woman have descended the stairs, and passed along the passageway. They face the entrance to the catacombs proper, the two squat columns hacked out of solid rock, the doorway beyond with its legend. The painted black letters seem wet in the lamplight, as though they might liquify and track down the stone lintel and doorjambs, joining there with the utter dark. The woman stands facing the nothing she has come so far to see.

"What is your name, young man?"

"August, Madame."

"A fine name. A good omen. I knew an Augusta, a long, long time ago." The woman turns suddenly. "August, do you see my candle?"

Even in the light of the sergeant's lamp, the flame cupped in her hands is bright. Too bright for a candle, it might be thought, with a weird and greenish halo. And when and how did she light it? But he answers, "Yes." Automatically, his eyes track the brightness as the bearer walks towards him. Everything else—the roof, the columns, the very lamp in his hand—fades away.

"Keep your eyes upon my candle. Do not look away."

Her voice echoes eerily within the chamber, but equally it seems to sound inside his head. His panic flares and he makes to run or strike, not knowing which.

"Remove your eyes from the light for even an instant and it shall go out."

He does not want it to go out—all around is dark and featureless. He does not know where he would run.

"Do not let it go out. We are deep in the catacombs, you and I. This light and my voice are your only connection to the surface. Watch it well, August. Listen only to me."

Back and forth the light moves, in a weird pattern. As he watches, his panic fades. The light fascinates—something he has never seen and yet, somehow, has sought since his childhood, sought through battle and bedroom, and all the petty boredoms of his life. He hears his own heart beating evenly as the light slows and finally stops.

"Are you listening, August?"

"Yes."

"You are watching me pray, by the light of my candle. After your heart has beaten a hundred times, you will help me rise and return to the surface. You will open the gate for me and wish me well as I go on my way. You will not lock the gate, but you will tell your lieutenant that you have done so. And you will forget I told you to do these things. Do you understand, August?"

"I understand, Madame."

"Good. Oh, and give me that bottle. It's colder down here than I thought."

As he rummages, the light leaves her hand and floats into the air, as the serpent staff uncoils and seethes along the rough, stone floor. With one hand, she opens her coat. When he passes the bottle over, she lodges it in the folds of her skirt. Then smooths it down, smooths it all down, and stands facing the dark portal.

"Secretaque altum flamma Baal vi et orientis silentio noctis ab Hecates..."

She leaves the sergeant standing, his eyes glazed and heart beating slow as funeral drums in his breast. With no further herald, she enters the Empire of Death.

***

THE MEMOIRS OF SIMON ÉTIENNE DE LANNERARY, COMTE BEAUCHÊNE

"It is the vanity of many a man, in his middle years, to set down the events he has witnessed and the trials and turmoil of his youth. Perhaps, oh Reader, you are of my blood. Perhaps you are merely someone curious enough to peruse these papers, however you came across them, hoping for a tale of the Revolution and the Terror. You must have already read many such accounts, but your appetite is unsated. You crave something you have not yet heard. In either case, I alone am qualified to tell how I contrived to survive the vicissitudes of our poor country. But to do so, I must revisit such darkness and horror as I have long set behind me, and confess to deeds that were not to my honour. Nonetheless, I find I am committed to this task. Perhaps it is as penance and a warning to others that I now set down all that I know of the family Dubois.

It was the autumn of 1788, and at the tender age of seventeen I was bound for Hell. My tutors at the Jesuit school in Dijon were united in their opinion that Paris was the infernal realm and, lacking their protection, I would fall easy prey to its devils. But I had been summoned, along with my sister Narcisse, to join our father, who was in the employ of the Department for the Inspection of Mines. The hardships of the journey reinforced an apprehension that my arrival at our townhouse in Saint Marcel did little to calm. I remember the water in the courtyard well made us sick for days, but Paris held our future, so we were obliged to adapt.

I was, with considerable reluctance, to uphold family tradition by joining the Department as a junior secretary. I had begged for a military commission, which we could well afford, but Father insisted we should build on what we already possessed—which was the nobility of the Robe. For her part, Narcisse was to wed. The gentleman's name was as yet uncertain, but his nature was not. He would be nobility of the Sword, and his family in need of the substantial dowry my sister would bring. This would ensure that I, as merely the third Count Beauchêne, would have the connections and graces to ensure our star continued to rise. The Dubois were merely one of the families with which we played an intricate game—offering succour whilst appearing to beg favour; the stakes increased, now Narcisse's exceptional beauty was on display in promenade and ball. Blonde hair and eyes a deep violet, at nineteen she could have been married a hundred times over, but that our father held out for the establishment.

The Dubois maintained a great hôtel in the Faubourg Saint Germain. The sight of this grand place, with its high ceilings and striped wallpapers, and massive portraits hung in gilded frames, taught me a stern lesson as to what the establishment truly meant. And so it was that I met Michel Marshal Ambroise, the Vicomte Dubois. Seven years my senior, he was of middling height, dark-haired and pale of face, with large, dark eyes. It was a face of sensibility; the kind young ladies might seek out in hope of discussing Rousseau. He wore his hair long and sometimes powdered, sometimes not—such a break with tradition was still daring—and dressed with an insouciance which became, I suppose, an officer in His Majesty's cavalry. His voice was soft but peculiarly resonant. All in all, he was the kind of man who need not exert himself to become the focus of a room.

Both of us had lost our mothers at an early age, and I felt a kinship with him despite the difference in our pedigree. I was willing enough to call him friend... no, that will not do. If this is penance, then I must admit I clove to him. He fascinated me, this sophisticate who seemed to possess all the secrets of the noisy and limitless new sphere into which my star had travelled. He would, I was sure, convey wisdom no other could or would, besides which even my father's instruction seemed quaint.

Michel accepted my company but insisted on calling me 'Savon' at all times. Close enough to my name of Simon to have the excuse of humour, but it was still the old put-down, 'soap of the commoners', which was another name for the dignity my grandfather attained. But I accepted it without demure, as he led me to the galleries and the opera, unveiled all the pleasures of the Palais Royale—oh, what a time that was!

I was considered handsome in my day. I don't flatter myself that my looks have survived! My eyes, though, they retain their blue—like my mother's, or so I was told. So yes, within weeks there was a younger, fairer version of Michel sipping coffee at the Café Foy, pronouncing on the horseraces, mocking the waxworks and affecting boredom at the prospect of yet another ball. I'm sure my tutors would have believed their prophecy fulfilled.

I should describe the ball at which our fate was sealed. It was held in the last days of summer, and the Dubois chose to make it a masquerade.

The night was cold—unseasonably so! But the Hôtel Dubois shimmered with the light of its many chandeliers, and the grand salon was draped in red and gold and cascades of white flowers—hot-housed roses and jasmine, gardenias and chrysanthemums all in huge china bowls. Their perfume, in the heat of all those melting candles, was dizzying, and ladies swooned in record numbers. The floor was an intricate parquetry. I remember from the amount of time I spent gazing down on crumpled skirts and heaving decolletage. China—the country—was fashionable, so the costume of many consisted of a silk gown patterned with blossom or cranes, and a bizarre, conical hat.

Not so Narcisse. As a play on her name, she appeared in Grecian drapes, with her hair pomaded into a floral crown. I recall thinking the legend of Narcissus was hardly a good omen for a marriage, but as I was dressed as a tree—at my father's insistence, a play on Beauchêne—I was scarcely in a superior position.

But picture, if you can! The bright hall crammed with silks and velvets, lace and fur, in colours I truly believe have passed from the world. At the centre, dancers line up for the allemande; pale, slim hands adorned with jewels weaving an elaborate braid with those tanned or trimmed for the night with claws. Wigs crowned with moon and sun sail upon waves of solemn discussion, of the upcoming harvest and of how, if it too failed, the king must surely summon the estates. The figure in cloth of gold is Necker, the king's treasurer, that in black cape and full mask the Archbishop of Paris. Servants in crimson livery circle with wine from Champagne, and along the end wall, under the glower of Dubois gone by, runs a table dressed in white linen and yet more flowers, from which peep silver salvers of fruit dipped in sugar or chocolate, and moulded creams set upon trays of ice and salt.

Now the music has changed to a waltz, and couples have broken from the line, spinning across the floor in a way the elders find daring. How is it that they do not collide and fall? Some spin through the huge windows standing open on the garden, where a chandelier has shattered and scattered discrete lights upon vine and bough, illuminating the faces of fauns. I stand awkwardly against the wall, encased in pasteboard and shedding voile leaves. I have no partner, despite a round of introductions, and Michel has abandoned me. But I see him leading Narcisse to the window where stands his grandmother, the dowager. I remember thinking that obtaining royal permission for this marriage would be a mere formality beside that of Augusta Athenais.

The dowager was garbed in voluminous white, as if to mock her prospective daughter-in-law. Plentiful pearls and a silver wreath in the Grecian style adorned her, and she supported her not inconsiderable bulk upon a cane. To my eyes and not a little envy, Michel had seemed to wear no costume, but a black velvet coat and breeches of the finest quality. As he bowed, I noticed for the first time that a wreath of dark, glossy leaves encircled his head, and gold curlicues rose from his shoulders, resembling neither epaulets nor wings. Narcisse curtsied in turn. In light of the dowager's fearsome reputation, I decided I should be with her, to offer what support I could. So, I started across the floor.

"But I am Echo," my sister protested, "she who pines for his love."

"A mere echo?" Michel's voice was soft but carried, somehow, above the music. "Never. Persephone, surely."

"The Queen of Hell?" the dowager chuckled. "Perhaps."

Narcisse looked startled, as well she might.

"And here's young Simon, looking thoroughly seasonal. Vicomte de Lanneray." The dowager rustled her satin and gauze, displaying a snowfield of bosom, and I bowed respectfully.

"A new branch, perhaps?" Michel bowed in turn.

All inspiration failing, I said I was glad to be here. Then enquired if the dowager was enjoying the ball.

"All the more for your friendship with my grandson." She pursed her wrinkled lips, studying me. "Narcisse, would you and Michel perhaps like to join the dance?"

But Narcisse herself stared at the dowager's walking stick. As the lady gestured with it, she gave a small gasp.

The dowager and Michel exchanged glances. "Perhaps my lady is in need of some air," he said.

"An excellent idea," said the dowager, and waved them away with her fan. "Bring me back some oranges and another glass of wine."

Michel's eyes lingered upon me a moment, then he offered Narcisse his arm. "It's all right," he said. "In fact, it is very well." Their eyes met and, after a moment, she went with him. As Michel turned, the gold curlicues resolved into a pasteboard lyre slung across his back. Orpheus, then, the poet who descended into the underworld to retrieve Eurydice after she was bitten by the snake.

"You have become Michel's friend," stated the dowager. "Has he spoken to you of our family's traditions?"

"Madame, I—I have great respect for your history. I hope it may inspire me to—"

"Not *that*. What I wish to know, Simon, is to what do you aspire?"

"I… to uphold the example of my father and grandfather, and bring honour to my family."

She nodded, but it were as though my reply disappointed her in some way. "To follow in your father's footsteps is certainly no shame: these days, the Robe offers a direct path to the highest dignities. And the Department for the Inspection of Mines is active within Paris itself."

I nodded, thinking that if I must have such conversation, then let it be with men, and she must have picked up on something. For she smiled and once again took up the cane. "Let's see if I can't find you some livelier company."

I saw then what had startled Narcisse: the dowager's walking stick was carved into a serpent's head. And as she led me towards the dancers, I realised Narcisse was now among them.

It was proper enough for them to dance, but there seemed something almost unseemly in it. The way their fingers touched and touched again. The way she looked straight into his eyes, as though she had suddenly obtained this right. Their lips moved, murmuring to each other there in the centre of the floor. Black and white, they turned about, gold and silver, a striking sight, provoking the murmurs of others. I saw my father and the Comte Dubois deep in conversation.

"They make a handsome couple, don't you agree?" Once again, the dowager eyed me. "But come, Simon, and be on your best manners."

I cannot help but feel I should have sensed danger, even then. Perhaps, had I been on my guard, it would have all turned out in some kinder way. But in another five minutes I forgot everything, for the partner the dowager found for me was the sixteen-year-old Artemisia Eloise, at that time heiress to the Voclain, and a sweeter young thing cannot be imagined.

Within the week, the contract was signed and the announcement made. Narcisse was to wed the Vicomte Dubois.

***

PARIS, 1819

The corpse-light floats before Patience and down the passage, exposing pitted detail and animating bony shadows against the wall. It was fortunate the young sergeant was sensitive enough to see the light—she can work without, though it is harder. But fortune attends the magus.

It was one of the first lessons Augusta ever taught her. *"We are workers in will, my dear, in the common parlance that makes us witches. But I assure you, our practice is nothing like your nurse's stories or the ones the nuns tell. You were convent-raised, after your mother passed? God imposes fate, but fate is ours to use like Ariadne's thread, guiding us to the results that we desire. Do you think it was accident that brought you to us, a young woman of your talent?"*

How astonishing it was, to be spoken to in this way. As if she were capable, even important. How strange it felt to respond, and yet so natural. Like a bird raised inside a cage that yet flies far and free when fate provides the opportunity.

She was beaten in the convent, by the nuns, for screaming in the night and stopping in the corridors, staring at that which no one else could see. Taught to be silent. She had expected nothing else from her marriage. But, to find people who shared her strange perversion, who called it a *gift*—no, that could be no accident. The Dubois had called her to them, and she would follow gladly but never blindly. For that, as Augusta said, was the only true sin.

Blindness and treachery. As far as she is aware, she is the last of the coven. For a long time, she believed she was the last of all those who were in the hôtel that day, but now she knows that two survived. Two survived, but it is she who keeps the faith.

How high the bones rise around her, like hedgerows gone grey and stony, with that barely present, yet pervasive sweetness in the air—hawthorn and privet, all withered to dust. It should perturb her. Even after all she has seen, she should feel awe passing metre after metre of this danse macabre. Consider the sheer labour involved in selecting and stacking the bones. And before that, the time it took for flesh to wither away, leaving the materials clean and disjointed. The time it took for them to grow in the first place. And yet, the cervical vertebrate might be severed in seconds. That took no time at all. Thury and his crew have made a special effort with the skulls; they centre every bank like a cluster of dead fruit.

There are rats down here, no doubt, and spiders aplenty. But Patience sees more than that. She sees her guardian serpent, an entity brought into being by repeated visualisation and empowering over the lives of twelve former bearers, from Augusta all the way back to Melisende. It slithers along the gravelled floor (carven ebony firm in her left hand, as the candle resides in her right), alert to any danger. Then there are the flickers and shadow-furls of other entities; minor gloms of corpse dust and memory, perhaps some true elementals cleaving to the stone. They scuttle and peek from behind the bones, recognising the power she holds.

Then there are the whispers.

Is someone there? Oh thank God.

Mama? Mama, it's dark.

Can that be you, my love?

Ahead the passage tees, and here the bones run floor to rough, stone ceiling. A cross stares at her, four skulls deep and three wide. The corpse light drifts towards it and she repeats the invocation: *By the mysteries of the deep, by the flames of Baal, by the power of the east and the silence of the night, by the Holy Rites of Hecate. Reveal to me that which I seek.*

The flame flickers for a moment, as though those eroded septums are puffing. Then the flame veers to the left. She follows. Her feet, encased in her sturdiest boots, crunch slightly at each step.

Marble and gypsum were cut here, to build the city above. As long as bone takes to grow, such tunnels take longer—centuries, as the streets of Paris rolled overhead. And this, opening around her, is one of those fabled chambers where Thury succumbed to a grisly fantasy. The greenish illumination sends shadows fleeing around a huge and circular pillar with a stone core, perhaps, but mosaicked completely in bone. Rings of skulls separate wide bands: the deep-grooved caps of thigh bones in the middle, giving way to smaller and smoother clefts that joined arm to shoulder or calf to knee. A Roman temple? No, for there is a real cross here, white limestone springing out from the wall. But it was Rome that these passages mimicked, the underworld carved by the ancients to match their myth. Despoiled Rome, then: defaced with crosses, and the rest of the great disturbed by creeping evangelists. Emperors and matriarchs, poets, soldiers, and slaves. But the ancients had other ways of remembering their dead.

Something brushes her face and lightly stirs her hair. Merely a draught of air. Several passages run off from here, to every point of the compass. The corpse light flickers once again and draws her towards the far-right corner, where it seems the air thickens with dust.

Please, can you help me?

I'm scared, I want to go home!

I am close, so close now. Just follow my voice.

She almost misses it. Just another shadow, it appears, cast by stacked pelvises. But it is a crevice, winding back into the rock—the corpse light hovers in a manner almost agitated. She glimpses sloping, undecorated walls and a low ceiling. The serpent coils about itself on the floor.

She knew her goal would not lie in one of the dressed passages. But the deeper she goes into the maze, the greater the likelihood of encountering rock falls and flooding. So long as she maintains her trance, attuned to what lies beyond the mundane, the chances she will lose her way are slim. But in these abandoned tunnels, rumours place at least one true ghost. Should she encounter it, she will be as vulnerable as the sergeant was, though rather better armed. That is the price, always. Sight ensures you will be seen, and changing fate, even in small ways, demands that you change in turn. For a yearning moment, memories of her life as Patience consume her—her friends, her work, the streets of London which while never *home* are still familiar, have become comfortable as a winter coat.

Marie's plea that she be careful, that Paris is still unsafe. Above all, not to succumb to those terrible fancies of hers. Yes, she has a knack for finding lost objects and soothing troublesome clients, and always knows when a friend needs aid. Her ability to create faces for the long-dead, for which there is no model, is truly uncanny. But to believe she can speak with them....

For a moment, it seems that she is mad to have done this.

But, for all her virtues, Marie could never *see*.

The serpent coils at her feet. The corpse light glows like a virid moon. She turns sideways, to work her skirts through the crack.

***

THE MEMOIRS OF SIMON ÉTIENNE DE LANNERARY, COMTE BEAUCHÊNE

As the year turned, I was obliged to take up my post in the Department, but that interfered only tangentially with my continuing explorations. Michel's marriage was set for the summer and we—forgive me, my Reader. Indeed, I skip past momentous events.

I attended, with my father, the meeting of the Estates General. I was there during the formation of the National Assembly and the declaration of the Rights of Man. But I doubt I have anything to add to your understanding of those solemn occasions. What I do remember is something I'm not certain I can convey. You may simply not be able to appreciate that initially, life proceeded very much as normal. Yes, there was now a National Assembly and yes, it insisted that its authority derived from the people rather than the crown. But it acknowledged the king: indeed, had high hopes of him. My father himself sat on a committee assessing the state of the provinces, and I joined in the discussions at the Hôtel Dubois, which were attended in those days as much by merchants and factory owners as by nobility. But it's not those things that return to me now.

I recall the spectacle of balloons rising into the air above the Field of Mars! Who had ever seen such a thing, before or since? Corded with gold, they were, and draped with crimson. The opera showed us the old gods; the waxworks brought us closer to the king and queen than I ever came in reality—during the grand audience he was a tiny figure, like a saint set under a canopy of gold. There were two of these displays, I seem to recall, both run by the old Switzer Doctor Curtius. The images of greatness populated his establishment in the Palais Royale, but there was the Cave of Great Thieves on Temple Street, where you might see the monster Gilles de Rais, and La Voisin smothering an infant. Michel, especially, was fascinated by these. We visited there so often I believed he pursued the old man's pretty, young assistant. But when such amusements palled, there were places where others might be found. Rough places, where drank the men who fought in America, who had seen Guinea and Algiers. Dangerous places, where black men wrestled and yellow men gambled. Dark places, housing the malformed and the mad. And in those places, did I not hear the rumblings of revolution, see premonitions of fire and blood? I saw things and heard them too.

I was trailing my father up to the comte's rooms when Michel drew me aside.

"Savon," he said. "I need your help. It's an errand for my grandmother."

The dowager had taken Narcisse under her wing, and the two were constantly off at the dressmakers and the jewellers. They even attended the establishment of Doctor Curtius, both for wax flowers and to have her own face sculpted, though I for one thought this overdone. I thought I might be directed to retrieve them home or collect a package, but there was something else on Michel's mind.

"Are you aware that the Dubois' have long been donors to Our Lady of the Woods?"

"The chapel that stands by the Cemetery of the Innocents?"

"Yes. Well, this is about the material they removed from the cemetery, the markers and so forth."

I knew all about the removal of the bodies from the Innocents—it fell under the Department's jurisdiction. All the detritus from it and the other old, urban cemeteries was being transported to an abandoned mineshaft on the outskirts of town. I felt a grim premonition of actual work.

"We seek the remains of an arch erected by my ancestress, Melisende Ambroise, in the 13th century. There's a reference to it in one of the old chronicles—obviously, the arch would have collapsed long since. But, if something survives?"

"I've heard there is a chamber down in the mines," I said, "where items of interest are preserved. Carvings and the like. Your arch might be there, or it might not."

Michel smiled. "Nonetheless, you can appreciate the advantage the presence of a junior secretary will grant me."

A carriage was waiting, my acquiescence assumed.

"Did you hear about the latest protest?" We threaded through the twisting byways, from Saint Germain toward Saint Michel. "It was two days ago. A crowd burst into Curtius's place at the Palais. They took the heads off the effigies of heads of Necker and the Duc d'Orléans and carried them through the streets!"

I had, of course, and opined the perpetrators were as mad as any of the wretches we had seen immured.

"Not mad." Michel sprawled back in his seat, like he might at a tavern. "But they may be deluded."

The carriage rattled on over the cobbles and, approaching the Luxemburg gardens, our way was barred by more protesters, all marching along in red wool hats and shouting incoherently about liberty and renewal. Michel watched them through a slit in the shutter until we were past. Then he turned back to me.

"Savon," he said, "if this goes well, there are other services we may need. But you'll have to show me your courage."

I bridled, of course, citing our previous excursions. But he shook his long, dark curls. "It'll take more than that if you're to join us. And I would like that, Savon. I should like to have a man by me who I can depend upon."

So help me, I thought he meant in the cavalry. Reaching across the seat, I seized both his hands and told him I would balk at nothing.

He smiled, gently. "What's the most frightened you can remember being?"

The sound of the carriage wheels seemed very loud, in the ensuing silence. I wondered where these utterances might be going. "A man does not give way to fear," I replied. "So, as a child."

"Did you hear your mother whispering, after she was dead?"

What a question! But he leant towards me, and his face was earnest.

"Listen to me, Savon. Anything is possible. Isn't that an amazing thought? You can have whatever you want, so long as you have the courage and are willing to pay the price." We drove the rest of the way in silence. When we arrived at the dishevelled yard that was our destination, he offered me a flask of what turned out to be the foulest liquor I had ever tasted. Bitter with herbs, the fumes stung my eyes! Nonetheless, I drank.

The rough-hewn steps dropped down into the earth, and after that came a passage. Michel held a lantern: privy to the word at the department, I had taken the precaution of a nosegay and high boots, but it was hardly enough. I had not realised what the tunnels were—what the clearing work entailed—and seeing it now for the first time, I thought I understood what Michel meant by courage.

Bones scattered every inch—the tunnels had been blessed, but this was less consecrated ground than a human stew. All the objections of the clergy, to what the government had determined in the name of public health, now made a ghastly sense. Coffin was stacked on coffin, and where these were lacking or had disintegrated, skeleton upon skeleton, some still bearing the leathery remnants of flesh. I saw hands clawed or clenched, and fancied this was to push off their fellow cadavers with no more nicety than in the usual Parisian crowd. But the worst of the stench was numbed not by the flowers but by the lingering burn in my nose and throat.

Michel appeared as fascinated by this as any other spectacle. He bent over a skull to which rags of hair still adhered.

"The pagans of Egypt knew a means of preserving their dead," he said, "and the Romans burned theirs—only they first took a mould of the face, so the dead might watch from the walls of the family home. During high days and ceremonies, a special caste of performers was hired to take on their guise."

"They were pagans. The grounds of the Innocents were sanctified by the bodies of the saints."

"So I have heard. But where are they now?"

A series of rough-cut passageways and stone rooms held stone angels and deaths heads, ancient medallions and pillars. There were also shrouded forms that seemed to be rather more than skeletons.

"Here are your saints, Simon!"

How could *this* excite him?

"Bodies a hundred years old, that look as though they were placed in the earth but days. The fat transforms, you see, into what the grave-diggers call corpse wax. But the scientists say it is closer in composition to soap."

I felt like I was choking. Seeing this, he straightened and set the lantern down upon a stone. "How courageous are you, Simon? Shall I be Eurydice?"

How he looked then I fear I shall remember till God calls me. The lamplight washed across his face, leaving his eyes as deep, black wells. With his black garb, he seemed to merge with the shadows as slowly he slid away into the dark. Daring me to follow. I left the lantern in its place and stepped through a gateway where it seemed no light could penetrate. I remember running frantically for the light, all my senses in confusion. Leaving Michel to wade through corpses if he wished, I seized the lantern and returned along the passageway, shrinking at the macabre sights and the startling appearance of workmen around corners and from out holes, with their stained bodies and reddened eyes. Their gruff barks spurred me on.

I sat in the carriage, heart still racing. When I finally saw Michel emerge, he seemed utterly calm, as though nothing had happened. One of the workmen followed him with something wrapped in canvas, and I assumed that his search had been successful. He passed the man four bottles and a sack of flour, and the bundle was secured to the carriage roof.

When Michel took his seat, he said that the inscription had not been forthcoming, but he was bringing that which might serve. I waited for an explanation of what I had experienced in the dark, but none was forthcoming.

***

PARIS, 1819
How can you not see me? I'm right at the edge of your light!
I'll be good I'll be good I'll be…
Come to my arms.
Thirsty.

Patience keeps shuffling forward, palms pressing stone, her coat rasping against the walls. Her lungs feel heavy: another potential danger, that the air will grow thin and stale. But the corpse light is bright as moonlight now, an intense virescence washing over the walls—this means her goal is close. By the mysteries of the deep, by the flames of Baal...

I'm thirsty, so thirsty. What cellar is this, that holds no wine?

Ahead, her serpent has halted and raised the first span of its length, hood flattened before a rough-cut gap.

It is small and plain: a monastic cell compared to the chapel she left behind. But here the corpse light hovers over a small pile of... material. Such a small pile. Really, it might as well be a cairn of rounded stones.

She understands now. Michel himself spoke of it: the side chambers where the original workers stacked the curiosities they found while demolishing the cemeteries. Fragments of sculpture and inscription, some things now moved to the Louvre. And so it became the place where Thury's workmen dumped what could not be used. What had not rotted clean... she does not look, not yet. She must seal the cell so she may work uninterrupted. Carefully setting down her instruments, she dips into her pocket for a paper of consecrated salt. Without pausing in her chant, she pulls it clear, trailing a thin, black stream across the doorway.

"By the Holy Rites of Hecate, let nothing pass that I do not invite."

There. She is safe for now. To exit will require more active measures, but she has time now, to prepare—

Thirsty

She turns around and there is the ghost, looming over the material and clearer in the corpse light than the man would have been by day. Pale eyes gleam in a slubby face. The rags of livery, once tawny bright, adorn a shrivelled form. Hands stretch like claws towards her, the nails broken and filthy, bleeding even now from the tips.

Have you brought wine for me?

She has sealed it in with her.

The paper in her hand still contains a residue of salt. She backs towards the door—her retreat will break the original ward, but if she is quick, she can repair it. And thus is she safe in the passage, while the ghost remains the master of her materials? Oh no, this must be decided now. She flings the salt in its face. The ghost flinches but is not put off—how could it be? Her life force, potent as only a magus's can be, must be the best prospect it has encountered since its lonesome and agonising death.

Now her serpent dashes forward, striking. It will defend her for as long as it can—she should have paid attention to its warning! But she has this interval to find a way to banish or contain the ghost, and indeed, she is armed. She has a flint striker in one pocket with a second candle; the other contains red chalk as well as her deflated purse. A hazel wand and a silver knife are concealed in her skirt, along with the half-filled bottle.

Ghosts are formed by obsession. The man who dies tormented by unfulfilled desire binds his spirit to the place of his death, and what obsesses this ghost is clear.

"You are thirsty?" Ripping open her coat, she works the bottle free. "Then drink."

Thumbing the cork, she tips part of the contents onto the ground, a libation but also bait. Her serpent writhes, injured, as the ghost attempts to seize the angel's share. She inscribes red sigils across the label, but the chalk grinds futilely against the glass. She digs in her pocket for the flint striker and does not flinch when it slices her hand.

Blood is a better ink and drink besides. She smears the bottle mouth, lets a little dribble inside. "Here," she says, proffering the bottle to the ghost as she jams her stinging finger against the glass. Over and under, drawing shapes so well-practised she has no need to look.

WOOF! The ghost is gone, and the bottle shakes, comes live in her hand. She completes the circle of sigils and jams in the cork, reciting the words of binding. Again and again the bottle rattles, nearly slipping from her hands. She grips it, the chant rippling seamlessly from her tongue. After a while, the glass surface grows burning cold, but the paroxysms are fewer. She has sealed the cork with a mix of blood and salt, and the ghost cannot break through. Eventually, she feels confident enough to set the bottle down.

"Yes," she breathes, her mouth dry. "That's right. My binding overcomes the anchor of death. I'll take you out of here, away from where your body lies. You will be a good servant to me, yes?"

No response. The dead do not lie; another of Augusta's lessons. Spirits that have passed beyond the world and time can be brought, by the power of the necromantic rite, to return and speak of the future. Even a ghost will not speak false, though its vision is occluded. Accordingly, she keeps her hand close, and when another, mighty rattle tips the bottle towards the gravel, she snatches it up. "I command thee, on pain of the torments and wandering of thrice seven years, by thy sighs and groans, *be still.*"

And the shaking ceases.

And now, after all this time, she is here, beside them once again. She had fantasised that, when she found them, they would be waiting for her, preserved as saints were said to be. But although the withered faces are fearsome, only a few wax beads have formed in the crook of the jaws. Only memory can conjure the barest resemblance to those she loved.

It will be enough.

It is harder for her to scrape out those little globules than she anticipated. Harder to stand and walk away once she is finished. But she does not mistake her path.

When she reaches the head of the stairs, the sky is gleaming a pale, rain-washed grey. The gate creaks open at her touch, and all the guards are sleeping.

***

THE MEMOIRS OF SIMON ÉTIENNE DE LANNERARY, COMTE BEAUCHÊNE

You will tax me now, oh Reader, with the fall of the Bastille. That I remember.

The news came through mid-afternoon, once we had returned to the Hôtel. The royal gaol, where only the most sensitive of prisoners were held, had been stormed by a red-hatted mob—seeming to me the very one our carriage had cut through. The inmates had been released and the guard slaughtered, and down on the street of Saint Antione, the rebels paraded with the prison governor's head. This time, there was no wax effigy. His blood spattered their hands and faces as they sang.

The colloquy in the comte's rooms, that day, was furious and plagued by uncertainty. Some spoke with dread of the prisoners, others denied they were of any real consequence. Most agreed that the king must act promptly and without mercy, but some feared this very thing, believing it would trigger more violence. A proper appeal should be made to the Assembly, placing the responsibility on *their* shoulders. All, it seemed, were fearful of the intervention of the Austrians, should France appear unable to keep its own house in order. From there, it was but a short step to cursing the name of Marie-Antoinette, whereupon all useful discussion ceased. I managed a discreet inquiry as to whether volunteers would be called on to bolster the armed forces, but the meeting broke up early, before the usual fortification of chocolate and pastries. Men went to join their families, and to assure themselves of the security of their businesses and stores. Some had already announced their intent to retreat from the city, at least to as far as farms and country estates.

It was strange sensation, I remember. The shedding of blood made the revolution real, yet still nothing had changed. I was aware there were those in the Assembly who demanded the abolishment of the ancient divisions of rank, but the servants still bowed and the commoners I encountered on the street still gave way before me. I was aware of the shortages of flour, meat and money, but had not yet experienced them. Rest assured, that was soon to come.

I was preparing for my own return to Saint Marcel when the dowager came to me.

"Simon," she said, "there will be another gathering this day. It is to take place after dinner and the attendance will be more— particular. This gathering you are welcome to join."

I remembered Michel's words and felt a rush of relief that I had passed the test. I remembered the great who had filled the ballroom, believed I was to be privy to *their* deliberations and perhaps even a part of whatever action was deemed the remedy to our country's ills. I dreamed, certainly, of attaining honour in battle.

The afternoon dragged on, heated and slow. Word arrived from my father, assuring me that he and Narcisse were safe. Supper itself was a subdued affair, and I was perturbed that there were no other guests.

It was Michel who took me down to the cellar. To avoid passing through the main hall, we went by the servants' stairs. Despite the heat, we wore heavy, hooded cloaks and I remember how the sweat oozed along my spine. The comte's cellar was large and superbly stocked, but as we neared what I considered the far end, a faint glow revealed a set of stairs whose existence I had never suspected, leading deep into the earth.

Michel handed me, then, a mask. It was a black domino, such as many had worn to the ball. "Put this on," he said, "and for God's sake, keep your mouth shut till you're called on, and don't say anything stupid when they do."

Setting foot upon the steps, I could not but recall the catacombs and what had transpired there. How right my premonition was!

It might have been a chapel, save there was no cross, or it might have been a crypt, save there were no niches in the walls. Ceiling and floor were of smooth, dressed stone, but it seemed tremendously old. Certain well-worn carvings might have revealed its character, but I had no chance then to study them. The source of the light was two braziers, which made the atmosphere suffocating, standing on either side of a draped trestle. Upon the floor, a circle had been inscribed in black and red, ornamented with outlandish symbols. Along the circumference stood perhaps ten figures, heavily caped and cowled in black. They all wore the same masks.

Behind the trestle, the dowager stood in her white robes and silver wreath, holding her serpent stick. "Simon de Lanneray. Will you swear upon your name and as you hope for salvation, never to reveal what you see and hear this night? Even in confession, to name only your own sin?"

Shocked as I was by this scene, I did not dare disagree. I swore further to obey her instructions and those of the operator as I would royalty, without question, and took my place in the circle, almost at the foot of the trestle. I supposed I stood beside Michel.

The dowager produced a massive silver chalice, which she held out in a grotesque parody of the sacrament. "In love and truth," she declaimed, and drank. The chalice was then passed from celebrant to celebrant, and when the cup came to me, I recognised the contents of the flask. I sipped but barely.

"In love and truth."

Slim hands took the cup from me, and raised it beneath the cowl. Then it seemed my very heart froze—for peering through the domino were my sister's violet eyes.

I was unarmed, and once again abandoned. Still, I would have seized her and carried her from that place, and the good God help any who came after us! But at that moment, the light from the braziers suddenly turned a bright and livid green, and the stench of the catacombs permeated the air.

"For the dead are risen from the grave," the dowager intoned. The circle repeated it and continued to do so, a low and echoing murmur. I froze, caught in confusion between motion and speech.

Behind her, a figure materialised in a black robe with the mask of a black dog. I recognised him immediately. In his right hand, Michel held a black wand topped with head of an owl, and in his left a bunch of some dark-leaved herb. As he approached, the dowager reached for the shroud, and I confess that I trembled as she flicked it aside.

The corpse of a woman it was, decency barely maintained by cloth so stained and tattered as to suggest long years in the earth. And yet, her flesh was still whole and firm, and of a waxy appearance. Every feature was visible, though her eyes were blind holes. I could see the nails on her fingers, the soles of her feet. Her hair was cropped, suggesting she died in illness or in shame. I understood, then, what Michel had thought would serve.

"By the mysteries of the deep," Michel intoned, "by the flames of Baal, by the power of the east and the silence of the night, by the holy rites of Hecate, I conjure and exorcise thee, oh spirit, to present thyself here."

He censed the corpse with the herbs, then touched his wand to its lips. "I charge thee, I conjure thee, I command thee, on pain of the torments and wandering of thrice seven years, by thy sighs and groans, to utter thy voice."

I had set aside the memory of the voices in the catacombs, as one might a nightmare. But now it returned, and once more I heard that terrible whispering, cries of terror and blasphemy, and sensed things moving but inches above my skin. The dowager made query of the corpse, and it seemed that one particular voice was driven to answer while the rest were held at bay. The words it spoke are scored upon my memory, along with that terrible sound.

The secret that grants mastery will be gained only by weathering the coming storm. Blood it shall rain and intolerance thunder, deception the staff of life and death the only truth.

"By the pangs of the double death," Michel spoke into the darkness. "In the promise of your release, how are we to survive?"

Like the drip of fluid from coffins, the suffocated scrape of nails, it came. *Not all shall live but some. The coven shall endure another five hundred years.*

Then all at once, it was over. The flames rose once more in the brazier—ordinary, yellow flames. Thank Heaven, they had covered the corpse.

They told me things, those sorcerers. That the dead could not lie and those who had passed beyond the confines of time could be brought to tell what they saw of the future or recalled of the past, through the conduit of their mortal shell. Then they let me go, relying upon both my honour and my shame to preserve their secret.

The next day, I told my father the wedding must on no account take place.

✻✻✻

PARIS, 1819

Well into the next afternoon, Patience wakes in the cellar of a certain old house on Temple Street. The widow who rented her the space had no idea that the ramshackle building once housed the Cave of Great Thieves.

The chamber presents little more in the way of comfort than the catacombs, although the skulls are fewer in number. It contains a pallet, a basin and jug, two small travelling trunks that sit against the wall with their buckles undone, and a bizarre collection of old wood and iron. The survival of this hoard through the wars and winters, with their insatiable hunger for fuel and metal both, suggests the place was boarded up and forgotten till recently. A mourning shawl of mould hangs beside the rickety stairway, where run-off seeps in from the street. Almost nothing remains of its former nature but a small, brick furnace that occupies one corner, chimney rising to the ceiling.

How long, she thinks, did I hide here, after my escape? A year? Two? Such displays, this place held! She remembers them more clearly than the real horrors which took place during that time. It was easier by far to contemplate the depredations of the Beast of Gevaudan than to register what happened beyond the walls. Having lost all she loved, she sought the company of pallid, wax figures, garbed in pillaged finery and crowned with stolen hair.

There was no figure of Melisende—thankfully, as all that remained commonly of her reputation was a ridiculous figure, part serpent, part lovelorn girl. But there was Margot de la Barre, the love potion held delicately between her thumb and forefinger, and La Voisin with a wax baby beneath her apron. Both had lessons of their own to impart, as she learned the wax-worker's trade. Now even they are gone, rendered down for candles or eaten by rats.

Patience recalls the day she was introduced to a bright-eyed young woman barely above her own age. The wax-worker curtsied but did not doff her turban, which preserved her hair against splashes and sparks, and could not be removed even for a patron's visit. Curtius's apprentice was widely believed to be his bastard, save by those who thought her his mistress, but as Michel handed her down the stairs, he described Marie as a genius.

"She gives bodies to the dead, allowing them to appear before us as they did in life. By any standard, she is a necromancer herself!"

But Marie was not a necromancer. She was an artist with a steady hand and a kindly heart.

Patience rises, carefully setting down the little pouch containing what she took from the catacombs. It had hung round her neck as she slept—no rat would dare the threshold, in the normal course of things, but the serpent, too, must rest after its exertions, and her new servant is as yet untried. The bottle sits passively in its nest of straw. The name of the occupant she has divined as Philibert, but she suspects she will discover little else. Although they may be commanded, ghosts as a rule focus entirely upon the desire that keeps them from moving on.

Not breaking her fast, save to swallow a little water, she washes from the same jug and performs a cleansing, scattering black salt in handfuls. She lays out all her tools, both artistic and arcane, then robes herself plainly with a wreath of fresh myrtle upon her brow.

Seated on the floor before the furnace, she meditates with hands clasped in her lap. The slash of the striker is only the most recent injury, cutting across old burns and the scars of other cuts. Then she commences chalking a massive circle upon the floor in red and black, ringing the furnace and bench, protecting the work to come with every sigil that she used upon the bottle and the great names besides.

As she works, the trance takes her. She sees the chamber, no longer as vacant and despoiled, but as a temple complete with demigods. La Barre and La Voisin lend her their power. The colours of the circle shimmer.

Now has night fallen—the grimy night of Paris and the great night of the world, that sets all things free. Now must she bow and sing, invite the subterranean deities to preside over her rite.

It is to Dis Pater, king of the underworld, that she offers the wine infused with gold, and to Proserpine new-budded flowers—it must be their Roman forms she conjures, as it is a Roman rite she seeks to mimic. She asks their permission to do what she would this night, and further, to petition the foremost of their servants—Hecate, the Queen of Phantoms. But when she comes to invoke that dread name, she pauses. For a working such as this, she must once again use her own blood.

"Accept this offering, oh thrice-potent." She draws the knife from its place: the sigils shudder and flare. "Thrice powerful, thrice lady of darkness. Lend me your power and more I shall spill in love, in vengeance, in your service." The hairs on her neck and arms rise as her voice gains the substance of steel, slashing the veil in twain.

Finally, with the wound clotting and all her body light and strange, she presents a cake to Cerberus, to stop his slavering mouths that otherwise would be crammed with souls. "The way is clear." She speaks again, and the echoes pick up the sound and carry it like bats through the tatters and down into the darkened caverns of death. "The way is clear. Come, take up once more your mortal mask."

The ground of the entire circle flares a shade that only the initiated know, the sum of all colours, the penultimate beauty of black.

The furnace is all dull garnets. In the basin, now, a mixture of pristine beeswax and—material. Wax has its uses in magic, even Marie admits to that. For nearly twenty years in Marie's employ, she has poured and sculpted wax to create the faces of kings, queens and politicians, soldiers and actresses. In this old workshop, she sets to a different task.

***

THE MEMOIRS OF SIMON ÉTIENNE DE LANNERARY, COMTE BEAUCHÊNE.

Do you know the first man to die under the blade of the guillotine? I find that people forget it was designed with common criminals in mind. He was the highwayman, Nicolas Pelletier. That was in the April of 1792, before the horror truly began. What I heard was, they brought the head to Curtius and he took an imprint of the man's face to add to his cavern of thieves.

You will forgive me, oh Reader, for jumping over the intervening years. This is in part for the shame those memories bring, but largely for their dullness. You see, I believed we were safe.

Initially, I was as shocked and angry as one might wish, having discovered the true nature of the Dubois. I went to my father, but at that time I took the oath I had made seriously and did not dare speak of particulars. My father refused to take my word—small blame to him, in the circumstances! That having failed, I attempted a duel with Michel, which was quashed so thoroughly by both our fathers it truly does not bear recall. I believe to this day that the amusement it caused in the district cost me my chance with the Voclain. Narcisse went to the chapel, in panniers so wide they brushed the doorframe, and left as the young Madame Ambroise.

But they spoke to me, Michel and the comte himself. They professed to understand my scruples; to share them, indeed. The meeting in the chamber beneath the cellar was not a common occurrence: it accompanied only the greatest of need and was accomplished without the slightest risk to either our bodies or our souls. Both assured me that Narcisse, now married, had other matters to attend to. As the months went by with no further disturbance—and a growing need to rehabilitate my reputation—I allowed myself to be lulled.

Add to this the increasing demands of my work. The fortunes of the Beauchêne had always been tied up in our 'beautiful oaks'—we had done especially well from the refurbishment of Cherbourg harbour. Now, the Assembly had need of what we could provide, and I found myself absent from Paris for months at a time—all under the aegis of the Department—overseeing the felling of trees and the rough cutting of timber, then the whole, arduous journey from Dijon with the laden carts. On returning, I was welcomed by my superiors and feted by the Dubois themselves. I came to take pride in these prosaic tasks.

There was one episode which should have troubled me more than it did. I was, in the autumn of 1791, sent to investigate the collapse of a building attached to the house of the Capuchins in Saint Jacques, which was quite near Saint Marcel. An old crypt had been revealed, and while I was there I saw a tomb of the 13th century, in which the body was as whole and sound as that which had featured in the rite. The monks were so excited! They believe it to be their founder. For my part, I inspected the vault and ascertained it did not connect to the catacombs proper, which made it no concern of ours. But the night after my visit, someone broke into that tomb.

In retrospect, it is clear the coven was as active as ever—perhaps more so, given the grim future that was predicted. I came to know, in later days, that what they sought above all were the writings of their diabolic ancestress. Have you ever heard the story of Melisende? Quite dreadful, even taken as a fairy tale. I don't believe she was truly half-serpent, any more than I believe she had conquered death. But the dowager believed. It was immortality she sought through these explorations and horrid experiments, to which the abbot's body was doubtless subject. A ghastly image! Yet I find it worse to contemplate the influence she held over her son and grandson, and whatever others wore those masks. I had my suspicions, and they were scandalous… but what of that? In the end, all their efforts were as futile as my own.

Yet another bad harvest pitched all levels of the city into hardship. The Assembly pronounced on the price of bread, but were powerless to make it available. Mobs roamed the streets, assaulting passers-by and breaking into buildings in any area not rigorously patrolled. The corpses of the starved and frozen were dumped in the mines and on the sites of the old graveyards, for the new Elysium constructed by the king lay beyond the reach of almost all. My great concern, as that fatal summer quickened, was that my father might decide to wed me to a cousin—the gangly, brown ornament of a remote farmstead who had never even dreamed of Paris.

And then the news came through. The royal family had attempted to flee the city, and been captured at an inn in Varennes. To this day I hold that the king would have returned voluntarily—it was his fear for his family, the gross disrespect that was paid his wife, that made him supervise their flight. But now they were locked in the Temple Tower, while the worst parts of the nation howled like wild dogs. You know who *they* were.

I was at the departmental office, as I recall. All we secretaries were playing cards, but instead of coins (as had once been the case) I was staking bottles from the comte's cellar against someone else's hard cheese. Michel burst in unannounced, in uniform and smeared with dust from stockings to cap. There was alarm expressed at his appearance, and more than a little resentment at his disruption of the game. He did not care.

"It's happened," he said. "The Austrians have taken Verdun—for the sake of love, go join your families!"

He was my sister's husband, the companion of my idle days. I went to him and took his hands once more. He said that his regiment had been called up and he was due this noon upon the Field of Mars.

We spoke of many things, that hour. Of family and duty, and regret. Then he departed to join his men, and I made my way back to Saint Marcel.

When I arrived at the town house, the servants were packing away our goods and chattels behind drawn curtains. My father greeted me in the drawing room with a glass of brandy.

My father. I can see his face yet, brow furrowed beneath his wig, jaw thrust forward. He wore his second-best coat: a caramel broadcloth with a lining of yellow silk. Amazing, is it not? The things that stick. We were both to return immediately to our estate, he said, with a commission for timber from the military. He had our passports and we must depart upon the moment. I told him it was my intent to volunteer. He replied that this errand was as great a service to France as any, and besides, if battle were joined, it would not be with the Austrians in a distant field. It would be, he opined in low voice, in the very streets of Paris.

All the more reason, I replied, for me to play my part.

He dug his fingers beneath his wig, which was a sign of the greatest perturbation. "I cannot argue with you, my son. All I can do is tell you what I refused to believe for so long. *Blood it shall rain and intolerance thunder.*"

The shock of it inclined me to mistrust my ears, but in his face I saw the truth. There had been three Beauchênes at that dread ceremony, and he had known from the start what kind of den Narcisse was to enter. He had known.

"Narcisse must come with us," was all I said.

He sputtered, said her fate was out of our hands, but I would not listen. I left the house and resumed my horse, making at once for the Hôtel Dubois.

That was the last time I saw him. Those were our final words on this earth.

The first withered leaves tumbled through the streets, and finally the change had come. All that had been hidden in Paris was now exposed. The rough men with billets in their hands, the black men bleeding, the yellow men screaming, the lunatics hooting in the streets. Such women as might have seemed alluring in the dark now showed pocked and wigless, assaulting respectable passers-by. Yet I arrived in Saint Germain without once being challenged. I can only assume that, in my agitation, they took me for one of their own.

This district was in a frenzy of a different kind. One of my fellow secretaries accosted me with drawn sabre, yelling that the counter-revolution had begun, and all loyal men must storm the Tower. Another pulled him away, claiming that this was no rebellion, but the Jacobins murdering their opponents in the Assembly. The Hôtel Dubois hummed like an angry hive, and no servant met me at the door. I staggered down the hall, my cries for Narcisse withering in my throat.

"Close and bar the doors." That was the comte, appearing at the top of the stairs in his gown and cap.

"No!" The dowager's voice filled the chamber, and the servants obeyed as if their master had not spoken. "Leave them open to any who seek admittance. If the mob come, you will say we have fled, but otherwise deny them nothing. Turn over the cellar to them, and the gun cupboard. If they raze and loot, do not resist. Come my son, you are not well."

The comte was shaking, his face a bad colour. A manservant aided him down the steps, and it was only at the bottom he saw me. "What the hell are you doing, Simon?" he cried. "You should be out the gates by now!"

"Not without my sister," I said.

"There's no time," said the dowager. "He must come with us."

I shouted wild things. I may have drawn my sword.

Then my sister was there at my side. "Come with me, Simon." Her voice was so firm and calm that for a moment I became a child, and Narcisse my anchor after our mother's death. As we walked down the passage towards the cellar, she begged me to tell her our father was clear of the city.

I snapped awake. "He awaits us now in Saint Marcel!"

"Then his fate is unknown."

"Narcisse, we cannot stay here!"

"Simon, the mob are going door to door—"

"Would you listen to the whispers over me? Come now—"

"No." She stepped away from me and in tones of absolute cold, said, "I'll hear no more. Leave if you will!"

She receded down the passage like a spectre in the opera, and after a moment I did follow her, through chambers and stairs that were all too familiar.

We were hiding in the ritual chamber when the sounds of looting filtered through from above. Shouting and whistling, cries of delight suggested the intruders had discovered the comte's remaining bottles.

The comte was here, with some of the maids and children of the household, and the elder servants, all crouching in the dark. In the light of a single taper, the dowager knelt at the base of the stairs as if in prayer. But as I watched she poured black powder from a vial, crossing the shaft from wall to wall. She murmured as she did so, words that seemed to have some great potency. The comte had a hand to his heart—I saw Narcisse bend over him, one hand on his forehead and the other on his wrist. Then without warning, Michel emerged from the blackness. His face was grave when he met my eyes, but he said nothing—only crossed to my sister, who threw her arms about him.

"But Michel," I said, "what do you here? Your men—"

Augusta was there, her withered finger pressing upon my lips. *"Silent."* In shock, I fell quiet.

The sounds of searching and *halloos* like a hunting party passed us by. We remained there for hours, silent and cowering like rats.

***

PARIS, 1819

The Hôtel Meurice has fine, new rooms overlooking the Rue Saint Honoré. 'Hotel' no longer means what it did—this is a place for English travellers to stay in comfort and pay for the privilege.

After completing her labours in the cellar, Patience slept for a day and a night. Then she rose and packed up her trunks. It was time for Patience Courtemanche to transform into such a creature as might approach a princess, whose brother might well be the Comte Beauchêne. To remain so for a week will devour the savings of twenty years.

How long since she occupied a chamber like this? All is clean and white, there is an enclosed bath and a dressing room as well as the bed. From the window, Patience glimpses the incipient green of the gardens surrounding the Tuileries Palace. She could walk the distance, weary though she is and with a bandage round her forearm, but for her purpose a carriage is essential. So is formal dress.

It is ritual in its own way, this toilette, reminiscent of her youth and yet so very different. She recalls the gown she wore at her wedding, how it was not so much a dress as a kind of tenting, first muslin then a stiff brocade draped over the hoop and panniers, secured by lacing over and above that of the corset. She recalls, suddenly and completely, the inertia attending her every movement, coupled with a complete inability to bend. Now even a royal audience only demands a gown of black-sprigged muslin, with barely more frills than a walking dress, that she can pull on herself, though a maid is required for the buttons.

"Your audience is with the Duchess of Angoulême?"

Patience nods as the maid prattles on.

"Oh, she is like a saint in Paris! So many good works and such kindness to all, after all she has suffered." The girl is of dark complexion and nimble, and above all else young. She helps Patience on with the black velvet jacket and exclaims at the quality. "Oh, this is so fine! You will do very well, I should think. Oh, but you should have seen the gown Her Grace wore for the reception of the Austrian ambassador—ivory silk with gold broidery. Her portrait was painted in it, you'll see it in the hall as you go in." Now the girl has moved on to Patience's hair, expertly pomading and pinning the curls into the front-heavy mass that will accommodate her new hat. She has already offered to dye her hair, claiming she can correct "whatever of nature's faults you wish!" But the figure in the mirror is already foreign enough.

A light powder upon her face and rouge upon her lips. More titbits of gossip from the girl, of royal charity and fashion, doubtless gleaned from previous guests at the Meurice. Finally, the Russian toque is pinned in place. Black, beribboned, with dyed ostrich feathers nodding like those on a funeral cortege. And there are gloves, to conceal her spoiled hands.

The ritual is complete. She is transformed, like a fairy tale, from serpent to woman. She dismisses the girl with a small gratuity, and remains seated before the dresser, gazing at herself. A faint scent steals around her, of roses and jasmine. It is the soap they provide here for guests, as they provide fresh, white linen and tea.

"Madame Narcisse Therese Ambroise," she says, feeling the unfamiliar words upon her tongue, "the Comtesse Dubois." Then she laughs. Facing into the mirror, she laughs and laughs and laughs.

***

The audience chamber, by no means the largest within the Tuileries, boasts peeling paint and a pervasive smell of mould. Like the once grand building itself, her hostess slumps in velvet and gilt.

The Duchess of Angouleme wears black that is ruched and puffed, with a collar of lavish white lace. On her breast sits the gold-framed miniature of both her parents, Louis XVII and Marie-Antoinette. She appears neither saintly nor elegant, only a tired and somewhat lumpy woman poured into a chair. The portrait in the hall presented a far more regal figure.

Patience curtsies. "Thank you so much for receiving me, your Grace."

The duchess shifts slightly, scrying her guest in the guttering candlelight. "I do not believe we have met before, Comtesse. Your eyes are an unusual colour, like amethyst. I believe I would remember."

"They are the one thing about me that has not changed, your Grace."

Those pale lips quirk. "We are none of us young as we were, but you keep the current fashion and lodge at the Meurice, no less! Tell me—did you steal away from Paris with the rest of your family's jewels?"

Surprised, Patience almost laughs. "If I had, your Highness, they would have been sold long since. I owe my current disposition, as I owe my survival, to good friends."

"Ah yes. Friends."

The roof here is high and painted with faded clouds. Two frowsy ladies in waiting hunker at the prescribed distance. A few paintings glower from the walls. The majority of the royal collection remains in the Louvre, the property of the people of France. One might think the Bourbon would reclaim them, along with the Louvre itself, but they have not. Perhaps they simply do not dare extend their hand where Napoleon himself refrained. And she has heard things about the duchess, from sources other than the maid at the Meurice. Returning to Paris after her long exile, Marie-Therese would not redecorate the chambers where she and her family lived before their attempted flight. During her periodic withdrawals from public life, it was said, she lay in those rooms with her gaze on the ceiling in the dark.

She is by far the most likely of her family to grant Patience the boon she requires. But first, she must convince the duchess of who she is. As the silence runs on between them, Patience marshals herself to speak. "The Hôtel Dubois is a ruin, I have heard."

"So many ruins." The gaze of the duchess turns inward as she fingers the miniature. "With God's grace, my uncle will reign long and restore Paris to its proper grandeur."

"Your Grace." She bobs once more. "I have also heard that there is Comte Beauchêne, who resides in Saint Marcel."

"Yes," says the duchess, returning to the present. "Oh, I see. You want to know if it's who you think."

"I had letters, your Grace, from people we knew. They said he survived the Terror but died fighting in the wars."

"The Comte Beauchêne, now let me think... Francine! Francine, was the title reassigned or was he recognised?"

"He had proofs and patents, your Grace." The elder of the women speaks with a heavy Austrian accent. "He was recognised and reinstated in his position at the Department of Mines, at a something lesser salary."

The duchess claps her hands—a shot that puts the echoes to flight like birds. "Does that sound like him?"

"Your Grace, it does."

"You have been in Paris now, this past week? And you have not gone to see him?"

"I… your Grace, he must believe me dead. To simply appear, on what might be a stranger's doorstep…."

"I imagine it would be awkward, yes."

Patience pauses a moment, then says, "I know I have changed, and possess very little in the way of memorabilia. Some small tokens, the letters I presented to the chamberlain."

"Proof and patents." And now at last, the duchess musters the energy to lean forward. "Two generations of Dubois died on the scaffold that day. How was it that you survived?"

And now she comes to it—the truth that is not truth, that must match whatever *he* has said. "Like my brother, only in a different way. Like him, I was trapped in Paris with my husband's family. It was my fault. He should have gone with our father, but he wanted to make sure I was safe." She pauses there, acknowledging one more senseless death. "The Dubois had loyal servants. Still, we spent much of the next year hidden in the cellars and the lower apartments: it was a very trying time. My poor father-in-law, he suffered from a congestion which killed him. We were forced to bury him in the garden."

Her Grace nods.

"As to what happened, the day of the arrests… there's no mystery, not really. I was not at the hôtel." She hesitates. "You may think ill of me, your Grace."

"I assure you, Madame Ambroise, I have seen very much in my time and heard, I suspect, far worse than you are capable of telling me."

"I had… I was at the cabinet of waxworks, run by Madamoiselle Grosholtz as she was then. The English use her married name, of Tussaud."

"The cabinet? The one that stood in the Palais Royale?"

"There was another—I know it sounds ludicrous, your Grace. But the Dubois were among the patrons of the show, and there was a thought, upon my betrothal, that *I* might be sculpted. Not as myself, of course, but as a nymph or some such foolishness." She smiles, remembering. "So I knew Madamoiselle, and she knew me. The dowager contrived a message be sent and she agreed to take me in. My husband agreed. There was a hope, you see, between us..." she trails off. The duchess, too, has never borne a child. "She sheltered me, and when she fled Napoleon's rise to England, I accompanied her, under the name of—"

"The false name, yes. I see. And you took the masks with you, as well."

So the duchess knew that the highlight of Madame's travelling exhibition was her royal parents' imagoes. Patience's stomach flutters, but she feels also the faint shifting of arcane energies, the pattern she established in the cellar pressing against the greater reality, changing it. Ariadne's thread guiding them both through the labyrinth.

At last, the duchess speaks. "Madamoiselle Grosholtz attended the royal apartments at Versailles. She taught my aunts to carve soap. A fine woman, who suffered as much as any of us. And she is still in England?"

"Yes, your Grace. Her son is with her now."

"I arrived in England in 1809." The duchess's voice is a soft reminiscence. "If you were there, you should have attended Hartwell."

"Tussaud would not presume. I did write to you."

"You did?"

"Yes. But there were so many other refugees from the wars by then. I assume the letter went astray."

"So many refugees." The duchess frowns, gazing back into that other place. "And men always pushing to the front of the line."

Patience nods, then waits silently.

At last, the duchess shifts her bulk and sighs. "Your brother thinks you dead. Well then, it shall be my considerable satisfaction to set him right. You are welcome to the Court, Madame Ambroise."

"I thank you, your Grace."

The duchess extends her hand, and Patience feels fate lock into place. She kisses the white glove, then lifts her chin to the proper degree. "I crave your indulgence, your Grace. But if I have a resurrection before me, I would offer a… a gesture of appreciation, out of my own pocket. An entertainment."

"An entertainment?"

"Of a very particular kind. Not for the public, you understand."

"I'm not sure I do understand."

"I will explain it all, your Grace, if you will permit. It would be in your honour, after all, and the honour of those we have lost."

She explains, and slowly in the decaying room, in the spore-soured air, the duchess begins to smile.

***

THE MEMOIRS OF SIMON ÉTIENNE DE LANNERARY, COMTE BEAUCHÊNE.

So there I was. For one hasty action, in defiance of my father, I had thrown away my opportunity for glory, my reputation and my freedom. For once Valmy was won, none of us might quit the hôtel for fear of our very lives.

I had been tricked like a country girl into a brothel, with fine words and a charming façade, thinking that a man who participated in such obscenities was somehow, at heart, still a man. But that is how Satan comes at us, not revealing the horror of his Fall, but step by step and shade by shade, such little things as seem as nothing yet expand the gape of the pit. He was a deserter, and that is the truth! The man I had admired, whose favour I had sought… and I, what was I but an able young man who had likewise not deigned to obey the Assembly!

I would have left that evening. Once the mob had passed, and with it the immediate danger to the comte and the ladies, I would have found my way back to Saint Marcel and thence to the Field of Mars. Perhaps I might even have attempted to cover Michel's absence—but the memory is confused. I can only assume I was given a drink which made me sleep. By the time I regained my senses, it was all too late.

So strange, the days I spent in hiding. So long and bitter were the nights. I know of all the great and terrible things that happened during that time, but again, it is like a nightmare. It was the hunger, perhaps, or madness of the kind that comes upon those in confinement. I can tell you we had servants with us, and that our lives depended upon their discretion. That we grew potatoes under the cover of roses, twisting wild and untended, and trapped pigeons in the despoiled upper rooms. As a great house abandoned by its family, the hôtel was looted again and again, and never once were we permitted to resist. I obeyed the comte until his death, even knowing the true source of every order that he gave. But I could not forgive Michel. I was trapped there with him, his grandmother, and their madness, day in and day out. They sought, as I have said, eternal life. The means to escape death, perhaps even after their mortal bodies perished. But all was illusion, a devil's trick—after all, who but the damned would seek to extend their stay in this vale of tears? Who but they would seek to return?

My father did win clear of Paris. He made his way, despite the invasion and roving bands of thieves, all the way to Dijon and thence to our family estate. There—though it was long, long after that I discovered the truth—he was set upon by his own tenants, and his body tossed into the river.

***

Simon betrayed the coven. Of that, Patience has always been certain. How else to make sense of her memories of those final days? And she had suspected—known. On some level, she had always known.

She had not seen why Simon should be brought into the coven at all. Oh, as a child she had loved him, her baby brother, had cared for him as best she could until they were parted. But he arrived in Paris a stranger, just another young man to whom the world was granted by birth. And he required the draught to see, whereas both she and Michel needed only their eyes. And Michel had such beautiful eyes. But Michel was also insistent: "You'll need his support, Cissy. You are Augusta's apprentice but I know how the coven works!" And she could deny him nothing, back then. She was in love, from their first dance in the ballroom. She supported his plea, and Augusta gave way.

She spoke to Simon herself, of the traditions and goals of Melisende's heirs, of the search for her lost wisdom. Michel made sure that Simon understood what was involved, before he was finally brought to take the oath. But as it turned out, he didn't have the stomach.

"He'll get used to it." Again, Michel stood his champion. "It takes time to adjust to feeling the energies, even longer to read them. In the meantime, he'll be a useful agent."

She had seen Simon's eyes as he staggered from the sanctum that first night. She had seen terror and disgust—and one thing more, though it took her a long time to realise what it was. And Simon kept his oath, though he behaved abominably otherwise.

In due course, he and Michel patched up their little spat, and became once again inseparable. There were nights Michel did not come to her, nights when Simon lodged beneath their roof. Young men will play their games, Augusta told her, don't be troubled by it. And of course, he brought them the body from the crypt of the Capuchins, preserved and whole, and of exactly the right century.

Augusta had been so excited. "Oh my dear, dear girl," she said. "This man may have known Melisende, or known of her. We may find the location of her writings; we may find *her*."

But that hope had proved false. Oh, the words they forced from it were terrible and strange, but nothing to the purpose.

By this stage, Narcisse herself had grasped the principles of the rite and was able to take Michel's place as officiant—to his great gratitude. She understood now why the bodies needed to be whole and as sound as possible; otherwise the drain on the operator was unendurable. Augusta said that circumventing this had to form part of Melisende's stratagem—so convinced she was that Melisende had cheated death. So desperate she grew, as the omens quickened.

And then the Terror was upon them, and finally she realised that what lurked in Simon's eyes was envy.

*****

She remembers the day when the whole of Paris went mad. When Simon burst into the hôtel like a whirlwind. Augusta received him grimly.

"You understand that if you stay now, you stay till the end. Like Michel, you'll be listed as a deserter. If you are caught by the guard, you will be executed."

"I don't care!" Simon's fist slammed the oak panelling like gunfire. His hair was dishevelled and sweat stood upon his brow. "Do you think I'm going to run away and leave you here?" He spoke the words staring at Narcisse, but she did not think he meant them for her. Glancing at Michel, she saw his lips trembling.

"Your studies have progressed," Augusta said, "but I tell you plain, Simon de Lannery, you will make a better secretary than a magus."

Her brother swore, punched the wall again. "Very well. But you will cede me that sword of yours. No, you will! Then go below. Bona Dea, Narcisse, can you take charge of him? I must see to the children."

She walked up to him, striving for firmness. "I am glad to see you. Come, brother."

But he shook off her hand like a horse fly. "You think I don't know the way? There are many things I know!"

*****

She remembers the day when the news came through that the king was dead. They carried him to the plaza in a cart, chopped off his head and took it to Curtius, so that his final agony might be preserved in wax. As the old comte wept and coughed blood, as the young men muttered together, she sought out the refuge that was hers and hers alone.

The winter sun was setting as she emerged from the servant's stairs. The old comte's chamber was filled with a cold, red light. She crouched by the window overlooking Ferry Street to see it better. No one else came here now. The grandeur that dazzled her when she first saw it was but a shadow, faded stripes and defaced portraits. The stains of rain seeping through the shattered glass and broken tiles. Like the comte himself, the house died slowly.

She thought of bright-eyed Marie, for she knew on whom the grisly task of fashioning the king's death mask would descend. The girl had the nerve and the skill (and waxworking was such a strange and intricate skill, fascinating in its transformations). The committee would not permit the royal images to remain on display in the Palais Royale, but this horror they must have.

For the first time, it occurred to her that her own bust would never be finished. Perhaps it was for the best. And then, she heard the creaking.

It set her heart to racing, her eyes to scanning every shadow. But she saw nothing. A beam; then groaning as the night air chilled the joists. No one else would come here. No one but her would dare.

***

She remembers the night when the old comte died. When Simon was given to lead the rite, for Michel refused and Augusta said that a man would be best.

Her father-in-law breathed badly throughout the day, and as the sun set entered a fit of coughing that did not pass. Blood burst from his lips and turned his left eye red. And now, Augusta would have her own son gaze upon the future. Where lies the greatest danger, now the storm has broken? Where lies their prize? How much further can they press before death swallows them all?

"For the dead shall arise from the grave!"

Her mistress was mistaken, Narcisse thought. It was better she attempt the feat than Simon, for whom the old man had but little respect. This was a lingering prejudice of Augusta's, and she feared it meant she had not gained her respect despite her work, despite her obedience. So she spoke the words, head reeling from the effects of the draught on an empty stomach. They were eating broth now, formed of starch scraped off the back of the wall papers, with potatoes and rose hips reserved for the children (the poor children, grown so pale and thin). But she was not so far gone as the spectacle of Simon's nausea escaped her, his obvious fear as he spoke the words over the comte's corpse.

"Trust your perceptions, Simon." Augusta urged. "Open your mind!"

Once more the voices rose from out the dark, lured by the bait of the operator's life. She knew how the spirits buffeted Simon's face, how his lungs seized as the warmth drained from his limbs. He *must* force the comte's spirit into his corpse, lest it become a ghost.

"Who comes against us?" he trembled as he spoke the questions. "How may we best prepare?" Then: "Father!" he shrieked. "Father, no! *He's dead!*" Flinging up his arms against a threat not even she could see, he stumbled backward, sacrificing all control. The binding threads flew wide and loose, stinging her face like whips. The voices of the dead swelled into a ghastly chorus; there were so many more now, than before.

"He's lost it." Augusta moved forward. "Narcisse, dispel them all! Michel, renew the wards! Bona Dea, if this doesn't work, I'll have to bottle him, my son…"

***

She remembers the final night.

Once more, she sought the solitude of the comte's rooms, the sidelong view of Ferry Street. It had been her only view of the outside world for so long now, she thought drearily of the Seine as the ocean and how she might set sail to Guinea and Algiers, where the snow never fell. And then the creaking came again, this time with a catch of voices. She rose and trod stealthily through the maze of withdrawing chambers. After so many nights, she knew which spots to avoid, and which would bear her weight without complaint.

In the despoiled bedchamber, Michel huddled in Simon's arms. They lay so close together, their faces buried against each other.

"My father didn't deserve this," he choked.

Simon murmured in reply, stroking those long, black curls. Those curls, which were *her* joy.

"I can't stand it anymore, everything is dead or dying, the entire world we knew and everything we love. All that is left is— is faces in wax!"

And yes, it was best that her own image never be finished. That her old self be melted down. For gently but firmly, Simon pulled Michel's head back by the hair and kissed him. Long and deep they tasted each other, then his hand moved to Michel's shirt.

Words came to her lips. "So, this is how young men play."

Michel looked up, blanching. His eyes were warm, brown pools, and she wanted to throw herself into them, beg him to make it *her* he came to for comfort. But Simon's face contorted—he thrust Michel aside and sprang from the bed. "You stupid bint, get out of here! This isn't your concern!"

"I think it *is*!"

He raged at her, shouting, punching the wall, dredging insults from the gutter. "What are you, Cissy? An ex-nun? Another witch, like the old biddy? You blasted women are going to see us all dead!"

A nun or a witch. It felt like cold steel entering her heart. But on what grounds might she protest? She had been nowhere in her life, save the hôtel and the convent. She knew nothing of this world, only how to summon the dead. Of course Michel would prefer Simon.

And then, something inside her exploded outward. *"SILENT. STILL."*

And they were. One on the bed, one standing a mere breath away. They froze, aware of her but unable to move or speak. The wonder of it warred with her incandescent rage.

She knew. She always knew that in truth, he wasn't hers. *She* was *Augusta's*, and their marriage but a means to an end, carried with grace but no more than the side plot of the grand opera. She left them there and fled as far and fast as she could—only not to Guinea and Algiers. She hunkered in the garden by the comte's grave, and only until the last of the light was gone. Then she came back inside to meet the consequences of what she had done.

"We can stay here no longer." Augusta seemed to have aged years overnight. For the first time, she thought her mistress resembled her dead son. "Not after all that racket."

She had not shouted or screamed, not put her fist through the rotting wall. She had stifled her voice as she had stifled her. Why should she be exiled?

As if reading her thoughts, Augusta sighed. "Whether Melisende walks immortal, or if her spirit whispers in the dark, I shall not know until I too am dead."

"Mistress, no!"

"Marie has agreed to take you in, so you can go there tonight. The rest of us will depart to other sanctuaries, and once a way from Paris is found… perhaps we will all go to Dijon, if your father has truly passed."

Of her father's fate she neither knew nor cared. "We can continue the search! *I* will continue!"

"Dare I hope you will permit Michel to see you to Temple Street? You cannot travel alone."

She nodded, not daring to speak for fear she *would* scream, or even weep. For all the power thrumming in her veins, she had never felt so lost—not at the convent, not at her mother's deathbed.

But for Augusta's sake, who looked on her with such weary eyes, she stood firm, taking the bag of magical tools across her shoulders, disguised with one of her maid's red shawls. Only when her mistress pressed the black staff into her hand did she finally break.

***

THE MEMOIRS OF SIMON ÉTIENNE DE LANNERARY, COMTE BEAUCHÊNE.

Why did we not flee before the guards came? We had time. It was nothing a sane man would not expect.

The Assembly had fallen as surely as the old regime. We were under the rule now of Robespierre and the Committee of Public Safety. They could provide no more bread and fuel than the ones they blamed for the lack, but they were willing to set the guillotine to task. First their one-time comrades in rebellion went to the scaffold, then the king and queen, followed any of rank that could still be found in Paris.

In the teeth of winter, the old comte died. This left Michel the master of the house, a responsibility he failed to fulfil as completely as he had that of captain or husband. It could not be long before the servants would finally betray us. And so, I laid my plans.

The first step was to get Narcisse out of the dowager's grasp. I am not ashamed to say I worked on Michel, appealing to his vanity and hopes for paternity. It was no wonder, I said, Narcisse had not conceived. No child could possibly thrive under these conditions. She must be found cleaner lodgings, above the ground, with better food. He brought this concern to his grandmother, and she agreed with little demur. I fancy that her son's death had sapped her faith and given her to think on more conventional immortality.

The place they chose to send her was the waxworks. I questioned the risk that she be recognised, but in the end could offer nothing better. She would not, I promised myself, remain there for long.

Have you, my Reader, ever experienced the mix of emotions that accompanies the onset of an event long feared? There is horror, of course, but also a weird form of relief. Imagine then, how the rattle of boots across the ceiling, the shouting of unfamiliar voices, descended to me. I was in the cellar, breaking down the last of the wine racks for firewood. I remember snatching up a billet as I ran towards the stairs.

Michel met me halfway, pulling the maids with the children behind him. His face was pale, but for once he used a firm hand. He was dressed and armed again as a cavalry officer, and carried my rapier as well as his own.

"They've found us," he said. "Simon, you must go to the sanctum."

"I'll be damned if I'll hide again!"

"It's too late," he shook his head. "They are breaking through both front and back. I beg you, Simon, save these innocents."

"How am I to do that?"

"I will cast the ward, but you must maintain it."

"I promised your father I would defend this house as my own!"

"Then do so, but in this fashion! They'll take all they find here to the scaffold, and perhaps we Dubois deserve it."

Above us, I heard the dowager screeching.

I took the arm of a little boy—the son of the comte's valet, I cannot recall his name—and did as Michel instructed. Once we were concealed, he left to join the battle above and I remained, my honour once more the ransom for those poor lives. For I did it. I knelt there and I spoke those words. Hours spent praying to the devil, until the last sound died away above. We remained in that place for I cannot tell how long—until the children were crying for water. Then cautiously we emerged and fled into the city under the cover of the winter night.

And that is my tale, oh Reader, for the most part. Once we were clear of Saint Germaine, the servants sought their families and I sought mine. But of my sister I could find no sign, merely guards, guards everywhere. I heard there had been arrests at the waxworks, and I understood. Narcisse *had* been recognised and questioned. She gave us up—the guards were used to breaking men, let alone young women. I have tried to confirm her fate. It seems she must have died an anonymous prisoner, her body dropped into the catacombs without record or ceremony. I pray constantly for her soul as I do for my own redemption. The Dubois died on the scaffold. I pray they came back to God at the end.

It stings that I could not save her.

Left with nothing, save a few remembrances—did I mention my father gave me his ring? I joined the army under an assumed name and fought in Vendee—a distasteful business, but I fulfilled my duty. Then, when the amnesty was declared, I presented myself to the new order under my true name. I fought in the second war of the coalition, I fought at Marengo and Ulm, and prayed most fervently for the restoration. When it came, His Majesty was pleased to confirm my title and restore to me my position in the Department.

I promised you a story you had not heard. I think we can agree, oh Reader, that I have delivered.

***

PARIS, 1819

Simon Étienne de Lanneray leans back in the old chair, which creaks beneath his weight.

"An invitation?"

The servant nods gravely. He wears blue and gold livery with the personal badge of Her Grace, the Duchess of Angouleme. The same adorns the exquisite white billet. Simon cracks the seal and reads the elegant script. His presence is sought at tomorrow evening's entertainment, a dance and supper cast as a masquerade.

Few in these days remember the Comtes Beauchêne, or think them worth parchment. His ancestral lands are worth nothing, the chateau ransacked, the woodlands long since destroyed by the passage of armies. He has his position in the Department, with a miserable stipend, but that could hardly be the reason for this.

A pulse of excitement beats in his temples. He glances at the desk where his memoir sits, the pile of neatly-inscribed pages. It was a strange fancy, that seized him as suddenly as a spring fever, to set down everything he remembered. Everything that he dared. For, having commenced writing, it occurred to him that many of his fellow survivors had published their stories and received good recompense.

But now he has other prospects. He is to attend Her Grace's ball as an honoured guest, and remind Paris of the oaks which once stood here! And then his hands clench, wrenching and cracking the fine invitation, for the venue is the Hôtel Dubois.

It seizes him by liver and craw—the awareness that has never truly faded, for all he has starved his senses, battened them down by every means. Now it swells again, as real as the sunlight beyond the drapes, that sense of the darkness lurking beneath the surface of all Paris. It lingers in his heart, where are buried the things that paper could not bear. Nothing could be worth returning to that place, to set the voices whispering....

Fortune favours the brave.

The words come to him from memory, perhaps. Their cadence is wrong, like a lyric misheard, but they calm him. Perhaps it was his father who used the phrase—yes, his father, that good old man. He breathes slowly, steadily, and the panic fades.

He turns back to the messenger. "Obviously, I should be honoured."

The man bows, and is escorted to the door by Simon's own servant.

Simon smooths the crumpled parchment, the old signet heavy on his hand. When his man returns, he orders a small brandy to ease his nerves.

The townhouse in Saint Marcel has seen better days, that is true. He wonders if the messenger noticed that the striped wallpaper was spotted, especially at the top. That there were lamps upon the tables instead of gas in the walls, and his jacket was an old broadcloth, as far from fashion as might be. But he is hardly the only nobleman to exist in such reduced circumstances, even among those who wait upon the Bourbon direct. Were his wife still alive, it would all be yet harder to manage. He can only imagine that harpy's response to such an invitation. The demands she would make! The clothes and jewels!

The spreading warmth of the brandy steadying his hands, he takes up the paper and re-reads it. Most crucial is the injunction he should attend to his own advantage. The duchess is acknowledged by all as a trifle eccentric, but it can still be no coincidence that the masque will take place at the hôtel. What can it mean? Has the question of ownership finally been resolved? The Dubois are extinct in the main line, but the flocks of second cousins and one-time dependents have been bickering over the property for years.

Could the judgement, perhaps, have gone in his favour?

How could he have hesitated? This is what he has been waiting for all these years, the chance to revive his name and standing! The final sentence bids him wear black, as he might to honour the memory of those long passed. Without hesitation, he plunges himself and his little household into the business of preparation.

The maid will lay out his suit and prepare his bath. His man is ancient as a mummy, and Picardian besides—he can polish his shoes, but he will not trust him with a razor. He will go out tomorrow and hire both barber and carriage. He will not count *sou* now his fortunes are finally on the turn.

A glance in the fly-specked mirror shows him not the beauty of his youth, but a man, rather—firm-fleshed and eyes an arresting blue, his hair grey but still long and thick in its queue. Beyond the duchess, women of rank and wealth will be there. It is a shame he dares not wear the medals he won under Napoleon, or those from the Assembly which are graven with a different name.

The barren rooms of his memory would not seem so fearsome, should he walk them as master. And as for the darkness, who is there in Paris who does not possess a black pit filled with his own ghosts?

***

The spring evening is cold and the rain has returned, veiling the district of Saint Germaine in a mist through which the lights of the houses sparkle and dance. It is, in truth, entirely fashionable.

Spangles are the order of the night; brights and scintilla amid black lace. The light from braziers sets them winking as the dance proceeds. The braziers are great iron things, as might warm a watchtower, but practical enough in a hall with stripped walls and beams bare of any chandelier. To those of the requisite sensibility, the scene presents a sombre magnificence, a kind of skeletal grandeur. Black skirts sweep across the floor. The draught from the many crevices sets the flames flickering, stirs the black feathers on a multitude of heads. Bourbon lilies spray white from cracked vases, around a dais where the orchestra (for once not distinguished by their coats), puff cheeks and pluck strings. And all are masked, yes; black dominos for the musicians and for the guests, something elaborate and bizarre. A strange fancy, and yet many have taken to it. On a circular table with a black cloth, there are bowls of wicked punch, and a cold supper has been laid in the manner of a wake.

What a daring idea this is, and yet so practical! Everyone has black in their wardrobe, at least one good dress or coat.

Everyone has a reason to mourn, even as they dance and drink and exchange sly glances, mask to mask. It has been noted that the Duchess of Angouleme never smiles at her parties, and glumly presides over balls. Now, it seems, her humour has finally found its match. Seated in her black gown, the inevitable portrait on her breast, her expression is dreamy.

Now the waltz is old and the polka—a violent, giddy thing—is the fashion, obliging couples to leap like grasshoppers. They spring about the floor as if they fear to slow, even for a second. Perhaps they are right, perhaps this interval must be seized and squeezed of every drop of glee, caught in chipped crystal and drained without stopping. Perhaps this reprieve will indeed be brief.

Simon de Lanneray hands his coat and hat to the doorman, his stick to the woman who is there for that purpose. He is clean-shaven and his hair presents a somewhat more vivid shade than it did this morning. Water of Cologne covers the scent of camphor that clings to his jacket and his waistcoat of fine, black brocade. His shoes are old-fashioned but polished to a mirror shine.

The announcement of his name causes but little stir. A colleague from the Department nods to him, then returns to his colloquy with an attractive redhead. Abandoned, as so often before, he heads for the table as though his only concern is a dry throat, and waits to be summoned.

"Excuse me, sir." A silken voice threads through cornet and violin.

He turns to see a woman in a black gown and a mask of silver flowers. She is mature, perhaps his own age, and her hair smokes upward through wreathes of silver leaves.

"Excuse me," she repeats, "but are you not the Comte Beauchêne?"

"Your pardon, Madame, but do I know you?"

"It seems not."

He cannot see her eyes—those of the mask are filled with black gauze. But he hears amusement in her voice. "Then perhaps it were more appropriate for our hostess to introduce us, or perhaps your father or brother?"

"In the normal course of things, indeed." She laughs, and it is a merry laugh that does something to disarm him. "But this is a masquerade. I might present myself as anyone, and anyone as my brother."

"So where does that leave us?"

"I wonder, are you married?"

Now he laughs, in surprise. "Bold question! But very well, oh mysterious one, I am the Comte Beauchêne and her ladyship passed away some years ago. I suspect this enquiry makes you one of the Dijon Comtois." *That pack of greedy dogs.*

"No." She shakes her head and smiles. "But I am myself a widow. Perhaps that leaves us the consolation of time."

Could she be a courtesan? It has been a long time, indeed, since he could contemplate such a luxury. But despite her forwardness, her manner does not quite suggest it. At the least, he is no longer alone.

"Are you enjoying the ball?"

She raises a cup and sips, considering. It gives him the excuse to take a good drink of his own. He nearly chokes, as the punch stings his throat and fills his head with fumes. Beneath the rum and pineapple lies a musty bitterness so potent it can only be the draught, must be the accursed, black draught...

But he has fought this battle already. There is nothing here in this decrepit chamber to threaten him—all of it lies in his head alone. So this is merely a heady punch, fortified with liqueur. Such things are also fashionable.

"I have but now arrived, as I think you know." The aftertaste, burning down his throat is almost pleasant. "It is a striking spectacle."

"You did not claim a mask yourself?"

He saw them on entering, he realises. A table spread with moulded, wax-gold shapes, no more to him than coats or sticks. It seems he was mistaken. For placed over living features, those shapes are revealed as faces frozen in grimaces of pain or fear. Their detail is incredible, extending to the individual contour of lips and creases at the corner of the eye. Wrinkled brows weigh shoulders smooth and white. Bulbous old noses, translucent in the light, extend far beyond the wearer's.

The woman sees him staring. "Mimes," she says. "After the Roman custom. At funerals, special priests wore the death masks of a family's ancestors."

"You mean, those are—for heaven's sake!" It is shocking, but he cannot take his eyes away. "Where would they even find such a thing?"

"The wax worker, Doctor Curtius, was forced to take many moulds—"

"Yes, I know… but this is morbid!"

"We have a generation, now, who never knew their grandparents." Spreading her fan in their direction. "Or parents, in some cases."

He takes refuge in the punch. "Well, I call it in extremely poor taste."

"When you have such strong opinions, perhaps we should take this discussion aside?"

He follows, for it is obvious she will not stay. Through a side door and into a hallway he recognises even with its stained plaster and exposed woodwork—his nerves twitch and he drains his glass. A servant looms on the periphery.

"Wine." The voice is barely a whisper, a rasping and eerie thing. "I have brought wine for you."

Thank God—any more punch and he'd be giddy. But before he can take up the offer, she speaks.

"I think you recognise me but are not sure. You wish to say a name but fear it might reveal too much of your heart."

"Madame, I assure you I am not so easily conquered!"

"I seek no conquest here. My sin is curiosity and a degree of nostalgia—for what might have been."

"Artemisia," he says. "Artemisia Eloise Voclain."

She smiles and, taking a lamp from the table, leads him deeper into corridors and empty chambers.

He yearns, now, to return to the ballroom. But the invitation said this would be to his advantage, and no one else has offered him so much as a greeting. Follow that lace train sliding over the stone, in that retreating circle of light, and anything might happen. And see? They are not alone—the servant attends.

Nonetheless, as they approach the cellar, he pauses. "Why bring me here, Madame?"

"You lived here, did you not? During the Terror." As though she has read his memoir. "I would see it."

If he retreats, it is back to the townhouse. To poverty and encroaching age. "I imagine there is little left down there save bats. They might catch in your hair, my dear."

"I wish to see where it happened. I would understand your sufferings."

She descends, and he finds himself stepping down, down, as if into dark water. She leads and he follows, until inevitably they find the sanctum bathed in greenish light.

In the deep place of his fears stand two figures, a man and a woman all in black, their faces wax. Like a man submerged, he turns slowly back to the stairs, only to find the servant is no servant but a shrivelled monster with gleaming eyes and claws the length of daggers.

"Still."

He knows, then. As the spell takes hold, freezing his arms and legs, he knows her name.

"You seem surprised, brother." Narcisse steps from his side, towards the brazier. "If the guards told you they killed me, they were lying."

This is impossible. He told himself none of it was real and it still seems so, that this is all just part of the masque. Or had it been him? Had it truly been his own voice whispering to him, inspiring him to write and follow his memories here? He strains against the binding, but it is as he remembers—someone else has assumed a hideous intimacy with his muscle and bone. It will be minutes before he can regain control.

But he can still speak. She has left him that.

"You betrayed us." Rolling his eyes, he takes in the nearest figure, the youthful body in tailcoat and straight trousers, so unlike his own breeches and stockings, the hair cropped in soldierly fashion. *Why did everything have to change?* Simon feels old, he feels weighed by more than his sister's spell. Damn her—he comes to the face and it is Michel. Honey-coloured wax rather than skin, but still his in each detail. Simon feels tainted bile in his throat. "What have you done?" he demands.

"Our clever Cissy," answers the apparition, "has solved the problem of how to summon the dead in the absence of whole bodies. Only a little corpse wax, as I understand it."

The voice is his. The eyes, the eyes....

"And a positive storm of energy."

The second voice is that of the dowager, he knows, he knows....

"Still, I doubt these vessels will last indefinitely. How did you decide who would host us?"

"I didn't." Narcisse's voice is cold. "Your masks were in with the others. I left it to fate."

"So, then." Horror weighs Simon's tongue. "You have forgiven her."

"What for?" Michel sounds mildly amused.

"For bringing down the guard upon us!" If he could but stamp, make fists! *Embrace him.* "Betraying us!"

"What are you saying, Simon?" Narcisse shakes her head slowly—in that blank-eyed mask she is less expressive than the dead. "We all know it was you."

"This," says the dowager, "is *unimportant.*" Her host is as young as the boy, decolletage and a cashmere shawl.

"Savon," says Michel (*Oh God, to hear him say it!*). "I know it wasn't you."

"Even now, you defend him." Narcisse's voice does not waver. "I did this, I raised you so you might look into the future and tell me what to do when the coven did *not* survive. I went to the trouble of bringing *him* here so that he might face your judgement."

"You have done," says the dowager, "considerably more than that."

Simon bows his head, down to his polished shoes. Once again, they have stripped away his armour and his honour. A nobleman reduced to service of the lowest kind, the slowest student in a devil's school. And yet, even now, he would do anything, no matter how vile, to be counted among them.

"What do you mean?" Narcisse asks her mentor.

"I mean that we cannot see into the future for you. We are here, in *time.*"

"Like a ghost. Bound to service or the place of death."

"Yes, but you have bound us to these glorious forms." The dowager admires the smoothness and plumpness of her host's white hand. "My dear, do you understand? If we contrive to balance the energies, we might remain indefinitely."

Those blank eyes turn to her.

"Do you understand?" Michel echoes his grandmother. "She means that you've discovered Melisende's secret."

"But it cannot last." For the first time, Narcisse seems uncertain.

"It *can*. If we combine our knowledge and our talents!"

"Does this answer your question, Cissy?"

Oh, that mocking fondness as he reaches for her. Simon braces, to see them kiss.

"The coven will rise again."

But she pulls away. "I understand what you say. But if we do this, let us not pretend I am anything more to you than a means."

"If we do this?" says the dowager, as Michel says, "Cissy."

"I loved you," Simon mutters, then raises his head. He looks Michel in the eye. "I love you."

"And I loved you *both*. In my way. Isn't that enough?"

The dead speak true, Simon thinks. *The dead speak true.*

"We don't have time for this!" The dowager rustles toward the brazier, in ribbons and gauze. "By my reckoning, these bodies must be made to *absorb* the wax." Peering, just for a moment into the flames, she steps back beyond the aureole of heat.

"I don't think we can melt our way in." Michel folds his arms. "What do you think, Savon?"

"I…" he stutters. *Who are these children? Whose bodies do they wear? Do I even care?* "I prayed in the sanctum, that you would escape them. That you would appear beside me once again."

"No such fortune, I fear."

"How *did* they find us?" Narcisse's voice is suddenly sharp. "You were arrested, held in prison. Surely they must have said."

"You would command me, then? As my summoner?"

"Michel Marshall Ambroise, Comte Dubois, I would."

Michel stands silent a moment. And then he speaks. "I was seen in the street and recognised."

Simon feels his own jaw drop. He struggles against his own surprise, but Narcisse recovers first.

"When? When was this?"

"As I returned from escorting you to the house on Temple Street."

And now she has no words. Her head dips towards her breast.

Simon feels a welling of some deep emotion he did not know he carried. It leaves him feeling light as air. The spell breaks, and he steps forward, arms opening.

"But the report was only investigated," Michel stares into his eyes, "because a man had been heard shouting inside the ruined hôtel. He was scolding a woman, saying she would be the death of him."

As if bidden by a harsher spell, Simon drops to the ground. Dimly, he hears the dowager speaking, driving them all to purpose. He does not care. Until he hears the dowager scream.

Looking up, he sees her body fold, crumpling to the stone floor. Narcisse stands with the dowager's mask held in trembling hands. Michel steps back, away from her, arms still clasped about his borrowed finery.

"I always liked the waxworks," he says.

"I remember." Narcisse advances slowly.

"The idea a body might survive, forever young and handsome. So concerned we were, with spirits, it seemed a—an oversight."

"And where do you think I got this idea? Oh Michel… but I'd not make you a ghost. Would you be bound inside a hollow shell?"

"I suppose not. Know this, Cissy. You are as beautiful now as when I danced with you at the ball."

"So are you." And still, she advances.

"Simon, help me."

Simon blunders towards him, cutting her off. The body is lean and muscular, in its military-inspired garb. The musk of it is sweet. It is not Michel's fragrance. It is not his body. *But I could do it*, he thinks wildly, *have him like a boy, for once the younger and the softer. I could show him this brand-new world.*

As he reaches for his prize, he dislodges a handkerchief from the waistcoat. It is embroidered, beautifully, with the monogram A.V. Andre, perhaps? Or Antoine? This boy has a name, and someone who loves him. Perhaps the fallen girl, perhaps his mother.

"Let me hold you," he gasps.

Michel stiffens as his arms close, but does not resist. His fingers brush that soft, shaved hair, then find the knotted cord.

"No!" Michel shrieks like a cat, like an owl. "No, Simon, please!"

The two masks, both miracles of portraiture, drop into the brazier. For a moment, their features seem to writhe. There is a flare as the fire catches the wax, and then it is done. He is alone with his sister once more.

***

The reek of wax fills her nose and mouth as the screams ring in her ears. Perhaps they will never fade. But Patience steps swiftly to the girl, bends down and checks her pulse and breathing. Both are strong, and some colour is already returning to her face. Bending over the boy, it filters through to her that Simon is sobbing. *And why aren't I?* she wonders, rolling him slightly so the head lies straight and his breathing eases. *Why in the name of Echo aren't I?*

Her back aches as she straightens, and for a moment dizziness almost claims her. *What have I done?* she wonders. *After all that I did to get here, all I sacrificed....* But the fact remains. Even amid the wonder at her own achievement, she saw Augusta playing with the girl's hand, like she might a fan. That was when she realised that if this were Melisende's secret, then she would not—could not—follow through. She could not have these lives on her conscience, or the lives that would follow should their first attempt at possession fail.

When Augusta lived, she thinks, *she starved herself for the children. Now she is dead, she would devour them whole. But even so, if there were some other way....*

She is empty now of all power. Tired enough to drop where she stands. Swaying, threads unravelling as the weight of oaths recedes. Only the links that bind her to Philibert and the staff remain. The memory of Augusta's eyes, the shock and betrayal there, stings her like boiling wax. If she had not betrayed them before, if Simon had not, then they certainly both have now.

But she has one more link, perhaps?

She turns to her brother, still slumped over the brazier where his lover's face once shone. "Well," she says. "It seems we are the coven now."

Simon's head snaps round. "Bow to *you*," he hisses. "Never!"

The blow catches the side of her head and she reels, stumbling. Her hand finds her temple, the other barks against the wall. "Simon?"

"It *was* your fault! Stupid girl, creeping round where you had no business! I suppose you think you're on the side of the angels, you white demon! Because we were men!"

"Do you think I would have cared less if you were my *sister*?"

He is on her then, hands squeezing her throat. And it seems that Simon too has learned new things in twenty years, for he has already cut her windpipe and her pulse is thrumming, as she bats uselessly at his wrists. She lets her hands drop as he sobs, "You killed him! You killed him *twice*!"

She finds the bottle in her skirt. She finds just enough breath to whisper, "Philibert. *I release you.*"

The bottle slides out and shatters. Simon screams as the ghost sinks his icy talons into him, the tips still bleeding.

Ah, a good vintage.

Then she is free and falling, jarring hip and hand as she lands. Coughing, too hard for the moment to see anything, think anything. It is only to give her time and breath. Any moment now, she will marshal her resources, pull out the salt and dispel the ghost as she freezes her brother once more. She will reason with him; she will save him…. As she tries to stand, her vision spackles, and blackness overtakes her.

When, finally, she is able to move without fainting or vomiting, she is alone.

Not alone. Her serpent has come and is wreathed around her, soothing and strengthening. Expressing anguish at not warning her in time.

"It's not your fault," she says.

A faint cry sounds from the girl, and she sees those plump hands twitch.

Slowly, aching now in every limb, she rises. "Come," she says. "We had better go."

***

Is someone there? Oh, thank God.
Mama? Mama, it's dark.
Is that you, my love?
Simon plunges blindly through the dark, hands scraping against rough stone, slamming into corners that barely miss his face. He must ignore them, ignore the faint, green gleam that kindles around calcite domes. Else he will see a little boy standing beside his mother's coffin, hand secure in his sister's grasp. His sister! Only a few, short years and Papa sent her away to the nuns. She had not wanted to leave him. Was that not the truth? He swore to childish gods, to sheep and twilight, he would bring her back and never let her go.

Pain explodes in his shin, and he curses. For a moment, all the dark is solid rock that comes crushing in upon him, filling his eyes, his lungs.

More wine, more.

"Go!" His own voice is hoarse. "Depart in Hecate's name!" Mashing his temples as though to stave in his own skull, blotting out the sensation of talons dipping through his skin, he shrieks and cries on the gods of honour and war, and at last the god of good, old-fashioned mines. "By Dis Pater, *avaunt!*"

And the ghost is gone, snuffed out as the last of the drug evaporates from his brain.

Now the darkness is quiet and still, still as the tomb. He was an idiot to run—and where, under God's black earth, has he run to?

In a rush of relief, he realises walls surround him and there is pervasive scent of wood and mould. In all likelihood, he is still in the hôtel.

Slowly, he turns about, attempting to match the bare beams and flaking plaster with something from his memory. The roof slopes, and a sharp chill pierces his skin—the wind snaking through partitions that bear not so much as a rag, although birds have roosted here. He remembers stalking the birds. He is in the uppermost rooms, where dwelt the valet and maids. As far above the ballroom as he had been below, for he cannot hear the music.

What has he done? Why, nothing. He did not betray his lover, for Michel was dead, had been these many years. He did not try to kill his sister, for that masked monster was not, could never have been her. His sister, that whore, rearing up in Michel's bed as he stood in the shadows and watched them…. He did not bring the guards down upon this house! So why is he shaking? Why does it seem as though his *jabot* chokes him?

Panic is the stain of a ghost's fingers, which unseen may still be felt. Which enter your heaving lungs, convince you that the walls are closing in, that you must run, run for the entrance, taking turnings you seem to remember but which led you deeper into the maze.

Simon wheels around, convinced now that the Revolutionary Guard are on his trail. He must find his way to the servants' stairs, which were set inside the wall. A labyrinth of tiny rooms, hung with web and scattered feathers and bones—and finally, the panel opens. He muscles inside the narrow shaft, cringing at the blackness. But he is of noble rank, if only of the robe, and will not give way to fear.

At his first step the rotten boards give way, and he falls down, down, all the way to Hell.

The impact shatters his skull and spine—a mercy, perhaps, as Philibert moves in to drink his fill. There among the damned he lies, a fear-frozen visage that over the years will turn inexorably to corpse wax, which the scientists consider is closer in its composition to soap.

⁂

Patience sits in the dark, in her room at the Hôtel Meurice. What a feeble darkness, this is; a pallor in disguise.

She has one more night here, amongst clean linen and scented soap. Then she must descend once more to the room on Temple Street so her brother will not find her. Her brother! The ache in her neck speaks bruises matched only by those on her heart. The only thing worse would be if Philibert killed him.

Tears stream down her face, though once again she makes no sound. For the working *has* changed her. It has left her responsible for reviving the coven from dust. For weaving what the years of war unravelled into a new pattern, strong enough to last five hundred years. She understands now: she must take her own apprentices and pass on the knowledge she has gained, together with the custody of the staff. But here and now she vows: she will never, ever breathe a word to them of what took place tonight, or the means by which the dead may be granted new life. That will be her burden, her constant and increasing temptation, as the years go by.

If I could *find another way….*

The snake regards her with eyes like mourning jewellery, and from it radiates a deep and abiding calm. *I came from her hand*, it seems to say. *Do you not realise that Melisende faced the same choice? Think you she had no coven, that* her *knowledge sprang from the void?*

She closes her eyes in hope that the black will claim her again, or at least numb her pain. But she cannot stop thinking. She will choose no aristocrats, no matter how gifted. No one who believes such power to be their right. The coven must work to ward and heal the land as whole. The signs all point to August, whom she met at the catacombs. The Gods alone know how she will find the young soldier, then win him over after what she did. But fortune favours the magus, and the magus is what she is.

Preoccupied, she does not register the knocking at the door. Until it opens, slightly, admitting a slice of light.

"Madame? There is a letter come for you, under the royal seal. Oh, mercy!"

Patience snaps alert, seeing the dark-complexioned maid whose hands were so sure as she chatted of duchesses and hair dye, pressed against the wall with a lamp trembling in her grip. Her face is waxen, her eyes fixed upon the serpent where it coils around the arm of the chair. Patience puts out her hand, to let the guardian crawl up her arm. "You can see it, can't you?"

Dumbly, the girl nods.

"Please, don't be frightened, it's all right. In fact, it's very well."

The girl does not scream, nor does she run. She watches the guardian, fear warring with fascination in her eyes. After a time, Patience judges it safe to continue.

"What is your name?" she asks.

"Michelle, Madame."

"Of course, it is. Of course. Mine is Patience. But I think my wait is over."

A NOTE AS TO SOURCES – The necromantic chant is derived from MS Sloane 3884, as glossed in *The Book of Black Magic and Pacts (aka The Book of Ceremonial Magic)*, A.E. Waite, London 1911. I have taken the liberty of reading "Banal" in the original text, as "Baal."

The Boneyard

Lisel combed her hair carefully and bound it back, then she trimmed her nails and fed both hair and nails into the fire. Her mother awoke in the fumes, and brewed tea. There were still bulbs to pack, so Lisel rolled them in a cloth and placed them in her satchel. She would not ask for help. Once she got the satchel on her back, she could bind her elbow to her side, and no one would notice that her arm did not move. All the volition that remained to her was in the upper part, barely enough to raise or lower the rest. The hand was inert. It had been without sensation for so long she had almost grown used to it, its malleable weight; but now, as she felt it neatly and casually for scabs or splinters, for the third morning running she could find no pulse. Her mother was watching so she looked up and smiled. She bound it fast and ate her bread, and when she left the hut, the boys were still asleep.

The light was a red wound opened in the grey. The horizon bled as if clawed by the thorny stems and dry hips, clutched for the memory it brought of roses. Soon her mother must harvest the hips, else they would be stolen. She walked in the tracks she had made in days before. She entered the Boneyard through the sheepshank gate. In the distance the alien walls of the towers rose impossibly smooth to bright lights like unwinking eyes; else the Boneyard ran on for miles. The eyes of the towers were watching, or so it was said; certain that even in the night they burned. She spread out her skirts in her place, next to a woman who made pictures in the dust.

The knucklebones were laid out in sets; some were human, some were goat. The bulbs she left rolled, with only one shrivelled round peeping from the cloth, and she had three dried eggs, perfectly whole with something that rattled inside them. The teeth were in a basket. She laid them out around her as the woman beside her laid out shapes of rust and chalk and powdered lichen. As the sun rose the haze thickened, or became more obvious, and even the figures of the living sifted in and out of sight down the long rows of stones. As the woman who made pictures rocked with a ceaseless, senseless ululation, Lisel sat with her face turned up to the sky and her hand under the folds of her wrap.

A dead woman bought a set of knuckles for a needle and three silver buttons, and walked away turning them over and over in her hand. Lisel resettled herself into waiting, into the long, dim awareness.

A dead man stood before her, bending down to show what lay in his spread fingers. She saw his strange, sweet smile. In his hand lay a vial of glass, begrimed and fragile but still whole. Its shape held nothing but translucence and a tiny, golden bead caught in the neck.

An egg. An egg for him. She reached out for the vial, and his fingers might have brushed hers, but like the rest of her they were coated with dust and that was protection. Dust was safe. He took up the egg and held it for a moment, cradling it, then he was gone.

How did they make their choices? It made sense that they would seek for their own teeth, their own knuckles. Across the row was a stall which had plaited bracelets of hair that had grown in graves, the proprietors claimed. That was hard to scavenge, and there was no need to doubt that men stole the hair of the living. The truly desperate would sell their own, even though that condemned them. Could the dead not tell the cheat until they held it in their hands? But even then, why the bulbs and eggs?

It was no use wondering. This was what she did, what she could do because the dead would come to her. She never sat here a day without their presence, though there were many who did. Sometimes she thought it might be the singing of the woman beside her. The dead never seemed to listen, but she would put a token on the woman's shawl at the end of the day.

"For the glass, what say you?" Face coated in dust and fingers hooked, this man was alive and eager, and in his hand he held a crow's foot. "I'm not dead." He had apples as well. There was a tale that no food which passed through the Boneyard could be et, but though she would not eat here, she was well beyond such niceties. She hid the apples under her wrap.

Slow the day passed for those who sat in the long rows; equally slow for those who watched in the towers, if that tale were true, but as shadows began to lip from edges and the world at last gained direction, a dead man came who stood and looked at her and not at her wares. It happened sometimes, there were strong dead and weak dead, and this one was there as firmly and nearly as the man she had traded with had been. But it was the scrutiny of a bird, something small and unreal.

"You have a dead hand," he said.

Her hand lay among the apples, no different really; an organic thing still sound and fresh but with no life. Still it responded with a phantom feeling; her mind itched.

"No," she said.

The dead man smiled. "I would buy it," he said.

"I don't sell them."

The shadows ran out from the towers and across the land. The night was coming. She sat stolidly, not looking at him. Speak only as spoken to, and never try to see them straight on. But the presence in front of her remained until it was time for her to roll up her stock and refill her satchel, taking every measure to disguise her arm, and join the slow, bustling crowd filing out of the Boneyard. Few exchanged words; all were burdened.

When she got home she crawled in the door, pulling the night wards into place behind her. The boys butted her like goats and cried for the apples. The only thing she had not sold any of were the bulbs, again.

"Keep them," her mother urged.

Her aunt had said that the dead bought bulbs; in any case, they could not be planted till spring. She began to unstrap her hand.

"You'll have to have it taken off," said her mother, "before it withers."

"I know."

She sat by the fire and held her hand gently, so that it would be warm.

***

The next time she went to the Boneyard, he came again.

The woman beside her had made faces, faces whose lips and cheeks were rain trails and whose hair was ash, echoing the broken roads and craters of the landscape beyond the Boneyard. She could feel his approach in the prickling on the back of her neck and in her dead hand, unreal. But he was kneeling before her and he had cloth. Underneath the soiling it was fresh and bright, the real old cloth that lasted in the ground, worth all the teeth and the bracelets of hair.

"Let me buy your hand."

"No."

He came back again with a cast iron pot and an unbroken chain with a lock; fabulous wealth laid down at her hem, food for the winter or a goat in milk, and the proprietors around her were watching. None tried to intervene or attract his notice away, there was no point; but they could see that she did not trade, see the eggs and the knuckles lying motionless around her knees and she, she could see him.

"Do you know why the towers were built?" he said.

She did not answer. The brilliant lights pierced through the sifting tan.

"When the world began to die, those with power chose people and placed them there to watch. They were to observe and record, to take samples and find out not what had happened, because everyone knew that, but what it was that had changed. Their descendants are still doing so. They never come out. What is outside is contaminated."

When she was a child, Lisel had sometimes cried that she had not been chosen, in a selection made lifetimes before she was born. Even now something in her stung. She muttered a child's incantation: "The world wasn't always like this; it wasn't the same."

"More people were alive and made more things. But the things don't keep us here. You can have them."

And she could feel the darkness spilling over the horizon. *What keeps you?* she did not whisper, and it was like her hand was aching.

"We have always been here, the ones who cannot leave," he said. "Still we wait. We want. But there are no distractions now. No medicine, no machines; you notice us now. And I say nothing has changed."

And at last he was gone, and she was able to complete the rite of filling her satchel and trudging out, out of the Boneyard with never a glance behind. Never glance behind.

She did not tell her mother, and in the morning her mother died.

***

It came upon her mother all at once. Then all working; now all stopped, and there had been no cry, no thrashing. Mother leaned in her wrap by the side of the door like a stranger caught in the coming or going.

She knew what to do. The boys were scared and wanted to run, but she caught them and tied the door shut. She sealed the cracks as best she could with mud and dung. Then she built up the fire with as many chips as she could find, and the boys looked on wide-eyed, then began to cough as she sat unblinking, gazing at the bright half-life of each separate hair.

It had to be done slowly, with little noise and no light, no smoke. Once night came, they would be safer from the near-hutters and casual passers-by who might notice something was wrong; but it would take a long time. She remembered the fire which her mother had built for her aunt, but this fire seemed to burn hotter upon her face. After a while the boys dozed, drunk on the stench. But she would hunch here and saw and crack, then she would rake and grind and finally scatter, so there would be nothing to scavenge, nothing to trade, so that she would not have to sit in the Boneyard waiting for the day she would look up and see her mother.

Her hand rested in her lap. The rest of her was alive. She felt it keenly, a deep, warm core to her, and that was what had got her the boys, of course. How strange, that they still seemed so much more her mother's. It had always been her mother that had cared for them. She had to go to the Boneyard. Her mother had fed and handled them, and now no more. No more mother to bake the bread and harvest the herbs, no more mother to scavenge through the broken ground for old graves—and still she must go to the Boneyard, for there was no one else, except the boys. Too young, though surely she had not been much older when her aunt first took her to sit and watch, and noticed that the dead came to her. There was a scratching at the door and at the roof hung with night wards; there always was at funerals.

It was done. Now, soon, she must do the same to her hand.

***

Did she miss her mother? Now her mother was dust and it seemed she could not even recall her face. The rose hips were stolen from the bushes one afternoon, while she was hunting the potatoes her mother had set. Three to feed, but four had been four hands, not two. She got the boys into the fields and gleaning, but they did not do it well. They did not like her, and would play and hide just to spite her; it was her fault that mother was gone. No one would help; certainly not now the word had gotten round of the death, and that she had sat in the Boneyard with a dead man, speaking as the sun rose and fell.

She had little left to trade. There would be nothing until she went to the Boneyard. But if she fed herself and the boys she did not scavenge, and if she scavenged they did not eat. The boys didn't understand; who else would look after them?

A woman who would trade her care for a roll of old cloth.

How desperate was desperate? If the desperate would sell their own deaths to keep hold of life, how desperate was that?

Lisel worked and the day turned to night, sweeping both horizons clear of all walls, all scars, all marks save the tower eyes. Men had tried to breach the walls where they went into the ground, had even tried to dig, but nothing ever came of it.

Even the people inside were really only a tale; none had ever been seen. She set the night wards in place as she crawled inside the hut and once more built up the fire. It came to her that her mother had not been old, not until her aunt had died, and that the last thing she had done was grind a day's worth of corn in the mortar that had ground her bones. Now it ground corn again, and Lisel leant nodding against the wall. She tried to remember the face of him who had given her the boys, and could not. That too had been a trade, nothing more. A cast iron pot and an unbroken lock, even one-handed those would buy her another man. She ground corn until she was sleeping, moving and yet not awake.

She thought the eyes were watching her, but that she had managed to hide her hand. Then she thought once more of the Boneyard, and it seemed to her that never once had she seen the dead speak to each other. Perhaps once she had seen a pair walking side by side down the row until they entered the stream of shadows and vanished. In her sleep, she realised that everything she had been told about the dead returning in search of their bodies was false. The teeth and hair were something they could touch, the eggs and bulbs the same, a mingling of life and death. That was why they came to the Boneyard and went through the motions of trade. That was why they came to her. He had come to her again and again, she knew him and could tell him from all the others, and what really was it that she feared?

On the day she had the boys she had bled. The sky was bleeding, a mass of bruised tissue thrust apart. She made the boys a dish of baked bulbs and shut the door behind her as she left.

As she entered the Boneyard, she looked at the towers and thought, *They will never find what has changed, for nothing has changed. They are blind.* And the child she had been smiled at that.

The woman who made pictures sang. There was a stinking seepage from one of her eyes, cutting down her withered cheek. Dust clotted the sores on her fingers and feet. On the hems of her wrap, Lisel laid out the last of the teeth and knuckles like an embroidery, and waited. When the shadows were streaming and the people passing to and fro were pictures in the dust, he came down the row like a memory.

"Please," he said.

"I will not sell it," she answered. Then she shifted those last muscles in her shoulder and brought her hand clear of the wrap. It seemed very new and tender, this hand free from dust and skin grown pale and soft in hiding. Curled like a bud she moved it at the end of her arm.

He said, "Beautiful."

She stood and reached out to him, teeth and knuckles falling away from her skirt and said, "Take my hand and walk with me."

KYLA LEE WARD

THIS ATTRACTION NOW OPEN TILL LATE

STRANGE SIGHTS AND SHADOWS

About the Author

Kyla Lee Ward is a graduate of the University of Technology, Sydney, who works in many modes, principally writing and acting. Reviewers have accused her of being "gothic and esoteric", "weird and exhilarating" and of having a "... real presence 'live' as she has too in these poems."

Her poetry has placed in the Rhyslings and garnered an Australian Shadows award. Her work up to 2019 is collected in two volumes from P'rea Press – *The Land of Bad Dreams* and *The Macabre Modern and Other Morbidities*.

This is her first collection of short fiction. A multiple Stoker finalist and nominee for Ditmar and Aurealis awards, her stories have otherwise appeared in the likes of *Aurealis, Borderlands,* and *Shadowed Realms* magazines, and in anthologies such as *Gods, Memes and Monsters: A Twenty-first Century Bestiary, The Lion and the Aardvark: Aesop's Modern Fables, The New Hero Volume One* and *Macabre: A Journey into Australia's Worst Fears*.

She is one third of Edwina Grey. The novel *Prismatic* (Lothian 2006) was penned with her partner David Carroll and mutual friend Evan Paliatseas, but somehow won an Aurealis Award for Best Horror.

Her acting career has been long and varied. If you know where to look, she can be spotted in *Underbelly Razor* and *Mad Max: Fury Road*. She is a regular performer with James Adams Historic Enterprises, bringing the delights of medieval combat and culture to schoolchildren, and has been your Guide to *Deadhouse: Tales of Sydney Morgue* (Blancmange Productions) for three seasons thus far. Composing the occasional script, her short film, 'Bad Reception', screened at the Third International Vampire Film Festival and she was a member of the Theatre of Blood repertory company, which produced her work alongside classic Grand Guignol.

A LARPer and role-player, she was a freelance writer for the White Wolf Gaming Studio as well as contributing to many magazines. Active in fandom since the '90s (when she and David edited the horror 'zine *Tabula Rasa*), her involvement culminated in programming the horror stream for Aussiecon 4 (the 68th Worldcon) in 2010.

She has travelled widely, seen much that is dark and strange, and now hosts regular true crime and ghost tours in her hometown. A practicing occultist, she likes raptors, sword play and the Hellfire Club.

To see some very strange things, including filmed performances, try HTTP://WWW.KYLAWARD.COM

Acknowledgements

"The Oldest Coffee House in Prague", "A Nightmare in Burgundy", "The Beautiful House" and "The Final Masque" are original to this collection. All other pieces first appeared as below –

"And In Her Eyes the City Drowned", *Weirdbook #39*, July 2018
- Finalist, the Bram Stoker Award for Superior Achievement in Short Fiction, 2019

"Who Looks Back?", *Shotguns vs Cthulhu*, ed. Robin D. Laws, Stone Skin Press, 2012

"A Whisper in the Death Pit", *Weirdbook #44*, June 2021
- Finalist, the Bram Stoker Award for Superior Achievement in Short Fiction, 2022

"Sakoku", *Agog! Fantastic Fiction, Agog #1*, ed. Cat Sparks, Agog! Press, 2002

"Should Fire Remember the Fuel?", *Oz Is Burning*, ed. Phylis Irene Radford, B-cubed Press, August 2020
- Finalist, the Bram Stoker Award for Superior Achievement in Short Fiction, 2021

"Gargoyles, As They Grumble", *The Gargoylicon – Imaginings and Images of the Gargoyle in Literature and Art*, ed. Frank Coffman, Minds Eye Publications, forthcoming

"This Attraction Now Open till Late", *Vastarian*, Volume Five Issue One, forthcoming

"A Tour of the City of Assassins", *Ticon 4*, Ticonderoga Online, January 2009

"The Boneyard", *Gothic.net*, September 2001

WWW.INDEPENDENTLEGIONS.COM

THE MAN WHO ESCAPED THIS STORY AND OTHER STORIES
by Cody Goodfellow
Collection – Paperback and eBook Edition
September 2019

CROTA
by Owl Goingback
Novel – Hardcover, Paperback and eBook Edition
July 2019

DARK CARNIVAL
by Joanna Parypinski
Novel – Paperback and eBook Edition
June 2019

CALCUTTA HORROR
by Alessandro Manzetti & Stefano Cardoselli
Graphic Novel – Paperback and eBook Edition
May 2019

COYOTE RAGE
by Owl Goingback
Novel – Paperback and eBook Edition
February 2019

APARTMENT SEVEN
by Greg F. Gifune
Novella – Paperback and eBook Edition
Juanuary 2019

FEARFUL SYMMETRIES
by Thomas F. Monteleone
Collection – Paperback and eBook Edition
January 2019

DARK MARY
by Paolo Di Orazio
Novel – Paperback and eBook Edition
December 2018

TRIBAL SCREAMS
by Owl Goingback
Collection – Paperback and eBook Edition
October 2018

MONSTERS OF ANY KIND
Edited by Alessandro Manzetti & Daniele Bonfanti
Stories by: David J. Schow, Edward Lee, Jonathan Maberry, Ramsey Campbell,
Lucy Taylor, Cody Goodfellow and many others
Anthology – Paperback and eBook Edition
September 2018

ARTIFACTS
by Bruce Boston
Poetry Collection– Paperback and eBook Edition
July 2018

KNOWING WHEN TO DIE
by Mort Castle
Collection– Paperback and eBook Edition
June 2018

NARAKA
by Alessandro Manzetti
Novel– Paperback and eBook Edition
May 2018

A WINTER SLEEP
by Greg F. Gifune
Novel– Paperback and eBook Edition
April 2018

SPREE AND OTHER STORIES
by Lucy Taylor
Collection – Paperback and eBook Edition
February 20
THE LIVING AND THE DEAD
by Greg F. Gifune
Novel – Paperback and eBook Edition
December 2017

TALKING IN THE DARK
by Dennis Etchison
Collection – eBook Edition
December 2017

THE BEAUTY OF DEATH 2 – DEATH BY WATER
edited by Alessandro Manzetti & Jodi Renee Lester
Anthology – Paperback and eBook Edition
November 2017

DREAMS THE RAGMAN
by Greg F. Gifune
Novella – Paperback and eBook Edition
November 2017

CHILDREN OF NO ONE
by Nicole Cushing
Novella – Paperback and eBook Edition
October 2017

THE RAIN DANCERS
by Greg F. Gifune
Novella – Paperback and eBook Edition
September 2017

WHAT WE FOUND IN THE WOODS
by Shane McKenzie
Collection – eBook Edition
September 2016

THE HORROR SHOW
by Poppy Z. Brite
Collection – eBook Edition
August 2016

THE BEAUTY OF DEATH VOL. 1
Edited by Alessandro Manzetti
Anthology – eBook Edition
July 2016

SELECTED STORIES
by Edward Lee
Collection – eBook Edition
July 2016

USED STORIES
by Poppy Z. Brite
Collection – eBook Edition
June 2016

THE USHERS
by Edward Lee
Collection – eBook Edition
May 2016

THE CRYSTAL EMPIRE
by Poppy Z. Brite
Novella – eBook Edition
April 2016

INDEPENDENT LEGIONS PUBLISHING
Via Virgilio, 10 – TRIESTE (ITALY)
+39 040 9776602
www.independentlegions.com
independent.legions@aol.com